ECHOES
OF THE PAST

MATT MORIARTY

An *A History of the Future* Novel

Cover Art: Tom Dusterberg - www.dusterberg.net

www.mattjmoriarty.com

www.createspace.com

ISBN: 1453776346
ISBN-13: 9781453776346
Library of Congress Control Number: 2010912929

With thanks to my family, who supported me and helped me the whole time…
And with thanks to John Overbeck, without whom none of this would have happened.

PROLOGUE

The early morning light poked through the holes in the tent to settle on the face of Francisco Jimenez. The young Hispanic man who had left his family and his home country of Mexico for a new life in the United States began to fidget in his sleep, a restful sleep, despite being far from safe in a refugee camp in northern Texas.

Finally, he couldn't stand the light in his eyes and, throwing off the thin blanket, sat up. Swinging himself off the bed, Francisco jumped as a mouse scampered out of one of his shoes, likely having sought shelter from the storm during the night. Laughing softly to himself that these insane storms were affecting even the smallest of creatures, Francisco finished dressing and left the small tent, careful not to disturb his tentmate.

He shook his head. Sometimes when it came to Adam, his tentmate, Francisco didn't know what to do. Supposedly, Adam used to be some big time cattle rancher, and he sure acted like a big shot; but the wars and now these insane storms and earthquakes had destroyed everything the man had owned. Despite that, Adam was still an ass. A big, arrogant ass.

That being said, Adam was one of his only friends in the refugee camp, at least partly because Adam spoke Spanish. That was a good thing, considering Francisco spoke very little English, but Adam was helping him with that.

"Francisco! Wanna come to the dining hall with me? We can finally get some breakfast!" Grinning, Francisco turned around to see his friend Pablo, as well as some other refugees, looking up confusedly at the Spanish. Pablo was one of his only other friends in the camp, as well as the only other Mexican.

After some discussion, they decided to head over to the dining hall, but as they did the earth gave a massive shudder, throwing everyone to the ground and flattening some tents.

"Francisco! Help!" Francisco turned to see Pablo trapped beneath a massive pile of rubble where one of the few remaining buildings had fallen on him. Swearing to himself, Francisco started hauling rubble off of his friend. But just as he was dragging Pablo clear, it started to rain.

"Well this is just great. Earthquakes, rain…and now lighting," he added as a bolt of white fire streaked out of the sky to set the dining tent ablaze. Seeing the hospital tent, he began dragging Pablo to it, but a blast right next to him made the world flash white. When Francisco could see again, Pablo was already dead. Wickedly strong winds began spreading the fire from tent to tent until it seemed the whole world was ablaze.

Collapsing to the ground and starting to weep, Francisco decided to end it all, but a bolt of lighting beat him to it, and there was a flash of light and then nothing at all.

And 2,000 years later, a young man bolted upright from a nightmare, drenched in a cold, cold sweat.

CHAPTER ONE

Shoren McCarter, an army commander of the Denver Empire, woke up in a sweat, breathing hard. Shaking his head in an attempt to drive away the dark dreams of the night, Shoren reached for his striker to light his oil lamp to help him see. After his lamp had been lit, he sat down in a meditative position and worked to sort out his dream. This was not his first dream about the Lost Times; for that was all the images could be from, though not even the most learned of scholars knew anything beyond rumors of that time. As he reflected on the dream, some of the words came back to him.

Shoren shrugged. Mexico? Texas? He had no idea where those words had come from, and most likely they were merely some fancy. They might never have existed. It didn't matter though; certainly no scholar could or would ever tell him.

He doubted that the continuously occurring nightmares were brought on by some anxiety over that long-destroyed era when men were as gods and the impossible happened every day. More likely they were due to his upcoming assignment as general of the Second Invasion Force that had entered the nation of Kirendad five months ago. They had been sent to ensure that General Mekal's forces were able to succeed in expanding their nation's borders all the way to the city of Koro, deep within the mountains.

Shoren stood up and crossed over to a table where a map was rolled out. Once again he traced the road that extended from Denver to Koro to the distant ocean.

Shoren frowned as he looked at the mountains his troops would have to pass through to reach Koro. Known to the ancients as the "Rockies," Shoren had never heard a more accurate name for the treacherous mountains. As he reflected silently to himself, Shoren smiled. Yes, "Rockies" was far superior to the name his own people had given them – "Mountains of Paradise."

Finally, Shoren decided to just go back to bed. The morning would come soon enough.

The morning did come, and Shoren had to get up early because he was expected at the Imperial Court. He got dressed in his finest uniform, which had been made for him by his fiancée Elina's family. Shoren frowned and shook his head, not wanting to worry about that today, even though he knew both she and her father would be there.

"No," he told himself, "you've got enough to worry about without adding that to the mix."

For in addition to taking command of nearly 20,000 men, he would also be charged with capturing the rogue general Rekii and sending him back to the capital for trial and execution. It was also very likely that others would be killed, other high-rankers and lords; but they would be hung in Kirendad, for only Rekii's trial and inevitable beheading were to be made public.

After all, they couldn't very well let a skilled general go rogue and then start looting and pillaging Kirendadi and Denver villages. The Denver tried not to slaughter such common people, especially in such a needless fashion. But that was neither here nor there. The most important thing today was to make a good impression on the Emperor, for such a chance might never come again.

A servant knocked on the door before sliding into Shoren's quarters with a basket of laundry.

"My Lord Shoren," he said, "I'm sorry to have interrupted you, but you must hurry if you wish to avoid being late."

Shoren sighed. He despised being back in the city with servants and courtiers fawning all over the place. They distracted and annoyed him.

"It's all right, Jon," he finally said. "Bring me my coat and I'll be going."

"Yes, my lord," Jon said while pulling the dress uniform's green and gold surcoat out of the ornate closet. "Shall I button it for my lord?"

"No! I can do it myself. Go away!"

"Uh, um. Yes, my lord. Very good, my lord." As Jon backed out of the room, he stumbled and tripped over a chair, knocked it over, and then fell, very hard, to the floor. Standing up, Jon picked up the chair and gathered up the laundry before slowly striding out of the room. He reminded Shoren of a bird with its damn feathers ruffled.

After Jon had closed the door, Shoren took a deep calming breath. He took another. He shouldn't have snapped at Jon. It wasn't his fault, but all the servants were annoying. Buttoning his coat and buckling on his blade, a long curved saber, Shoren walked out of the room. Catching sight of one of the clocks set in the palace hallways, he started running. If he hurried, he might not be too late.

He was on time to the Imperial Court, though just. Shoren rushed up to the herald standing by the great blue, gold-trimmed doors marked with the black and gold eagle that is his people's symbol. The herald glared at Shoren as he arrived and impatiently pointed to a bench where he was to sit and wait. Shoren declined to sit and chose instead to walk up to the much shorter and scrawnier herald and ask him when the audience of the officers to be sent on invasion was to be.

"I do not know, sir, nor do I care. I would imagine that it will not be held for quite a while. His majesty the Emperor is receiving the Uavadan ambassador, Lord Karl, from the city of Parowan. Lord Karl is here to establish a trading deal with our nation."

"And I wonder why the Emperor is dealing with this instead of the Merchant Advisor," Shoren said coldly. "He should be dealing with the invasion first. The officers need to organize and set a timetable so that we can leave. Every delay means…"

"I know what every delay means. You military types never concern yourselves with the gold needed to run a nation, let alone one as glorious as Denver. Parowan is the strongest of the Uavadan city-states, so the Emperor meets with the ambassador. Sit down and wait. I have no time to speak with you."

Shoren, who had been told to arrive just after dawn, ground his teeth and sat down. The herald, who supposedly had better things to do than talk to a high ranking commander like Shoren, was now telling one of the servants to fetch him some wine. Shoren snorted and rolled his eyes. The arrogance of the heralds and high nobles who frequented the palace was sometimes amazing but always irritating.

After several long hours a herald, not the one Shoren had argued with but one much younger, informed him that it was time for his audience.

"Finally." Shoren grinned and stood up. "I think I was just about to fall asleep there."

The herald shook his head. "I would hurry. The Emperor's patience is not what it was, now that the Uavadan audience is over."

"Thank you. I'll keep that in mind." Shoren hurried over to where the herald was ready to announce him. The herald tapped his staff and shouted.

"The Lord Shoren, legion commander of the third cavalry and member of the Order of the Mountain is here for his audience with the Emperor."

The Emperor nodded. In a reedy voice he said, "Send him in."

Shoren walked forward across the polished marble floor to the front of the dais, right on top of a massive golden thunderbird inlaid at the front of the steps, and bowed in the traditional fashion, bending low at the waist. He waited a few seconds and then straightened. The Emperor looked down at him, and then motioned for the officers who would be part of Shoren's staff to stand behind him. After the gesture, all one hundred of them, all in varying uniforms, ran from between two of the massive marble columns to join Shoren in an orderly fashion.

The heralds then began to announce the commanders of the other forces that would be traveling alongside Shoren and his men, as well as the commander of the occupation forces that would help to absorb Koro into the Denver nation and guard from retaliatory attacks from the Kirendadi. Among them were legion commanders Ronnald Zaar and Juan Dolger. Shoren looked up and heard some of the last announcements.

"...Major Curtis Sten...commander of the seventh sub legion..."

When the last officer had been announced, the Emperor motioned again, and all the officers walked forward in a line strung out to face the Emperor and the great Eagle's Throne. The throne was massive with a back and armrests that looked like huge golden eagle wings spread and encircling the seat, as if to present the Emperor. The front feet of the throne were like massive talons. The throne was inlaid with black opals for the eagle's eyes and talons, and rested on a long red carpet with red cushions.

Four guards wearing chain mail stood at each edge of the dais, each wearing a long, knee-length red surcoat over his armor. The surcoats buttoned up the left side so that the gold and black eagle was visible. Each guard carried a massive two-handed sword in a sheath on his back, as well as a ten-foot pike in his hands. Each wore a golden helmet with cheek guards made to look like an eagle, with a crest of horsehair on top like a mane. Since they were members of the Protectors, the Emperor's personal bodyguards, the horsehair crests were made in alternating bars of the imperial colors, red and black.

To the west side of the audience chamber, Shoren noticed a large gathering of the nobility and their servants. When Shoren looked to the east side, he groaned audibly. Not only was there a large gathering of the bored nobility, come to see the commanders in their fancy uniforms, but even the high ranking merchants were there and the guildmasters! After scanning both sides of the chamber, Shoren would have liked nothing better than to disappear inside his surcoat, because there, next to those blasted craftmasters, stood Elina and her bloody noble family, all looking like damn idiots in their bright red and blue coats. Those two colors, especially as bright as they were, were the colors of Elina's family. There stood Elina, grinning, happy to see that Shoren, who she believed would come back and marry her like a bloody fool from some stupid story, was the center of attention. When Elina saw him looking at her, she waved. Shoren was saved from further torment when one of the officers behind him cleared his throat, drawing Shoren's attention back to the matter at hand, whereupon he realized that the Emperor had asked him to come forward and kneel.

The Emperor gave another command, and several servants stepped out from behind the Emperor's dais, each carrying a basket with many sealed scrolls inside. Each servant went down the line, giving the scrolls to the recipients. When they had finished, each soldier held three scrolls. When each servant had stepped back behind the dais, the Emperor stood.

"Each one of you now possesses three scrolls. The first scroll, which has the thunderbird seal in red wax, contains your orders. The second, with the sword seal in blue, is your proof of rank, and the final scroll contains my personal blessing. You have your commands." The Emperor spoke some more, and named Shoren as high commander of the Second Invasion Force, but not a general. This bothered Shoren somewhat since a generalship was permanent and his current rank wasn't. It had angered Elina a lot more, and Shoren smiled to remember her rant about "fools who don't know real talent." The Emperor also named the other leaders of the invasion, each with a specific job to do.

When Shoren walked out of the Imperial Court, he looked through one of the windows, and saw that it was almost midday. Shoren was just about to retire to his quarters for the midday meal, but then he noticed another officer, Commander Tomas of the infantry, walking up to him. Tomas was tall, even taller than Shoren, with short-cropped hair and a short brown beard. Tomas was generally known for being more concerned with winning battles than with the carnage that resulted, and he knew his business. That's why he was taking command of the infantry divisions directly under General Mekal. He also was known for being blunt and straightforward. Many nobles thought him almost barbaric, despite his education.

"Greetings, 'High Commander' Shoren. I must say, you have a tough job ahead of you. Lord Ryon and High Lord Daved are joining me at my manor for the midday meal, and I thought you'd like to join us? We could also discuss our tactics in the upcoming battles," he added, winking at a gaggle of noble heiresses to show just what kind of battles he meant.

Shoren snorted and accepted, albeit a little warily. He unbuttoned the green and gold cavalry surcoat and loosened the collar of his shirt. Shoren also eased his dress saber in its scabbard, wishing he had his ordinary sword. Luring a rival into one's home and then killing him was not unknown, especially among the high-rankers in the military, and while Shoren didn't think Tomas would try it, he didn't know the man very well and he had been the target of such a plot once before. He had been able to survive, as well as kill his would-be assassin, but the lord's family still held a grudge, and he didn't want to have to go through that again.

Shoren and Tomas left the throne room together and walked out of the main hall and toward the front gates. They passed some of the private audience chambers, passed by the rooms for the many nobles and visiting ambassadors, and finally walked out to the great front steps of the Palace in the Mountains of Paradise. Tomas led Shoren to his carriage, where several important looking men waited. He saw Ryon, but not Daved, both of whom were his friends. He didn't recognize anyone else.

"Tomas, my friend! We've been waiting for ya'!" exclaimed a thick-necked, balding man who was probably in his late fifties. He embraced Tomas in a huge bear hug. "Major Jared said we ought to go to yer home straight away, but I told him we'd best wait for ya, 'cause otherwise we'd miss out on this magnificent carriage, and the wine in it! Ha-ha!" His white and red surcoat was unbuttoned and rumpled, and his shirt was covered in old wine stains. Shoren also got a good look at his sword, which was not a dress sword; no, this was a true war sword, four and a half feet of good Denver steel, with a plain boar hide hilt. After Tomas had seated himself, he turned and introduced the man as Major General Josef Nixon. Shoren gaped. This was the Major General Josef Nixon in charge of the entire Denver Imperial Army? The man who had defeated the horse riders of the Great Plains when they invaded twenty-five years ago?

"High Commander Shoren? I'm pleased to meet ya." The giant stuck out his hand and Shoren tentatively shook it. "Well it's good ta' meet the man who'll be winning the war for us, or just about. Let's get into the carriage and on to the manor! Ha-ha!"

Shoren, Tomas, Josef, and Ryon all settled themselves into the carriage and were off on the bumpy road, away from the Palace of the Mountains of Paradise and toward the noble district of New Denver. When the carriage hit a particularly bumpy spot, Shoren opened the red and white patterned curtains and looked out at the city.

Denver was set in a valley and surrounded by mountains, so until ten years prior there had been no wall protecting the city. Denver had stood for over 2,000 years without walls, but its sacking by the horsemen from the Plains changed that. Even so, it had taken the bureaucrats fifteen years to decide to build the walls, and then only because the horsemen threatened again. As Shoren looked past the cobblestone streets he could see the workers still building Denver's great stone wall that surrounded and protected the city.

Shoren could also see the gray stone of the homes and inns and stores that dotted the landscape, the peaked roofs that let the snow slide off in the winter so as not to put too much pressure on the roofs rising up high into the sky. Shoren saw his favorite inn in the city, The Golden Peak, shining like fresh-fallen frost thanks to its polished granite exterior, and he smiled to see that Frenk's inn was busier than ever, thanks to the surplus of soldiers awaiting marching orders. Shoren's attention was then caught by Tomas's own manorial palace, far smaller than the mountainous Imperial Palace but still impressive.

The carriage rolled to a stop in front of the massive front steps, where Shoren and the other guests alighted, handing their coats to the servants who were waiting for them, and labored up the massive front steps into the main foyer. Shoren looked around and smiled, for although on the outside Denver buildings often seemed gray and drab, all being built of the same gray granite, on the inside all Denver folk more than made up for it by decorating their homes with massive tapestries, gilt decorations and colorful rugs. Everywhere Shoren looked he saw another work of art which was nothing more than to be expected. He even saw a painting of the legendary Cheyenne Mountain, where the guardian spirits resided.

Shoren turned to Ryon and snorted.

"You know, this place is really nice, but I almost think I'd rather be in a tent, in the field."

Ryon laughed incredulously. "Shoren, listen. We are in a really nice palace, with lots of good food, good wine, and pretty serving girls who are also pretty willing, hobnobbing with a bunch of dumb aristocrats who couldn't tell a sword from a sneakblade, and you would complain."

"See! That's why I always beat you when we dueled at school. You never pay attention. I did say almost."

Ryon frowned. "You didn't always beat me. I won plenty of times."

"You won twice. The first time I tripped over a rock and the second you had your sister watch, and in the middle of the fight she started whistling and calling my name. That's cheating. Of course, she did feel bad and she came over later to apologize…" he grinned.

Ryon smirked. "Yeah, and then you embarrassed yourself in front of my father because you didn't know which fork was for the salad."

Shoren shrugged. He'd never really cared for the luxuries and niceties of noble life. His father, the current Emperor's cousin, had wanted to raise Shoren to be a politician but had died when Shoren was only four. Shoren's mother was just as shrewd as his father, so she tried to teach Shoren the ways of plots and schemes. She called it an art form, but Shoren never really caught on. What's more, Shoren was a bit of a willful child, so when he was just twelve years old, his mother sent him to the finest military school in the land, Fort Tyrris, which was named for the legendary Aramain conqueror. When Shoren was eighteen, his mother arranged for him to go to the Salt Lake Academy, the military school that most Denver nobles were sent to. Shoren left the school in just two years and promptly joined the army, where he quickly rose through the ranks, partly because of his natural ability and fine education and partly thanks to his mother's constant scheming.

"Um, Shoren? Are you coming?" Tomas' question pulled Shoren out of his reflections, and he walked into the granite feast hall. There Shoren saw that the lords Ryon, Josef and himself weren't Tomas' only guests. He also noticed several non-military nobles, chiefly the great and mighty Lord Tobis and his wife, the Lady Emela. Both were vicious schemers who delighted in bringing down high-ranking opponents and taking a petty revenge on any slight, be it real or imagined. Shoren had absolutely no idea why they would be there; but it wasn't his place to question Tomas' choice of guests, even if it was those two.

Ryon nudged Shoren in the ribs with his elbow, causing Shoren to realize that he'd been frowning.

Shoren forced a smile. "Happy now?" he asked under his breath.

"Look, Shoren. I know you don't like those two, but at least keep smiling. If you don't, they'll take it as an insult and try to embarrass you. Just keep the conversation light and meaningless, and talk to them a little bit or they'll be insulted. But most of all, don't say anything you wouldn't want the whole city to know by morning."

Shoren shrugged and groaned audibly but continued whispering. "All right, all right. I'll be careful. Keep the mood cheerful and don't say anything stupid. Got it."

"All right. Good. I don't want to have to save you again, not after you said those things to…"

"Shoren! Ryon! How good to see both again!" Tobis said in greeting, oozing insincerity. "It's so excellent you could make it to the feast. I know how dreadfully busy you must be, working so hard to protect our people. I hope everything is well in hand?"

Shoren wanted nothing more than to cut that ingratiating, lying smile off the two-faced fool. No. Silly as Tobis might seem, he was no fool. Shoren forced another smile.

"Oh, all the preparations are made. The Kirendadi are tough folk, but the might of Denver cannot be triumphed over."

"Yes. Well, it would seem as though the army has given you a wonderful opportunity wouldn't you say?"

Ryon spoke up. "Shoren's earned it. I can tell you that. He made top marks at the Salt Lake Academy, and has served with distinction in any number of battles since then."

"Yes. Well, I would like to know how you plan to deal with the rogue. What was his name…Rekii?"

Ryon watched curiously as Lord Tobis continued to make a point of talking to Shoren. He wondered why the man would do that. The conversation was taking up all of Shoren's attention, that was sure. Ryon also realized that the other nobles were talking among themselves, and Tomas and Josef, while engaged in a deep discussion, were occasionally glancing at Tobis and Shoren, who was now sitting and already on his second cup of spiced wine. As Ryon started to take his seat he saw movement out of the corner of his eye. Damn them all to the black spirits. He should have known.

"Shoren!"

Ryon's shout caused Shoren to whip around, and as he did several servants with Tobis's family colors charged forward, bearing knives and swords. Assassins!

Shoren whipped out his sword, only to realize that he'd brought his dress sword. In that split second, they were upon him. Shoren crouched low, swinging his sword horizontally across the first assassin's neck, nearly severing his head. He had just enough time to parry and see that Ryon was also engaged with an assassin. Josef was trying to capture a fleeing Tobis but was being held off by Emela, who had grabbed Josef's sword and was now swinging it wildly. Tomas just stood dumbfounded.

Shoren was desperately trying to hold off two assassins when his light, softly made dress saber broke off at the hilt. Shoren backed up onto the table and promptly fell off the other side right on top of Emela. He struck her in the face with his elbow and took Josef's war sword. Just in time, too. Now that he had a proper combat sword, he had the upper hand. It was a simple matter for Shoren to cut the legs out from under the first man on the table and then to slice off first the hand and then the head of the second.

Now that he was safe, Shoren looked around. Tomas had apparently come to his senses and was holding a terrified Emela at the point of his sword. Ryon stood over the corpse of the other assassin, bleeding from a glancing cut on his ribs, and Josef stood over the unconscious form of Tobis whom he had beaten with a chair.

Tomas walked up and grabbed Emela by the hair and shoved her face at the corpses and Shoren.

"What's going on?" he shouted. "Why would you do this? And in my house! I want answers now!"

Emela started to shake. Tears rolled down her cheeks.

"I'm sorry, so sorry. Tobis made me do it! We had to try it. Shoren, I'm so sorry!"

Emela grabbed Tobis's hand and tried to pull it off her hair. Unable to make it move, she grabbed it with both hands but was still unable to pull free. She struggled for a few more minutes but finally just stood there limp and unable to move. She looked sullenly at Shoren as he crossed over to her. When he reached her he spoke, his voice hissing softly like a blade being pulled free of its scabbard. Soft and dangerous.

"Why would you try to kill me? I have done nothing to you." He hesitated a moment. "Unless of course…" he drawled, "you won't say, in which case maybe I should just kill you now."

Emela shook so hard she collapsed onto the floor, causing Tomas to release her hair. He did lift his sword to her throat though, clearly indicating that he didn't trust her. Emela glared at him before trying to push his sword away. When it didn't budge, she turned to Shoren.

"I'm not saying anything unless you can guarantee that nothing will happen to me."

Shoren smiled. "All I can guarantee, Lady Emela, is that if you choose to say nothing, both you and your darling husband will die."

She cringed. "All right, all right. I really don't know anything. When Tobis wakes up, ask him. All I know is Tobis owes a lot of money, but someone was willing to erase all his debts if he would kill you. I don't know why. Ask Tobis."

CHAPTER TWO

Tobis and Emela were chained together in a dungeon, awaiting interrogation. The dungeon lay deep within the bowels of the Imperial Palace. The walls were all solid gray, bare stone, and in front of the couple sat a plain wooden table, upon which sat a simple bowl of water. Both Tobis and Emela could see that the original light brown of the table had been permanently stained red with blood. All in all, it was a frightening scene.

Tobis and Emela sat in silence in the dungeon for hours, having been told that to speak before they were told to would result in dire consequences. While neither of them knew exactly what that meant, they could imagine, and that imagining was enough to still their tongues. The couple was battered and bloody, their fine feast clothes in tatters. Tobis was forced to sit very still, for whenever he moved his head he tore the half-healed scab that formed where the Major General Josef had beaten him with a chair.

Both Tobis and Emela looked up when the large iron-bound wooden door opened suddenly. Once again, Tobis's head started to bleed. Two Imperial Guardsmen then walked in, red surcoats swishing with their spears at the ready. The two men looked around the room and then at each other, both nodded and one motioned to the door for someone else to come in.

A man walked in. His face was hidden by a deep cowl, and his clothes were plain and dark, though finely cut. The man had black leather gloves on his hands, one of which caressed the hilt of the short, curved blade at his hip. Tobis and Emela smiled. Their employer had come to save them.

"Well, well. So here we have the two would-be murderers, Tobis and Emela. No longer lord and lady, for your titles and land have been seized. But you may get them back." The man hesitated. "But that's not likely. You may be executed. But that's not likely either."

"My lord, what is going to happen to us?" Tobis asked. "Are you saying that you can influence that decision one way or the other?"

The man tipped his head. "I believe you were told to remain silent. But it's all right. I won't punish you. Instead, I'm going to ask you a question. One question, and one question only."

"What is the question, my lord?" Tobis asked tentatively. Emela looked at the man and shivered with fear at his smile.

"Oh, the question is a simple one. Who am I?"

The couple shivered. Emela answered. "We don't know, my lord. Even if we did, we wouldn't tell anyone. We'll keep your secret. I promise on my honor as a Lady of Denver."

The man snorted. "Honor. What a ridiculous notion. All I wanted to know was if you knew anything to tell. Now that I know I'm safe, I intend to keep it that way."

At this, both guards stepped forward with ropes. They walked up behind Tobis and Emela and laid the ropes across their necks. They then crossed the ends behind the pair's necks.

"Please, my lord, please! We won't ever tell anyone, I swear!"

"Yes, my lord!" agreed Tobis. "No one will hear anything from us! Nothing at all!"

The man smiled again. "Oh, you can be sure of that. But feel free to scream and plead all you want. Down here, no one will hear you."

The man gestured, and all protests were cut short by the application of extremely tight ropes. Finally, the noises stopped and two pitiful corpses sat where once sat the two most powerful nobles in all of Denver. The man smiled again, and reflected for a moment how dangerous it was to use such people, but they were the only tools he had. For now.

"Take the bodies. Burn them. I don't want anyone to know what happened to them. And I hope I don't have to say that revealing any of this will result in your deaths. Your extremely painful deaths."

The two guards nodded silently as they unchained the two bodies from their chairs. The man turned and walked out the iron-bound door, his black cloak swishing behind him.

CHAPTER THREE

"What do you mean you don't know what happened to them?" "Shoren, I'm telling you the truth. I've looked into the matter, and neither hide nor hair of Tobis or Emela is to be seen anywhere. I don't know where they've gone, and my inquiries into the matter have been met with silence. I would have to assume that they died under interrogation, and the palace is just too embarrassed to admit it. They could have escaped or been rescued, but why would anyone keep that from me? They probably died."

Shoren was talking to Mercio, one of the commanders of the Palace Guard. It had been a week and a half since the attempt on his life in Tomas' palace, and Shoren still didn't know anything about why Tobis and Emela would have tried to assassinate him. Of all the people to try to kill, why him? Shoren hadn't done anything to warrant killing, or at least, he didn't think so.

"Well, thanks anyway, Mercio. I have a meeting with Major General Josef about some last minute details. If you find out anything, send me a letter. I'd really like to know where they are and how they disappeared…as well as the rest of it." The last Shoren had muttered darkly to himself.

Mercio waited a moment to see if Shoren was going to say anything else, maybe reveal just why it was he had come down on the Palace Guards like a spastic hawk a week ago, demanding to talk to everyone who had seen Tobis and Emela taken to the dungeons. When Shoren had learned that the pair had seemingly vanished without a trace, he had gone berserk, screaming wildly about the ineptitude of the Guards, an act that had gotten him into numerous duels.

When Shoren didn't elaborate further, Mercio walked away. Shoren watched him go and shrugged. Mercio *was* one of the Palace Guard commanders, so he did deserve a little respect. It was just that Mercio was probably looking to use Tobis and Emela's disappearance as a means of showing the incompetence of his superiors, along with an oh-so-subtle hint that he hadn't let their incompetence keep him from doing his job. After all, someone has to fill all of the sudden vacancies. Shoren sighed. He did have to meet with the major general. Shoren looked at the sun through a nearby window. It was already half finished with its climb to its peak. It was definitely time to get going.

Shoren looked around again, to see if anyone had been watching his private conversation. No. He was sitting in his favorite tavern and inn, The Golden Peak, and was being left alone, as was typical for a tavern like the Peak, more likely to be filled with mercenaries, foreigners and soldiers than anyone of any rank. Except for Shoren. Taking another look, Shoren smiled. This tavern was probably safer than any of the more elegant taverns and inns, likely due to the fact that here everyone knew that everyone else was armed and more than willing to use their weapons.

Shoren stood up and gave his plain brown wool coat a tug. He checked his sword, his true battle sword this time, not his new dress sword. It was made of the best steel that could be found. Most people simply bought Denver steel, but Shoren's sword came from afar. According to the merchant he had bought it from, the blade came from all the way across the Great Mississippi River, and even further east. Shoren didn't know if the merchant had been telling the truth, but he did know that he had carried the blade with him in every battle since he bought it, and the curved, single-edged blade could still cut through almost anything. Here though, more important than the sword, were Shoren's knives. He had three of them. One on his belt, a shorter one hidden in his left boot, and another short one strapped to his wrist. It was a good thing that his coat ran all the way to his boots, Shoren reflected, as he pulled the collar of the coat around his ears before stepping into the cold Denver morning. Otherwise someone might get a good look at the sword, get some other street toughs together, and try to take him. A sword meant either a soldier or money, and any mere soldier couldn't afford Shoren's sword. Street toughs would also be confident that even if a rich man could use the blade, he couldn't kill five or six drunken thieves. Shoren would have little difficulty doing that, but he didn't want to draw attention to himself. Corpses did tend to do that.

Another thing. Most of the cutpurses and footpads were related to many of the legitimate business owners. Often a band of cutpurse brothers or cousins would lurk around their father's or uncle's business and steal from and kill the people who happened by. Shoren knew that Frenk, owner of the Peak, had several nephews like that, and Frenk probably wouldn't appreciate it if Shoren killed them. He wouldn't stop serving Shoren, but Shoren's ability to hold a private conversation in Frenk's tavern would be at an end.

With that thought in mind, Shoren stepped outside. Out of the corner of his eye he noticed a filthy young man in ragged clothes looking at him from the alleyway. At Shoren's cold glare, the man grimaced and slunk away. Shaking his head, Shoren made his way to the stables. When he got there, the stable boy brought out his roan mustang already saddled and bridled. Shoren thanked the boy, gave him three copper pennies for taking such good care of his horse, and rode off. The care was expensive, but at least it meant that Shoren would never walk out of the tavern to discover that his horse had been stolen. It also meant that the stable boy would feed his horse the grain normally reserved for Frenk's horses – the non-moldy grain. Of course, pennies didn't always work with the stable boy, who was Frenk's fifteen-year-old nephew, but the threat of fist, boot and blade helped. When Shoren looked at the boy, he could still see the small scar on his cheek from the last time Shoren's horse hadn't gotten clean grain and water. Shoren believed the boy had learned to keep his word. Well, at least he had learned to keep it with Shoren.

Shoren patted his horse on the neck and started to lead the animal away. When he got to the more open streets in the palace district he would mount. Here though, in the narrow streets, he had to lead the roan. His horse's name was Guerrero. That was an ancient word meaning "warrior." Guerrero was Shoren's warhorse, the horse he used in battle, so Shoren needed to take care of him. Guerrero snorted and shook his head.

Shoren patted his neck again, but soon discovered just what Guerrero was snorting at. Eight filthy, ragged men were spreading out around him. Each carried a rusty sword and a shield. Three of the men also brandished spears and the others long, sharpened sticks. These were no drunken louts. They carried ropes and lassos. Horse thieves.

The men around Shoren said nothing. Shoren also said nothing. Any attempts to talk his way out would fall on deaf ears. Shoren gripped his sword. One of the men stepped forward. In one smooth movement, Shoren pulled his blade free and slashed the man's throat. The other men rushed forward in a flurry of action. Shoren ducked one man's swing and then stabbed him in the belly, only to notice that three of the men were trying to capture Guerrero. One of the men managed to get a rope around Guerrero's neck, only to get a hoof in the face. When Shoren was able to see the man again, his entire head was a shattered bloody mess.

Shoren hissed as a blade cut across his shoulder. He twisted and had to slam his sword into his attacker's neck, where it slipped. The sword slid out of his hand when his attacker fell back into his friend. Another one of the men saw them and dropped his rope to rush Shoren. Quick as thought, Shoren pulled free his knife and threw it. The knife was a blur as it slid into the man's chest. The remaining three men stood up and waved their weapons. One man hurled his spear. It missed, but Shoren fell while deflecting it. Looking up, he saw the point of a sword about to stab him, and a short prayer began to materialize in his mind. *Dear spirits, bless us now as we die, bless us as you blessed us in life. Accept my soul into your eternal embrace and protect me from the black spirits who do me harm. Save those I could not save, and bless those I could not...*bloody hell. Shoren saw the man's surprise and rage as a gleaming long sword thrust through him. The dying man fell to the ground, and Shoren suddenly found a hand right in his face. He gripped and recognized his savior. Josef stood there, grinning, sword in hand, covered with blood, and bodies all around. After a few minutes, Shoren grinned too. Josef shook his head.

"Damn, Shoren. I'da thought you'd have been able to take 'em all on, if it weren't for dat blasted spear dere at da end. But I tink you did well. Except I had to save your ass dere at da end, aye? Heh-heh. But I'm thinkin' you'd have done better to keep your sword dere at da…"

"Josef, don't think me ungrateful. Please. But…what are you doing here? A man of your importance doesn't belong down here. Not in the slums."

"Well, Shoren, many would be saying da same ting about you. I'd like to be knowin' meself. I'm sure you ain't down here for da pleasant scenery. But what you be doing down here be your business, me friend, and not for me to know. But I'd be asking you to keep your nose out'a me own business if you'd like to be doing da proper ting."

"I'm sorry. I'm sorry. I just thought I'd ask."

"Well, now dat da formalities be out'a da way, maybe you'd be tinkin' to buy your friend a drink, aye? Maybe at dis Golden Peak? Mayhap while we drink, we can talk over da last-minute orders? We will. I be wantin' a drink."

"Yes, sir. I'll have to see about Frenk cleaning up this mess. Hopefully I didn't kill anyone he's related to. If that's the case I might have some difficulties in the near future, even if he doesn't round up a mob for revenge. Frenk might even stop serving me."

With that distressing thought, the two walked inside. As soon as they did, they ran into Frenk himself, a scrawny, weasel-looking fellow with shifty black eyes, with his greasy, unkempt black hair hanging down to cover his face like a mask. Frenk slunk up and started screaming at the two soldiers the instant they walked in.

"Murderers! Murder! You have killed my son! Murderers! Get out of my tavern. I'll call the Watch! How dare you call yourselves soldiers! When the army gets done with you I bet you'll…" The scoundrel's tirade was cut off as Josef wrapped one of his huge meaty hands around Frenk's throat.

"Now just ye listen here, you little scheming weasel." Josef's voice came out low and dangerous. "Dat rat ye call a son dats lying out dare in da street jest now tried to kill me friend. So good riddance I say, and if you be tinkin' to dispute it, well dis sword could drink some more blood tonight.

"Ah, yes. One more ting. If you be tinkin' ta call de Watch down here, I may just have dem check out your tavern here. Jest looking around I be see'n many tings dat be illegal. Why, over dere I be see'n at least four women for hire right over in dat corner. Enough to land you in prison at da very least! Plus, I be hear'n dat you sell bad whiskey and bad grain for da horses, and I've even heard some tales o' guests, rich guests, disappearing when dey be stay'n at your inn. Now, I can't say what happened to dem, but dat along wid da rest be enough to land yer head on da chopp'n block. Wouldn' you be say'n so?"

The last question he directed toward Shoren, who nodded his grim agreement. Frenk just paled and pulled himself free and scuttled off to the back of the inn, muttering apologies the whole way, and promising them the best mead "on the house."

That situation taken care of, Josef swiveled his glare all around the room. Shoren heard muttered curses as men and women alike knocked down tables, chairs and each other in their hurry to get out of the sight of this huge, angry general who looked like he made a habit of decapitating criminals for sport. Which, Shoren reflected, knowing Josef, the man probably did.

As the two men seated themselves at a newly vacated table, a nervously sweating Frenk came up to them and proffered to each a large tankard of mead. Shoren took his with neither comment nor flamboyance, but Josef took his with a huge toothy grin that he flashed at Frenk, causing the poor man to nearly drop the tray in terror. Shoren just shook his head.

Once the mead was set down in front of them and Frenk had scurried away once again, Josef started out the conversation, moving immediately to advice and last minute orders.

"Well, Shoren, at least dis does save ya da ride all da way back up to headquarters. Anyway, da Emperor has decided that I'll be providing yer troops wid an escort dat will take ya to de edge o' Denver. I convinced him o' dat so dat I can at least see ya off to take care o' yer business wid Rekii. Also, yer troops are being beefed up wid anuder thousand of my infantry. Dey'll be wid ya just in case tings turn south, but I'm hoping ya'll be sending 'em back to me alive, right?"

"Josef, you know that I want to send your troops back to you alive. I'm just hoping to take Rekii out with as few deaths as possible. Sadly, I think that many of the soldiers, your own included, are going to die."

"Ahh, well. Da important ting is for you to capture dat bastard Rekii and get your troops up to da invasion force. I not be allowed to tell anyone dis, but de Kirendadi have chased General Mekal's forces all da way back to the border. If he loses, we'll be fightin' 'em here, in our country. Maybe it'll teach 'em to be careful who dey pick fights wid, eh? Especially wid stone hard, skinny bastards from da mountains. Anudder ting. Don't be trusting yer officers, 'specially not da lords. Each of 'em will stab ya in da back, if'n ye not be careful enough."

"Thanks, Josef. Although I already knew that last bit, about not trusting anyone I don't have to. I had probably better get some sleep. You too. We're leaving tomorrow."

"All right, Shoren, all right. Just let me finish my mead first. I'da never be wanting ta waste such good mead." The big man let a grin split his face. "And it's free, too! Ha-ha!"

CHAPTER FOUR

Captain Frank Miller leaned back in his saddle, surveying the carnage below. Everywhere he looked he saw the corpses of women and young children, all slaughtered in a hail of gunfire.

Frank had seen similar scenes, both in the Third Korean War and the Mexican Gulf War. This time it was different though, probably because both the killed and the killers were American. He sighed inwardly. It was more than six years since the bombs fell, and he was tired of waiting for help. No one had come to save them, but then again, it could just be that there was no one left to do any saving. Ah, well. It was unimportant. What was important was what he and his fellow marines were about, finding these killers and putting a stop to them.

He jerked his head, and the three other marines turned their horses. All three checked the ammunition for their rifles and pistols, secured their helmets and body armor, and rode quickly to catch up to Frank. Not for the first time, Frank thought that at some point they would have to find some other way once all their firepower ran out. Frank shrugged. That was a question for another day. In fact, he and his men were chasing the bandits not only to stop the killing of women and children, but also to gather up some more bullets and explosives. One of the other marines, a corporal named Robert, spurred his horse until he rode next to Frank.

"Sir, I've not asked you about this before, but we've been tracking these men for three days. Maybe it would be best if we just went home."

"And let more people die just because these psychos are hard to find? You're a marine!" Frank realized that he had been snarling and had his fist raised. Just because the world was going to hell didn't mean that he had to cause division in his own ranks. He calmed his voice down and said, "Look, I know this is tough, but we have to catch these guys. If we don't, they'll probably just come back and kill more people. Do you understand?"

Robert lowered his eyes and muttered under his breath, "Yes, sir."

Frank looked back at the other men. "Do the others feel this way?" he asked, still keeping his voice low. "Because if they do, maybe it's time to turn back. Otherwise, we keep going."

Robert saluted. "Yes, sir." He then added in a lower tone, "Even though I think this might be a mistake, you still have my support, sir."

"Thank you, Robert. I know I can count on you."

"Yes, sir. Permission to withdraw, sir?"

"Yes, and thank you for bringing me your thoughts. This is a team, after all, and everyone has something to contribute."

Robert nodded, but didn't say anything. In fact, he looked a little relieved to have been able to have his say. With that thought in mind, Frank looked at the ground and suddenly noticed horse tracks. He raised his hand and the other three men stopped. Frank quickly motioned for his men to dismount, which they did, immediately gathering around him.

"What is it, sir?" That came from Private John McCarter, a young marine who had barely finished his training when the nukes hit. He was still young, but in no way inexperienced, not any more.

"Horse tracks." Frank pointed at the spot where he had first seen them. He then motioned with his arm to indicate where the tracks appeared to go. "I saw them back there, in the mud. It looks to be about six or seven horses, and the tracks look fresh. John, I want you to watch the horses. The rest of us are going to follow these tracks and see if we can find some more traces." By the time the marines got out a "yes, sir," he was already pulling equipment off his horse.

Once all the weapons had been gathered, and the horses secured, Frank led the two remaining marines into the woods. The other man was a private they had found wounded on the roadside, nearly four years before. The man had opted not to give his name then, and he had kept it that way, preferring to be called "Tiny." Tiny was about six feet seven inches tall, with shoulders to equal any two men's, and was completely out of his mind. Though Frank wasn't sure, he thought he recognized Tiny from a short time he had spent as a guard in a military prison. He believed Tiny to be a man by the name of Charles Nixon, who had been given three consecutive life sentences for killing a superior officer in a reportedly brutal fashion. The officer in question had been sleeping with Nixon's wife, but the military conveniently ignored that fact.

Frank led Robert and Tiny into the woods, staying to the sides of the muddy trail where they had found the tracks. When the tracks led to an area that wasn't so muddy, they simply seemed to vanish. The three marines fanned out to find some other sign. Frank saw what he thought to be an empty beer bottle, but Tiny made the marine sign for "sounds this way." Frank and Robert quickly hurried over to where Tiny was standing, looking at a small clearing. In the grove stood seven men, each with lots of guns, lots of ammo, and drunk as lords. Frank smiled a wolfish smile. This should be easy.

Just as Frank raised his rifle to shoot, Tiny motioned for him to wait. He then pointed out to Frank five more men who were not drunk, each of them with a high-powered rifle and numerous grenades, all with eyes to make a winter day seem warm. Frank nodded and made the signs to shoot those men first. They lifted their rifles and opened fire. One man jerked as bullets riddled his body, dead before he hit the ground. Two others died in a similar fashion, but the two survivors quickly started returning fire, with the seven drunken men raising their weapons, some even firing in seemingly random directions. Frank started to fire into the group of drunks, but immediately realized that one of the drunks was aiming an RPG or Rocket Propelled Grenade right at his own position. Frank's eyes opened wide but he lowered his rifle and leaped out of the way just as the woods around him burst into flame. Frank sat upright just in time to see the man load a second grenade and look right at him. This was not good. Not good at all.

John jumped as he heard the explosion, but immediately got hold of himself and settled the horses, which were terrified by the explosion and gunfire. Once he had the horses calmed down, a second explosion terrified them all again. With a muttered curse he grabbed his rifle and looked toward the source of the explosions. He longed to help his comrades, but Frank had told him to stay with the horses.

That was unfair. Even though he was very young when compared to the others, he had still been a marine for six years. Now sure, for most of that time the United States of America didn't exist, and by default neither did the marines, but he had passed the training, and once a marine, always a marine. Screw it, he decided, he was going to help Frank and the others whether they wanted it or not.

Now that John had finally made the decision to help, he had to figure out a way to do it. He checked his ammo and grenades, then carefully made his way in the direction of the explosions. After a few minutes, he was able to see the fighting, and winced as a bullet buzzed past his ear. He could feel his heart thumping in his chest. Despite having lived for six years always on the hunt, tracking and killing those who would threaten their new community, John had seen relatively little action. Frank had always had him providing covering fire, or guarding the horses, or people, or whatever. He had killed some men, but only a few, and it had never been in a firefight like this.

Another bullet flew past. His breathing heavy, John could now see the fighting. Frank was on the run, with what seemed to be a huge drunken man struggling with some sort of rocket device, but John didn't recognize it. Suddenly, the man raised the device and fired, shooting off a high-tech rocket that sped toward Frank with lethal speed.

"Holy shit!" Then, with more of a whimpering tone, he began to curse under his breath "shit, shit, shit, shit…" He finally recognized the weapon, an Anti-Personnel Movement-Tracker RPG. Each rocket had an internal computer that latched onto a target, and as long as the computer detected movement, it could chase its target. Pretty much the only way to escape it was to trick the computer into hitting something else, like Frank was doing, causing the computer to send the rocket right into a small cluster of trees. John could even see the computer brain detach itself shortly before impact, a money-saving technique that allowed a used computer brain to be reset and attached to a new rocket, making the whole system far less expensive.

This was bad. John could also see Robert and Tiny, both of whom were engaged in firefights of their own, each pinned down and unable to help the other, let alone poor Frank. "Bad" did not even begin to describe the situation. John spared a glance at Frank, and things were even worse for him. Frank had fallen, and it looked like he had twisted his ankle. The big man with the RPG had seen this and was busily working to load yet another round! The man's drunken state notwithstanding, it appeared to John as though he was having a difficult time with it. Oops. Never mind. He just finished and was doing his best to get a level shot, a shot that wouldn't miss.

John raised his rifle. The big man's head was in his sights now, just waiting for a bullet. *Well,* John thought, *never let it be said that I ever refused a request.* As though it had a mind of its own, John's finger tightened, and then squeezed. Just a short burst. Ammo was scarce. He didn't miss, and the big man's head exploded like an overripe watermelon dropped on the floor. Bullets suddenly sprayed in John's direction, but he was already moving. Once again, as if of its own accord, his finger squeezed the trigger and another man fell, and then another, and another.

Less than a minute passed, and he had already reached Frank and was pulling him out of harm's way, and the men who had pinned Tiny and Robert down were now shooting at the new threat, shooting at him. This of course freed Tiny and Robert to turn the tables on the attackers, and begin to cut them down with heavy machine gun fire. John was exultant. He had saved Frank and freed Robert and Tiny to finally shoot back. He was a hero.

Suddenly John realized that he was on the ground! Well, wasn't that odd. He tried to push himself up, but his arms were jelly. He was wet, he realized, covered in some warm, sticky liquid. He could see some of the liquid on the ground and it was a bright shiny red. He could hear some gunfire, but it was distant, far away. After what seemed a long time, he couldn't hear it at all. He could hear other sounds though. Voices mostly. He couldn't make out the words, and that was odd too. He should be able to understand them. Frank appeared over him, and John smiled.

Good, he thought, *at least Frank made it. Hey! There were Tiny and Robert too! We all lived! Well, that's good. Maybe, we can celebrate later, with some of the liquor back at the bar. Hey guys, I did good today, didn't I. Yeah. I'll do good next time too. And after that, and all the times that come. Yeah.* John coughed up some more blood.

With a start, John realized that he had actually been saying all these things aloud. That was odd. He thought that if he was talking at least he ought to notice. He realized that Frank was shouting, and Tiny wasn't there anymore. No, there he was. He had out all sorts of medicines and supplies, and he was working on John's stomach. *Oh, John thought to himself, I must have been shot. I didn't know it because I've never been shot before. It's good Tiny's working on it though. Tiny was always good with medicine. He likes to help people.* In fact, John remembered Tiny saying once that if he hadn't been drafted he would have finished medical school and become a doctor. *Yeah, good old Tiny, always helping people.*

"Ahhhhhhhhhhhhh!" John let out a huge scream as Tiny pulled a bullet from his stomach. Tiny frowned. He had two more to take out, and John was losing blood fast. Tiny set his teeth and began to pull out a second bullet. John let out another scream as this one came loose, even louder than before. Tiny nodded to himself. If John continued to scream so loudly, it meant he was still conscious and aware of what was going on. Finally, Tiny was able to pull out the last bullet. As it came out, John let out another bloodcurdling scream. As Tiny sat back on his heels, Robert moved in to clean the wounds with antiseptic, and then to bandage them. With all this done, Tiny looked over at Frank and then Robert. Frank had been cut in several places by flying shrapnel, and it looked as though some had stuck in his skin. None of it looked serious, but Tiny would have to look at it more closely. Robert, however, had been shot. There was a large bleeding wound on his left shoulder, but it looked as though the bullet had skimmed the top. That was lucky. He looked back at John. John looked to be unconscious, but his breathing was regular. There was still the chance of infection, and the large loss of blood was a concern, but Tiny and Robert had closed the wound and the antiseptics should have cleaned everything up. Tiny looked to Frank, who was saying they should probably just rest here for a bit, that they were in no condition to travel. Tiny had to agree. He looked back at John, unsure if John would even live. At least the bullets hadn't hit any major organs. Tiny looked down at himself. He had been hit by shrapnel too. Not a one of them was ready to travel, let alone fight. Hopefully they wouldn't encounter anyone on the way home.

CHAPTER FIVE

Major General Josef Nixon grimaced as he looked at himself in the mirror. Ten years behind a desk had not been kind to him. He had managed to get his heavy mail on, but the banded metal breastplate was simply too tight. Surely it hadn't been that long since he had been out in the field. Maybe he could just put on a dress uniform instead… No! He would get this blasted armor on. No matter what.

With a grimace, Josef rang the bell that would call a few of his servants. The door to his room quickly opened and three maids ran in. Once the three saw Josef in his mail, holding the steel breastplate, each of them tried to hold back smiles. They weren't quick enough though, and the smiles did nothing to improve Josef's mood.

"Well!" he barked, waving the armor in their faces. "Help me into this thing!"

Without a word, the three women positioned the armor over Josef's chest and one of them began pulling on the straps. The straps refused to budge; a second maid pulled with the first to make it move. The two girls made a grand show of struggling to tighten the straps, with one girl's foot on Josef's back for leverage and the other girl pulling on her. The third maid grinned at this, but turned to gather the rest of the armor, the helmet, the gauntlets, the greaves, the girdle and scabbard, and finally the boots. The large shield she just left leaning against the wall because she wasn't sure if she could even lift the thing.

Finally the breastplate was on, and when Josef mentioned that the bulge in the middle was because the armor must have warped, his maids agreed. Yes. Of course, metal does that. He muttered a curse under his breath and ignored the suddenly wide eyes and fake-shocked looks he received. The girls had been maids there long enough that they were used to it. He harrumphed loudly though when the two girls who had tightened the straps on his armor began talking quietly about the values of clean speech.

Once all the armor was on, with his helmet gripped in one hand and his shield in the other, Josef walked toward the stables, the girls following him, telling each other how dashing he was, all dressed up in his fine armor. The other servants all around smiled when they saw Josef stalking toward the stables with the three chattering magpies following him. Finally, Josef turned and told the girls that if they wanted to make themselves useful they could find him some breakfast. The girls looked almost hurt at the request, and when Josef turned his back, one stuck out her tongue at him.

Josef reached the stables and made sure all his supplies were ready, and then began to saddle his massive charger, known to the ancients as a Clydesdale. Once his horse was fully saddled and armored, the three young maids brought him breakfast. He sighed.

"I hate fruit." The girls had brought him a bowl of fruit and nuts – blackberries, strawberries and cherries, and also melon slices and walnuts. All in all, it was a healthful meal, about as plain as it was healthy. Josef muttered another curse. "I want some meat! Maybe some eggs too. Not this, this...fruit! Ah! Why bother?"

"Well, if you had given us time I'm sure we could have found you some meat and eggs. But you have to be ready to ride soon, and we don't want you to be late." With a significant glance at the bulge in his middle, she added, "Also, Lina, Lisa and I thought you would appreciate some healthy fruit."

This all came from the oldest of the girls, Mari. She claimed to be twenty-five, but she was probably as young as twenty. The other two were even younger. Josef had hired the three "sisters" only a year before, when he found them on his doorstep, fleeing from a life of "professional companionship." The man who had been controlling their lives had tracked them to Josef's home, and once Josef realized what had been going on, he had resolved to help them.

He remembered that night as though it was only the night before. The girls' master had come barging up to Josef's door, demanding to have his slaves back. Actually the man said the three girls were his orphaned nieces, but were ungrateful, lazy girls who thought they could squirm their way into the house and bed of a rich man who would make them into ladies. Josef remembered his response as well.

"Really, and I be supposin' dat dese three girls be lying to me, heh? Dey be telling me a different story, one where you be forcing 'em inta the beds o' many rich men, all for yer benefit. Unless ya can be convincing me otherwise, de girls be staying here wid me."

"What lies have they been telling you? They are my nieces, and I would never do anything to harm them! Sir, you have to hand them over to me, or I will be forced to contact the authorities."

"I be de authorities ya blasted fool! I be Josef Nixon, major general o' de Imperial Army! Get off me property, or I'll arrest you, send you ta trial, and den kill you! Wid me own sword!"

The man growled at this and drew his sword, clearly desperate. His eyes darted in every direction, hoping for a way out. When he saw none, he pointed his sword at Josef.

"This is just more proof that the throne is trying to cheat an honest businessman! Give me back my girls or suffer the consequences! I am a powerful man in this city and I can have you arrested. This is your last chance!"

Josef said nothing, only smiled. He was wearing both the short sword and the long sword that was the standard of any infantryman. He bared his teeth. The short was better for these close quarters. He drew the short blade at his hip, ignoring the larger and more impressive sword strapped to his back. Without hesitation, he plunged into combat.

The other man barely had time to react to Josef's attacks. The short sword striking past his defenses was like a viper. The man couldn't bring his large, unwieldy sword to bear upon Josef, and very quickly the short blade stabbed through the man's stomach. Josef pulled the blade out slightly, adjusted the angle and stabbed again, up into the man's chest. With blood dripping from the man's mouth, Josef leaned in and whispered in his ear.

"A powerful man ye may be, but now ye be lying dead upon my sword. I'll be leaving ya in de worst part o' de city, so dat yer brothers may see ye and know fear." Josef smiled the smile a lion smiles when he sights his prey. "Ye however, will die alone, tonight, on a rainy street. Pleasant dreams."

Josef turned away and went inside. From that day on, the three girls would be his maids. He recalled the words of his dead wife, who said that when you save someone they become your responsibility. He hoped she would smile on his efforts to cleanse the city of scourges like that man. After that night he embarked on one of the most relentless hunts Denver had ever known. Josef hunted for the slave masters with an intensity bordering on obsession. Thanks to his efforts, slavery and the slavers had been all but wiped out in Denver. Once Josef had seen Shoren safely off, he intended to remove the "all but."

Josef's mount tossed his head, jangling his harness and armor, and bringing Josef's mind back to the present. He finished his breakfast, reflecting that a meal of fruits and nuts wasn't so bad. He then mounted his horse and rode out to where his infantry was gathered. Whenever he saw Denver foot soldiers he had to smile.

The men were standing shoulder-to-shoulder, shields locked and weapons at the ready. They wore steel armor that would have been familiar to Julius Caesar, with a long sword at the hip, a short sword strapped to their backs, and a crossbow and quiver full of bolts. The Denver Legions were perhaps the most adaptive and flexible soldiers of any military, able to travel upwards of twenty-five miles a day.

Everywhere Josef looked soldiers were getting ready. Horses were being saddled, weapons drawn and re-sheathed, and officers all about heckling men to move. Josef easily picked out the commanders and galloped his horse to take charge. The commanders deferred to him instantly; he was the major general.

Josef would only be taking a small contingent of infantry to the border, for their main purpose was to provide reinforcements in the event Shoren needed help in his fight against Rekii. Once Shoren was finished, Josef's troops would remain at the border, guarding against potential Kirendadi raids. The hope was that their presence would prevent the Kirendadi from taking retribution on Denver.

Josef realized that the sun had almost broken the horizon, yet the newly risen High Commander Shoren was nowhere to be seen. His troops were already organized, and the supplies for his army packed, but the man himself was not present. That did not bode well for this expedition.

☆ ☆ ☆

Shoren was still in his rooms in the Royal Palace, putting on his armor. He moved quickly, but he did not allow his only servant, Jon, to assist him with the armor; instead Jon packed Shoren's few personal effects. Shoren had spent most of the early morning meeting with his staff, discussing a report on Rekii's numbers. The other generals, especially those few of the nobility who had seen no actual combat, wanted to bring more troops. With some trepidation Shoren revealed what he knew from Josef about General Mekel's situation, about the many defeats, and about the Kirendadi oath of vengeance.

Shoren's staff had agreed to the current troop level, but only after they realized that their commander was not going to budge and that arguing further would only delay the inevitable outcome: marching with the troops they had. This left Shoren rushing to put on his armor and pack up his few belongings. Thankfully, Jon had done the packing. The rotund little man had even laid out Shoren's armor and had brought his master a small but hot breakfast of oatmeal and dried fruits.

"Delicious, Jon! This is truly good. It is an excellent example of the culinary arts. The palace should give the cook a raise."

"Thank you, my lord. Actually, I cooked the oatmeal. It was a little difficult to find the fruits, but I thought you would like them, my lord."

Shoren cocked his head and looked at the short man. "Really? Well, I'll give you a raise then. I may just have you cook for me instead of eating the camp rations. That would surely be a pleasant change."

"No, my lord, I cannot accept a raise for simply doing my job. Besides, I would never want to rise above my station." The man looked horrified at the very thought. "Money is for lords and merchants, not a humble serving man, my lord."

"Nonsense. You do a good job, and you get good rewards. You do a better job, and you get better rewards." All this came while Shoren was struggling with a gauntlet and trying to eat at the same time.

He waved a spoon at Jon and continued, "Stop all of that 'my lord' business too. It's really irritating."

"As you say, my lord. I'm sorry, my lord, it's just habit. My lord."

Shoren sighed. Jon would probably end every statement with "my lord" now, just to annoy him. Servants had their ways and you had yours, but a balance was required or you would end up with poorly trained servants that you had to constantly replace. Shoren wished that somebody would just call him Shoren though.

Shoren shook his head and gave his green commander's cape a tug. He supposed he could always just not take any servants, but then he would have to set up his tent and belongings, clean his laundry, and deal with any number of small chores that servants normally took care of. Shoren laughed. He could just picture himself down at the river knee-deep in water with the washing women cleaning his clothes.

Shoren slipped on his helmet, belted on his sword and quiver, shouldered his horse bow, and glided out of the room. As he did, the members of his staff who had not yet departed joined him, demanding his attention with their petty complaints about rank and status and the privileges of their lineage.

Shoren sighed and tried to pay attention, but – after a fleeting thought that if he had been allowed to choose his own subordinates he would have selected men who had risen to officership through talent and skill rather than money and calculated schemes – he blocked out the prattle. Such men desired army positions only for the political power they brought, unlike the soldiers who, like Shoren, had been in the army since before they had lived a full decade. They were the true army, once rank-and-file soldiers who rose to officership and then became generals, commanders and beyond. Why, even Major General Josef had risen in such a manner.

Wishing was pointless however. While it was sad that Denver's corruption spread even to the army, allowing incompetent officers to achieve positions of incredible influence and authority, there was nothing that could be done. That was one reason most soldiers distrusted officers they were unfamiliar with, and why they were loyal to their commanders and the military. Not to Denver, but to their fellows.

Most nobles viewed soldiers as nothing more than a convenient tool for advancement.

Shoren shook his head. *Enough of that.* He was already at the stables, his horse saddled and bridled, ready to ride. Shoren mounted Guerrero with practiced ease. His staff was not too quick to mount, some of them being largely unfamiliar with horses.

Charlz Smied was having a particularly rough time getting into the saddle. He was young, only about fifteen or so. Whatever his age, Shoren believed Charlz to be much too young and inexperienced to be in the field. Charlz' parents, however, wanted the boy to go along, for a dual, if unstated, reason: They wanted their heir, Charlz' older brother Jamz, to establish himself in Denver without Charlz' interference, so that Jamz could carry his arguments with his own weight; after all, he had a brother in the field.

Once everyone was mounted, Shoren turned his horse out of the stable, with a spoken command to form up behind him. As he did so however, he noticed the heir to the throne, his cousin Richerd McCarter, seated on his horse at the end of the stable. Richerd made the military hand signal for *Come and speak to me. Alone.* With a muttered oath, Shoren nudged his horse to meet Richerd.

"Well, well, well. Shoren. I would hope that you would get to your army soon. They seem impatient to leave." As Richerd said this, his black-gloved hand caressed the hilt of the short curved blade at his hip.

"What do you want with me, hmm? I do need to get to my army, and you need to attend your father. I'm sure he would be displeased if you were late for a session in the Throne Room."

"Shoren, my father is not yet even out of bed. He grows weaker day by day. I will soon ascend the throne and gather the support of my greatest nobles, the ones with the most promise."

Shoren's voice grew flat. "I will support the throne, cousin, the throne and Denver. Denver above all. The army code."

"Well, just stick by your army code and kill those you're supposed to kill. Good-bye, Shoren." Without another word Richerd turned his horse and rode away. Shoren grimaced and wished that Richerd would involve someone else in his endless scheming.

Even Elina was tied up in it. A few days prior, she had implored Shoren to support Richerd. She had asked him also to return home quickly, as though a war could be finished simply by the desire of the commander! She feared for his position, and for her future position in the Imperial Court.

Elina had come across Shoren while he was walking in one of the garden mazes of the Imperial Palace. He had just ended a meeting with his subordinates over the supply trains needed to supply the army, a very dull and dry matter. Shoren had only meant to walk the gardens and clear his head before he went back in to finalize the details, but here was the Lady Elina coming toward him with one of her maids, Jenni he thought, in tow.

Once she saw him she descended upon him like a hawk on a rabbit. Well, Shoren wasn't exactly a rabbit, but that's how it seemed. Once she reached him, she grabbed him by the sleeve of his shirt, green to indicate his status as a cavalry officer, and shooed her maid away. She fixed him with a hard glare, but ruined it by running her fingers through his hair.

"Shoren, Shoren, Shoren. I hear it's almost time for you to leave for war. Isn't that what you're doing here, in the Palace, planning your war?" She almost seemed to purr. When he opened his mouth to speak, she put a finger to his lips to silence him. "I hope you don't focus everything on this war and forget your place here in Denver. I've watched you squander away many opportunities that could have greatly advanced your position here. You won't let that all go to waste, will you?"

Shoren backed away from her. He certainly didn't want to talk to Elina, or anyone else for that matter. He just wanted to walk the gardens and forget all the scheming, just for a few minutes.

She frowned. "Well? Aren't you going to say something?" She hit his chest. "Maybe you'd like to say that you're sorry for ignoring me! Maybe you'd like to apologize for going off to war again, leaving me back here wondering if you're going to come home? Would you like to say that? Every other noble girl is married, Shoren. I'm the only one who's not. What am I waiting for? For you to finally 'be ready'? For you to come home from war like some great hero and then ask me? Or maybe you intend to destroy and squander everything your family has gained for you first, so that we can live like commoners? Is that your plan? Is it? Answer me!" That last came out in a shriek.

Shoren caught her hand before she could hit him again. That punch had hurt. "No, Elina, I don't want to squander my position." He held up a hand as soon as she opened her mouth. "I need you to watch it for me. I have no talent for the scheming and backstabbing of the court; my true skill lies in war. That is what I was meant to do. And it's not my war. I wish I didn't have to go, but it is what it is. There is nothing we can do to change it. As for marriage, maybe after this is all over. Once the war is done, we can get married. If that's what you want." He sighed. Shoren truly did not want to marry Elina, but there were very few other options available to him. Actually, there truly were no other options. He shrugged. At least it made Elina happy.

Elina positively beamed. She grinned up at him and stroked his face. "Thank you, Shoren. I'll make you proud. I'll advance our family, but I want a promise that you'll marry me."

Shoren tried to make his face look tender and loving, but he couldn't quite make it happen. He settled for a wry smile. "I promise, Elina. When I come back from Kirendad, we'll get married."

Elina looked at the ground. In a small voice she thanked him. Shoren guessed that he hadn't even managed a smile. Finally, she looked up. "There's something I want you to remember. Support Richerd. I don't like him, but he is the current heir to the throne. I know that he's gathering support for his ascension, so try not to offend him. Please?"

"I can't promise to support him, Elina. I can only promise to support the heir the Emperor names."

Elina sighed. "I suppose that's all I can ask of you, Shoren. But at least promise me that you won't oppose him. He does stand the best chance of getting named, and he will remember any opposition."

"I can promise that. Not that I'll be able to support or oppose anybody while I'm off fighting the northerners."

She seemed satisfied with that and leaned up for a good-bye kiss. Shoren hesitated, but gave her a kiss, albeit a mild one. She backed away, looking slightly disappointed, and called Jenni to her. Her maid quickly caught up to Elina as she strode down the garden path.

Shoren sighed but walked back into the Palace, knowing that awaiting him were endless discussions over amounts of grain and feed, over a thousand little things that required his supervision, if not his input. It would be boring, but at least he would have the meeting in the garden to occupy his mind. Elina, his new fiancée Elina, had given him many things to think over.

Shoren's mind was drawn back to the present by the sounds of the army making ready to leave. Idly, he wished his people possessed the secrets of the ancient flamethrowers or thunder lances. At least his own people's repeating crossbows were known only to Denver workers.

Shoren looked out at the army, beginning to set up in marching formation. The infantry with their huge shields locked together – each man disciplined to the point that he could execute the most complex of battle maneuvers in his sleep – was able to march longer and faster than any other comparable infantry force. Although most commanders set a pace of twenty-five miles a day, Shoren had known the infantry to march upwards of thirty-five miles a day, forty when pressed.

Denver cavalry too, was something else. Although not as effective as the Kirendadi raiders, let alone the horsemen from the Plains, Denver light cavalry could tear apart almost any enemy without once meeting sword-to-sword. Their light horse bows gave them the ability to decimate any heavy infantry or cavalry. Denver heavy cavalry were great huge men, on massive horses, covered in armor, each man a living arsenal. Cavalrymen had massive steel swords, mighty lances, and even carried some shorter spears to break up the enemy from a distance.

The Denver forces even trained huge mastiffs to charge at the enemy to break up their shield formations. The dogs were huge, easily two or three hundred pounds, and covered in leather armor, with steel spikes sticking out. They were trained to break up enemy formations so that the Denver soldiers could reach them already shattered, and could then tear the enemy to pieces. Once the human soldiers arrived, the hound masters would sound their whistles to call the dogs back, safe and sound.

Not all the soldiers were wearing their armor today. Only the guards at the edge of the formation would do so, because they wanted to move quickly, but also be able to defend themselves if they were attacked, as unlikely as that seemed in their own lands. Once Shoren's troops reached Kirendad however, all the soldiers would be armed and armored all the time.

Once the formations were set up, the columns began moving down the ancient highway that led to Kirendad. The highway followed the original route from the Lost Times, even though it had been built over many times since then. The road eventually splintered off into many different directions, toward the Great River and beyond, and even to the ocean. Shoren would be following the road to Laramie, a small village left over from the Lost Times. Denver itself was such a place, even though it was no longer on the original site. Laramie was on the original location; a town that had not moved from its former position but had instead persevered through the ruination of the ending of the Lost Times and throughout the two thousand years since.

Laramie was on the border of the empire and was currently occupied by Rekii's forces. Shoren's first task would be to liberate it from Rekii and then to set up the town as a base of operations from which he could find and destroy Rekii. Laramie was about a hard week's march away.

CHAPTER SIX

Willem watched from his vantage point in the mountains that guarded the road to Laramie as the Denver soldiers made their way down the road. He couldn't see how many of them there were, but he knew that they would be enough. He had little doubt that the soldiers would be able to retake Laramie, but what they did then was anyone's guess. He shrugged. That's why he was a scout, not an officer. He didn't have the head for such planning. He did know that he had to report this to General Rekii right away. Willem jumped on his horse and sped off toward Laramie, knowing that Rekii's troops needed to make ready immediately.

✧ ✧ ✧

Shoren looked down at Laramie, his staff gathered around him. Ryon edged his horse up behind Shoren, looking like he wanted to say something, but uneasy about doing so. Shoren had been studying the landscape around Laramie for almost two hours, and what he saw, combined with the scouts' reports, indicated to him that Laramie would be a tough nut to crack. He thought that he should be able to simply knock down the town's walls and ride right in. It was not the taking that worried him, it was the keeping. As easy as it would be for Shoren to capture Laramie, it would be just as easy for Rekii to recapture it.

Finally Shoren turned to his staff. "I know how to capture the town. What we need to do is to knock down the walls and then ride in. However, first we need to cut enough logs to repair the timber walls so that Rekii cannot retake it. I want the men to start cutting down the logs now. Get to it!"

As his senior officers hastily made off, Shoren turned to Ryon and whispered to him that he should take his cavalry around the hills to the other side of the town so the army could come on it from both sides. This would allow Shoren to capture the town that much sooner. The sooner he could capture it, the sooner he could fortify it against any attacks from Rekii. Ryon rode off to take his cavalry around to their designated position, and Shoren rode back to his tent. It wouldn't be long now.

✡ ✡ ✡

The rogue General Rekii sat in his camp chair, glaring at the scout who had just informed him that the Denver army was now on his doorstep. The man looked frightened and had delivered his whole report bent over at the waist, the way people bowed to the Emperor. Well, soon all people would bow to him that way. Rekii waved a bejeweled hand, and the little insect scurried away.

Rekii now turned his attention to one of the trophies on his fingers, a favorite of his. It had come from a noble somewhere in the mountains, a man who had believed that his title made him better than others. Rekii chuckled as he remembered the way the soft man made him think of a little pig, ready to roast. The noble had certainly squealed like a pig the first time Rekii poked him with his knife, but this gem caught his eye, and instead of poking the man again, he decided to take it. The fat pig refused, yelling something about family ring this, ancient treasure that. Rekii decided that if he couldn't have the ring, then he would just take the whole damn finger. That had been amusing, even though it took a few stabs to hit the finger, and the pig's fine carpets got all bloody.

Well, Rekii realized that once he had this ring, he didn't want the pig's other jewels to feel left out, so he cut them off the pig as well. Then Rekii decided that the war dogs might appreciate a bit of pork, so he gave them the fat piggy. The man's screams had been most entertaining. Then of course, he started on the man's wife and children.

Rekii shook his head. As amusing as it would be relive those memories, he knew that he needed to figure out a way to keep the Denver from catching up to him. Idly he wondered just how many there were. He thought the scout had mentioned it, but clearly not. Rekii made a mental note to cut out the man's tongue since he was obviously withholding information. He turned to his senior officers.

"I need a more detailed report. I need numbers, of horses, infantry, and siege machines. I need the names of commanders, and I need to know everything that can be found out about the man in charge. I also want to know if they're here for me, or for the Kirendadi. If I'm just an appetizer, then maybe we can slip out unseen."

"Sir, we have reports from all our scouts in the field. My clerks compiled them into a single document for your perusal. It seems that they are here for both. This Shoren is here for your head, but once he has it, he is to travel north and join Mekal. As for numbers, he certainly has more than enough to take us apart. I would suggest that we fortify ourselves in the town. That way if they want it, they'll have to bleed for it."

Rekii turned to his advisor, a man with a horrible habit of speaking out of turn. He would have to die at some point, but not yet. He still had his uses. Rekii smiled as an idea began to form.

"No, my dear Markus, not fortify, but abandon Laramie. From these reports it would appear that the foe commands upwards of twenty thousand men, more than a match for the mere five thousand we possess. What we must do is simply abandon Laramie. He can have it. There are plenty of other little towns to plunder. Why bother holding on to one, especially when it's almost dried up anyway? It's high time we left, so the fool takes the town and swells his ego while we make good our escape." Rekii scratched the scraggly beard on his chin thoughtfully. "But let's make it look as though we intend to keep the town, make him think he's worth my time to fight. I want to leave behind only a few hundred men, just enough to make it look convincing, but not enough to significantly weaken our forces. While this Shoren defeats us, we can slip away during the short battle. I think we should travel to the northwest. If we do that, then we can not only escape, but also travel to other, richer towns with as weak defenses as this one had. Come, Markus, let us plan our escape, and decide who shall be sacrificed to the oncoming beast that is Denver's army."

✲ ✲ ✲

The sun was just going down, leaving shadows across Shoren's face. He looked out at the town that was about to find itself under a very short siege, then at his troops who were preparing the catapults, and finally back at the town. Those catapults would be ready very soon. He saw the soldiers gathering the ammunition together, and Shoren was still unsure what kind would be best to use.

The ammunition came in several varieties, ranging from simple stones to massive clay jars full of various pressurized, very flammable liquids. Shoren knew very well the damage one of those flaming missiles could inflict on timber walls, but he saw that such weaponry posed a risk of setting the whole town ablaze. The large stones would take longer to eradicate the walls, but he settled for those anyway. He decided that if he needed to he could always use the flaming pots, and besides, it might be best to save those for when he encountered the Kirendadi. He didn't doubt that he would have to besiege someone there too.

A messenger came running up with a slip of paper in his hand. He bowed.

"Sir. A message from Commander Ryon. His cavalry is in position."

Shoren nodded. "Send a messenger hawk back to him, telling him to wait until the attack starts. He needs to be watching because we'll not be using anything flammable that will light up the sky. Send it now."

The messenger bowed again and left. Shoren mounted his horse and rode back to the main army. At this point the messenger had long since sent a hawk. Shoren stared at Laramie for an age, but abruptly broke the silence and raced his stallion to the head of his sprawling army, drew his sword and waved wildly above his head for all to see. The trumpeters gave a long blast from their horns, Shoren roared, and his troops roared with him.

"We are Denver soldiers!" he shouted, when the deafening cries died out. "We fight to protect our people! We fight to defend our lands, and we fight for honor!" He paused as more cheers went up in the multitude of men massed together. "This is what we have done for generations! We have fought Kirendadi, Uvadans, Powhoans, Navajo, Teshions, the horsemen of the Plains. We have even fought the Aztlans. But we have never fought a traitor. Until today! Today, we fight for our honor, the very core of our being!" The entire army was silent, and for a moment Shoren was at a loss what to say. Then his eye caught the inscription on his sword, the first words on every soldier's lips each day, and the last he speaks before he slumbers, and if he can manage it, the last he says before he leaves the world of life. Shoren screamed it, and the world screamed back. "Semper Fidelis!"

With the words of the ancient battle cry to support him, Shoren let his sword come crashing down. The catapults let loose with their payloads of heavy stones, and Shoren watched as the first stones smashed into the timber wall. The timber flexed and repelled the stones, and Shoren frowned. *This*, he thought, *could be a problem.* He watched as the second wave of stones was also repelled by the timber wall, but these bounced and began to roll back toward his infantry. Shoren quickly ordered his men to move back, even though the formation had already broken. His troops almost weren't quick enough; one man missed being crushed by inches.

Shoren grabbed the nearest trumpeter and ordered him to sound the cease-fire. The message was relayed and the catapults ceased their work. Shoren could see the operating crews standing around in confusion until the trumpeters sounded to switch ammunition to the pressurized flammable liquids. Just for good measure he had his troops step back before the new missiles were launched. The bombs exploded upon the walls, ripping them apart. Laramie was now open to attack. Shoren hoisted his sword, let out the ancient battle cry once more, and ordered the charge.

✧ ✧ ✧

Lord Ryon was leaning back in his saddle when a messenger came running up, bearing a note from Commander Shoren. It confirmed what he already knew, to pay attention to the attack and intercept anyone who thought to escape to the north. Ryon frowned. He considered sending a message back to Shoren to tell him that his scouts had seen people moving in the woods, but they turned out to be nothing more than terrified farmers. Of course, that was when they had found anyone. For the most part they hadn't.

Abruptly, Ryon heard a great shout, and heard stone crash on wood. He could hear more shouting, silence, and then suddenly the night sky lit up like daybreak. He heard another explosion, and then another. What was Shoren doing? If he kept on like this, the whole town would burn down! The sky lit up again, and Ryon turned to look at the woods near the base of a nearby mountain and swore. He saw figures, surely Rekii's soldiers, marching at full tilt into the forest. He swore again.

Ryon grabbed at the sleeve of one of his lieutenants, but quickly took control of himself. It just wouldn't do for a captain like him to pluck at the sleeve of an underling. He ordered the lieutenant to take a hundred riders and chase down those troops. The man took control of his hundred and rode off. Ryon thought for a moment, and shouted after him.

"I want some alive! Officers preferably!" The man acknowledged his order with a wave of his sword. Ryon turned his attention back to the town and grimaced. It appeared as though the defenders had chosen to stand their ground instead of flee. Ryon also noticed that the gates had caught fire, along with almost everything else.

Shoren was not happy. His decision to burn the wooden walls had set almost the entire town on fire, but Rekii's forces had not charged out to meet him as he had expected. Instead they had chosen to remain in buildings and shoot arrows at Shoren's forces, and it was becoming increasingly difficult to distinguish an armed enemy from a villager desperate to protect his family. Too often villagers appeared to be soldiers, with Shoren's soldiers realizing their mistakes only after innocent villagers had died. The casualties were mounting.

Shoren and his staff had moved closer to the fray throughout the battle, mainly so that Shoren could see what was happening and give orders, although that was also becoming difficult, thanks to his noble officers, who expected to have been turned loose during the battle, to plunder, rape and pillage as they pleased. Shoren had not permitted them what they saw as their rights as victors and they had complained profusely when they read the order denying them their fun. Shoren had already had to take the head off one man who had insisted and finally begun edging away toward the town. Mainly as an example, Shoren had severed the man's spine at the neck, leaving his head hanging by a few tendons. But he declared that the noble had been an incompetent officer, a potentially capital offense. The other nobles quickly became much more compliant with Shoren's orders.

Shoren could see where the traitors had barricaded themselves in the small houses and stores and were unleashing crossbow bolts and arrows from the second story windows. Many were using the legendary repeating crossbows, a Denver design that put a hand crank on each crossbow, enabling the archer to pull back in a few seconds, meaning each bowman could shoot seven or eight shots a minute. Now, ironically, Denver's invention was being used against its own army.

Shoren swore and galloped toward the burning gates. His nobles followed him, albeit warily. They didn't want Shoren to accuse any of them of incompetence. Shoren ignored them, slowed his stallion to a walk, looked around, and drew his sword. He then dismounted and motioned for the other nobles to do the same. As they were jumping off their horses (or falling, depending on the noble) Shoren walked up to the back door of a tailor's shop and kicked it in.

Almost immediately he stumbled on a mannequin that had fallen in front of the door. He kicked it aside and was rewarded with two very nervous-looking peasants staring at him. They were holding knives. The woman seemed steady but the man was shaking so hard that Shoren had to wonder how he was able to keep hold of the knife. Shoren put out his hand in what he hoped was a calming gesture.

"Put down the knives, people. We don't want violence here." Shoren regretted the words as soon as they were out of his mouth. Half the town was on fire, people were dying left and right, and he didn't want any violence? Unfortunately, or maybe fortunately, they didn't seem to understand him.

"Saldenutuk! Saldenutuk! El mael Saldenutuk tiene mi notankan! Decie este seutaka morir mi notankan! Mori! Mori! Por favor!"

For a moment Shoren was at a loss. He backed away from the couple and put his hands out as if to ward them off.

"Could you repeat that? In Denver, Kirendadi, English, anything!"

The man stopped. He looked nervously at his wife. He spoke.

"I speak English."

Shoren sighed. He had known those classical language lessons would come in handy someday, though he wondered how a simple merchant knew such an ancient language. He shrugged; it didn't matter.

"You speak in English?" The man nodded. "Good. Tell me what's happened."

The man thought for a second. "Three soldiers came to our house. They took our children! They said that if the Denver attacked them they would die, but our children would die first. Please help us!"

Suddenly the attacks by the townspeople made sense. Rekii's soldiers had told the parents that if the Denver attacked them they would kill the children. That left the townspeople no choice but to defend Rekii's soldiers by attacking the Denver, who inevitably killed them. That provided Rekii's soldiers with some extra protection but also meant that at the end of the battle there would be fewer people who could give Shoren information about troop numbers, supplies, escape routes, or anything else of importance.

"There are three soldiers upstairs?" The man nodded again. "Ok. We'll go upstairs, kill them, and get your children back."

The tailor fell to his knees and began thanking Shoren profusely. Shoren motioned for him to go back to his wife and tell her what was about to happen. When the tailor was finished, she started babbling tearfully in her own tongue until Shoren snapped at her to be quiet.

Shoren then speculated on how exactly he would kill the soldiers upstairs. He thought for a moment, looked over at two of the most ineffectual and pompous nobles in his retinue, and got an idea. He sauntered over to the two of them. With a twisted smile on his face he clapped both on the back and hauled them over to a corner of the shop where he could discuss his battle plan. The two arrogantly sniffed at the others. They were planning the heroic attack; the others weren't.

"How would you two like to lead the attack upstairs? I'll follow of course, with the others, but you two will have the glory of being the first among my retinue to meet the enemy. Think of the honor and the prestige."

One of the two looked over at the tailor's wife. "Mmm, she's a pretty one isn't she?" His partner nodded. "I bet she'll be mighty grateful when we rescue her children, don't you think? I'll bet she'll be willing to do anything we ask." With a wary glance at an irritated Shoren, he continued. "And if not, we can demand it of her. Denver laws still apply out here. We've done her a service; so she gets to service us. It's only fair. Right, commander? You can't say it isn't in the laws."

Shoren sighed. Then he grinned. "If you two do as well as I expect, you can have whatever you want. I'll even promote you. I might even let you keep her." He finished, with a nod of his head to show who he meant.

The tailor sat watching as the three men argued in a corner. He watched in particular the man who had spoken with him just moments before. He had an indisputable aura of command about him. He was, without a doubt, the leader.

The man the tailor saw in front of him was tall and lithe, almost knife-like. He was holding his helmet in his hands, a simple steel headpiece with little embellishment, although the cheek-guards were worked in the shape of a thunderbird, the symbol of Denver. His armor, like his helmet, was made of blue steel. The cuirass was made of banded steel, his legs and arms were protected by steel plates that curved around each limb, and underneath was chain mail.

The leader seemed to sense that the tailor was watching him and silenced the other two men. He turned around and the tailor found himself looking into his hard green eyes, the eyes of a man who would brook no opposition, who was both calculating and utterly ruthless. The man slipped his helmet back onto his short-cut blond hair and then, with his free hand, reached up to draw the short sword strapped to the back of his armor, thought better of it, and simply gripped his other sword in both hands. This sword had a long, slightly curved, single-edged blade.

Shoren motioned for the two nobles to go up the stairs. They looked at each other for a moment before drawing their swords and creeping up the stairs in what they obviously imagined was a stealthy manner. Shoren groaned audibly and followed the two men, who immediately began running up the stairs to the door. With a wary glance at Shoren, the two opened the door and charged.

Shoren stood behind the open door and watched as two of the most ludicrously stupid people he had ever encountered began a shout of "Die, traitors!" as they attacked three armed, well-trained men and were immediately cut down by crossbow bolts.

Those mechanical crossbows were the weapons of choice for any Denver archer. They were complicated devices, and difficult to make. Each crossbow had a wood and metal frame with a string made of five strands of twisted steel. A crossbowman would brace the butt of the crossbow against his stomach and use the hand crank to pull the string back. The first noble was killed by two bolts to the chest while a third bolt took the other man in the neck. One man, heavy-set with a large nose set beneath wiry brown hair, struggled to reload his crossbow, but the other, small, skinny, blond, one eye sewn shut, dropped his in favor of a sword, which he drew as he advanced on Shoren. The soldier by the window did not engage Shoren however. Instead, he ran to a corner in which lay several large burlap sacks. They were moving.

The man gave one of the sacks a mighty kick, producing a muffled shriek. As the two others advanced on Shoren, he cut open the sack and pulled a young girl out by her hair. She was bound and gagged, but she twisted about, making it hard for the man to keep his grip.

The blond man leaped to engage Shoren with a slash at his legs. Shoren warded off the attack using his own sword and immediately switched to a horizontal neck slash that the man avoided with a back step. Out of the corner of his eye Shoren saw that the girl had managed to spit out her gag and had the man's hand firmly between her teeth. He dropped the knife, slapped the girl with his other hand, and began kicking her fiercely.

Shoren saw the big-nosed man finish loading his crossbow and swing it in his direction. Instinctively, Shoren hurdled toward one-eye and grabbed and ducked behind him. Big-nose's crossbow emptied itself into one-eye's back. As one-eye slipped to the floor, Shoren twisted around to see the third man gripping his knife, about to scalp the girl.

Shoren thrust his sword into the man's throat, and the poor girl, now blood-spattered, began screaming wildly, her desperate eyes focused just behind Shoren. Shoren tried to calm the girl, making soothing gestures and noises. He frowned. *It's not working*, he thought to himself. *Maybe if I…aahhhhh!*

Too late he remembered big-nose and his sword, late enough for big-nose to stab through a gap in Shoren's armor into his side. Shoren grabbed his side, trying to stop the blood from gushing out. He dropped to his knees, allowing big-nose to knee him in the face and send him flailing back onto the floor. With a twisted leer, big-nose reached for the girl.

Shoren pushed himself up off the ground, saw big-nose with his knife at the girl's throat whispering to her in the same language she spoke. Whatever he said terrified her. Her mouth opened and her eyes grew wide as she tried to squirm away from the man, but he gripped her hair so hard that she couldn't move.

Shoren struggled to get up only to receive a foot in his face for his efforts. Big-nose started to slit her throat slowly, and blood began to pour from the shallow cut that was getting deeper as big-nose cut more. As if out of nowhere, an arrow flew into big nose's chest. Another tore his throat, and one more flew by, brushing his hair but ultimately missing him. He was already slumped onto the floor, dead.

Shoren felt someone lifting him off the ground. Turning, he looked into the face of his rescuer and for a moment couldn't move, so deep was the shock. It was Charlz! The fifteen- year-old kid who couldn't even mount a horse had just casually killed the man who had laid low his commander.

Shoren sat down on a rickety chair and breathlessly asked Charlz where the others where.

"They're downstairs, sir. None of them wanted to come up here. They just assumed you had the matter in hand. I heard the screams though, and I didn't think they sounded like you were doing fine. They sounded like trouble." Suddenly he looked away and blushed. "I think our men thought you were the cause of the screams, sir. The men were talking about how it wasn't fair that you would take your pleasures but deny them theirs. Sir."

Shoren frowned. "Get the other children out of their sacks, Charlz," he said, vaguely waving his hand around. "No one wanted to come up here?" Charlz nodded. "What about the men I left to mind you? Not that I'm complaining, but why did they ignore their charge?"

"Uh, that's them, sir. You took them up here with you. They're dead."

"Oh." Shoren clapped him on the back. "Well, good job. I really appreciate it. Now release those other children as I told you. Uh, how's the battle…going?"

"It's over. We think there may have been only something like five hundred of Rekii's men. In the end, the villagers killed more of our men than did the traitors." He frowned at the bag he was untying. "That's understandable though."

Shoren nodded and with some effort stood up. "Get those kids out of those bags. Make sure everyone's all right. I'm going to have a little talk with my assistants about duty."

Don Alejandro watched warily as High Commander Shoren and the boy, Charlz, walked down the steps, followed by four children, three of whom looked like they had lived less than a single decade. The commander's armor was rent open on one side with blood seeping out. Charlz was supporting Shoren with his arm.

When the four children saw their mother, they cried out joyfully and ran to her open arms, jabbering away in their strange tongue. The woman hugged each tightly in turn, running her hands through their hair and checking for injuries.

Turning his attention back to the commander, Alejandro was struck by the way young Charlz stood and by how, even though the high commander was leaning on his newfound friend bleeding out his lifeblood, he gave each noble a steely look. There was something dangerous in Shoren's eyes. A flash of fury.

Shoren leaned away from Charlz and stood on his own, but with a steadying hand on the stair rail. Finally, he spoke.

"We are here for a reason. That reason is to protect our citizens and to destroy the traitor Rekii. As you can see, I have been wounded in that endeavor. The two men who fought with me upstairs have died while helping me reach that goal. Why they died is not so important as how they died. Those men died because they were stupid. They charged when they should have gone quietly, attacked immediately when they should have waited. Not only did they die because of their actions, but they almost got me killed as well. Thankfully, they won't be getting anyone else killed."

Suddenly, Don Alejandro was certain that Shoren had sent the two nobles upstairs to die. He may even have killed them himself. If Shoren could get two nobles killed, what then was there to stop him from killing more? Alejandro was filled with a sudden desire to be anywhere but where he was. He knew though that he couldn't leave. A transfer would never be allowed.

"Unfortunately, because of their actions, I was wounded. I almost died. There was screaming. I heard it. Each of you heard it, and each of you is honor bound to help those in need. That's part of the oath you take when you become an officer. However, the only one who came to my aid was Charlz, a fifteen-year-old boy, not even an officer. He's given no oaths. He's honor bound by nothing.

"According to Denver law, which all of you have attempted to use in order to get me to allow you your rights, as you put them, I can execute all of you. I should. I may yet. But I won't…for now. But, if one of you doesn't find me a surgeon, immediately…"

Like all the others, Don Alejandro, an important and high-ranking noble, practically fell over himself trying to get as far away from Shoren as was humanly possible. Maybe, just maybe, he wouldn't wait for a transfer.

✣ ✣ ✣

Commander Ryon watched as the lieutenant and his hundred men chased after the other soldiers. The riders were almost upon them when the hidden figures turned about face and unleashed a mighty barrage of crossbow bolts in their direction. Every one of the men died in a heartbeat. Ryon swore. He spared a glance at Laramie, just to make sure the gates remained closed, and saw that even with the town on fire, Rekii's men were still not attempting to flee.

Ryon shouted a command to his other captains and they in turn passed it on to their men. "Attack. Chase them down. Let none survive." Ryon brandished his sword high above his head and let loose the ancient battle-cry – "Semper Fidelis" – and the soldiers charged onto the open field.

At first Ryon's raiders rode in an arrowhead formation, but they quickly split apart into two groups so that the traitors could not cut them down. Rekii's infantry quickly gathered in a circle in order to huddle behind their huge rectangular shields. Ryon gave a command to unleash a volley of arrows from their horse bows. The arrows arched skyward, and Ryon quickly lost sight of them in the night sky.

Although unable to see, Ryon could tell by the cries and shouts of the infantry in front of him that the arrows had found their marks. The horsemen around him quickly began slicing up the survivors, who were attempting to flee. One man, he looked to be an officer of some sort, began shouting for quarter. The soldiers around him began dropping their weapons and shouting too. Finally, those few who refused to surrender had either fled or died.

Pulling his horse up next to one of his own officers, Ryon gave the command for the prisoners to be rounded up, but he wanted the officer, the man who had begun shouting first, kept separated and brought to him immediately. Then he was going to take his prize to Shoren.

Markus Veratter, a medium-ranking noble and second-in-command to General Rekii, sat tied in a chair before High Commander Shoren. He sighed. First he had to deal with that well-paying maniac Rekii, then he lost a battle, and now he was in the hands of the Denver commander, who was very likely to hang him. This just wasn't a good tenday.

"So what exactly are you going to do with me? Community service, perhaps?" he began, knowing full well that death was the only lawful punishment for treason, and rightfully so. People should obey their superiors, he smiled to himself, fully aware of the irony of this self-accusation. That was what got him in this mess to begin with. "Well, if you decide on imprisonment, I'd like somewhere with a view."

Shoren looked at him, smiling. "Actually, I think community service is a great idea. In fact, if you tell me everything you know, if you cooperate fully, it's in my power to grant you a full pardon. Much preferable to a cell with a view, wouldn't you say?" He laughed at his own joke.

For his part, Markus just stared incredulously. This man would pardon him? How did he have the power? Only the Emperor could do that. Unless…unless he had special imperial powers granted to him for the duration of this campaign. That would make sense. Maybe this wouldn't be such a bad tenday after all.

"Of course I would prefer a pardon! And all my men, you'll pardon them too?"

"That depends on your level of cooperation. If you tell me what I need to know, I'll grant you and your men a full pardon, and a reassignment to this army under my command. If not…" he trailed off, leaving the consequences of refusal quite clear.

Once again, Markus was stunned. Reassignment! He had never imagined such a thing could happen. Not only would he not be executed, but if he played his cards right, he might be able to return to Denver with honor. Best to be cautious though.

"What do you want to know, and what do you mean by 'reassignment'? What would we have to do?"

"You would have to give me all the information I want about Rekii and his army, and you'll have to help me fight him. When this is all over, I'm going north to fight the Kirendadi. You'll have to fight up there too."

Markus sighed and fidgeted in his chair, briefly pulling against the rope that held him. Fighting the Kirendadi was going to be difficult. They were barbarians, but they were dangerous barbarians. They were a horse culture, akin to the Plainsmen, but more warlike. He knew that any fight against them would be difficult and dangerous, but far better than the alternative.

Markus looked up. He smiled. "Well, sir, I have to say that is perhaps the greatest thing I could wish for. However, I want you to write out the pardon for my men and me. If you would allow me, I would like to try to contact my other colleagues under Rekii. I know of several who would be amenable to what you're offering."

"No. Even if you were right, it would only take one person for you to be wrong about to destroy everything. No messages. I'm also going to assign some aides to assist you."

Shoren turned around and motioned for two young men to step forward. They did. "These are your new aides, Charlz Smied and

Rasti Makees. They will be your aides for now. I trust them implicitly. I hope you will find them to be equally trustworthy."

Markus shrugged. "Well, High Commander McCarter, I think that is an excellent idea. If someone would just untie me…?"

Rekii leaned back in his chair, wiping the blood from his tomahawk. He had won it in the war against the Plainsmen many years before, and even now he used it for punishing failure, or for letting out his anger. A person needed to be able to express his emotions, lest their suppression lead to mental instability. Rekii stared at the screaming messenger on the ground. The man needn't bellow so; he still had his left hand.

"When I get my hands on Markus, I'm going to kill him. Slowly. I can't abide a betrayal. Not just that, but he surrendered two hundred men. Damn him! I hope he burns!" Suddenly Rekii looked thoughtful. "Maybe he will burn…" Then he grimaced. "If somebody doesn't shut that man up, I'm going to kill someone! Maybe…you!"

Without warning he hurled his tomahawk directly into an aide's forehead. Then he drew his sword and thrust it through the still-bleeding messenger's jugular. Blood splattered everywhere. With an irritated sigh, Rekii motioned everyone out of the tent before retrieving his tomahawk.

Three terrified woman were standing outside, cut and bruised and wearing cast-off rags. Rekii had been enjoying them ever since he had taken them from their homes in Laramie. He leered at them before telling them to clean up the bodies. He pinched one on her way inside. She just scurried all the faster. Rekii smirked.

Rekii and his aides looked around at the valley where they were camped. Rekii frowned before addressing his staff. "Everyone, we can't be sure about whether Markus betrayed us or was captured. Either way, he will probably talk about this place. We should move, find a safer place to wait until we can find another place to strike."

Rekii produced several maps and laid them out on a table, using his tomahawk and three scalps for paperweights. As they stood there discussing the direction of their flight, a cold wind began to blow.

The same wind blew through the mountains and down into Shoren's camp, disturbing Markus' cloak as he made his way back to his men. His most important goal was for his comrades to survive. Shoren had closed one door, but Markus had yet another plan. And if Shoren found out, well he had a third plan, and another after that. He shivered. It would have to be enough.

CHAPTER SEVEN

John McCarter sighed as he fingered the captain's bars on the collar of his jacket. He had worn them for nearly twenty years, ever since Frank's death. Robert had been killed in an ambush, and Frank nearly killed as well, but he had held on long enough to give John the collar pin. His friend Tiny had died later, of disease, John still didn't know which one.

Thinking of his friends usually made him think of the first time he had been wounded, probably ten years before Frank died, fifteen before Tiny. After John had recovered, Frank had given him an old, somewhat rusted Purple Heart. It wasn't until later that John discovered that it had been awarded to Frank once. The ribbon had long since been destroyed, but John had put the Purple Heart on a chain and had worn it ever since.

A cold wind ruffled John's gray speckled hair and beard. He could see the hundred men with their spears and bows and swords. For the most part the weapons were poorly made, but their little town seemed to have run out of ammunition almost overnight. They had to find better weapons and fast. These few survivors of long-lost Denver had to be able to defend themselves.

As John watched the hundred men, a thought came to him. In the academy he had studied Roman military tactics. Maybe they could be applied here. Yes…large shields combined with some sort of sword and bow; especially if they could use some kind of crossbow… There might be something in the library.

There was laughter in the town, and John paused to watch a small group of children chasing a chicken around and around. He shook his head. *I barely remember the old America anymore*, he thought, *but I still keenly feel its loss. The children though, they've lost nothing. They just live. They've never known anything different. What was that!*

John realized that the children were screaming and he saw why; the chicken they were chasing had been pierced by an arrow. John grabbed his rifle, his few remaining clips of ammo and a very long knife. It was time for battle. First he had to figure out where the battle was.

There it was, and it presented John with one of the strangest sights he had ever seen in his life. Men on horses with bows, lances, axes, and a few guns were fighting men wielding swords, spears, and the occasional sub-machine gun. It looked just like an old western! Those men were Indians! Sioux!

John had heard that the tribes of the Plains peoples had begun to move out in force onto the plains, likely in preparation for what was coming, but he had never really believed it. Supposedly several businessmen, mostly Sioux, mostly casino owners, had seen the war coming before anyone else and had gathered their people together in order to survive and bring back the old ways. John had never believed it, but here was proof before his eyes.

What they were doing down here in Colorado John had no idea. It didn't matter. John raised his rifle and, with the ease born of long training and longer experience, casually shot two men out of their saddles. Suddenly, the raiders opened fire with their own guns. They mostly had low-caliber, semi-automatic weapons that could be fired with only one hand – better for horseback attacks. The attackers had pulled back for a try at reaching the other side of the town. The young men of New Denver were there first, opening fire right into charging Sioux. The raiders released a last volley of arrows and shots before fleeing.

John nodded as he came down the hill. It made sense. The raiders weren't looking for a firefight; they were looking for free food. Likely they were having a hard time finding food and thought to take it from a seemingly defenseless town. John was troubled though. He himself had finished his ammunition, and near the end, most of the gunfire had stopped.

John finally limped down the hill, his old wounds taking their toll on him. He was fairly surprised to find few casualties. Only a few raiders had died, about seven, with probably thirteen Denver deaths.

Damn few wounded though. One man, a very young man, was badly hurt. He had taken an arrow right through the left shoulder.

John felt his own left shoulder, rubbing his hands over yet another old battle wound. After a moment, his hand came to rest on the Purple Heart hanging around his neck. John unclasped the chain and held it up so that he could look at it in the sun. He walked over to the young man.

With a start he realized that it was Sam, his youngest daughter's fiancé. That only made this more important. John waited until after Sam had been laid up in bed. Once he was stable, John walked up to their impromptu hospital and shooed away the healers. Sam looked up at him and grinned.

"Well, sir, I suppose the wedding will have to wait until after I'm better. You should be happy. But now you can't say I'm no soldier. I've got to have impressed you now! I mean look at this thing!"

John laughed. "It looks worse than it is, trust me. But if you let yourself get shot just to impress me, well, I'm sure I've got a bullet somewhere that can do better than that arrow. Besides, you're marrying my youngest daughter. Trust me, if you weren't impressive, you'd be dead." He paused. "I have something to give you though." John pulled the Purple Heart out of his pocket. "I've told you about Frank Miller, the captain? Well, he was awarded this in the Second Korean War…" Looking at Sam's blank face, he amended what he was going to say. "It was awarded for being wounded in action, before the Collapse. He gave it to me, after I survived a vicious stomach wound shortly after the Collapse. Now I'm giving it to you. I hope you keep it as sacred as I have."

Sam took the Heart almost reverently and stared at it for a long moment. Finally, he clasped the chain around his own neck and looked up. He tried to speak, but was overcome with emotion. He took a moment and with tears in his eyes said, "Shoren! Wake up! You need to wake up!"

Shoren looked around groggily. What was going on? This was the second dream he had had about that John McCarter. This was really strange. After a moment, his hands found a necklace on his table. Hanging from the gold chain was a simple metal heart. It wasn't purple, but the dream set him to wondering. He shook his head. There stood Charlz, looking impatient. Shoren put aside all thoughts about hearts and survivors and motioned for Charlz to say what he needed to say.

Charlz was breathing heavily and was wearing a hastily donned uniform, shirt untucked, coat unbuttoned, and his sword nowhere to be seen. Shoren motioned again.

"Sir, you wanted to know if Markus could be trusted. Remember how I told you he couldn't? You disagreed. Well, I was walking to my tent after the sword lessons from Ryon, and I saw a man sneaking around. I followed him right into Markus' tent. He told Markus something about how Rekii's camp was abandoned and how he couldn't find some people, I don't know. But after that Markus pulled out a map and began looking at it, asking the man all sorts of questions. Finally, he asked the man if he still had the message. The other man said yes and pulled out some kind of pouch and gave it to him. I told you he couldn't be trusted."

Shoren nodded. "Yes, you did. Go wake Ryon and tell him to meet me here. Get the Black Guards. We'll want them here too."

Charlz nodded and turned to run. Shoren turned away immediately to get dressed, but for a moment he paused. Shoren first pulled on his cotton padding before the chain mail suit, but as he looked at the pieces of armor laid out on the cot he sighed. Finally he reached for the lacquered bands of steel that would cover his torso, but another hand quickly pulled them away. Shoren grabbed his knife and put it at the throat of the intruder, only to realize that the blade quivered centimeters away from the neck of his manservant Jon.

"Jon! What are you doing up?"

"Well, sir, I wouldn't be a very good manservant if I didn't know what my lord was up to at all times, would I? You need to be done fast, and you need my help. Put the knife away, please? My lord."

"I swear you call me that one more time and I will cut your throat."

"Didn't your lady mother tell you never to swear? Besides, if you cut my throat then no one will help you with your armor and Markus might get away. My lord."

"Do you hear everything that goes on around here? And don't say, 'My lord.'" Shoren waved the knife at Jon again, but the man just pushed it away while he finished pulling the straps on Shoren's breastplate.

"Actually, sir, I don't hear everything that goes on around here. Just everything that pertains to you. My lord."

Shoren growled at the man but said nothing further. That was probably a wise decision, considering the circumstances. Without the distraction, Jon was able to put on Shoren's collar guard, shoulder pieces, arm guards, gauntlets, and groin, calf and knee guards in just a few minutes. Shoren quickly pulled on his own boots. They were leather riding boots, but covered in steel strips to protect his shins in battle. Jon took the helmet from its stand and handed it to Shoren, who set it down and waved vaguely at the shoulder belt and sheath. Jon had forgotten. The manservant quickly recovered though and slid them over Shoren's head perhaps a little hastier than he should have, because he had to adjust them once they were on. Rising above his right shoulder was a two-foot short sword, and also attached to the baldric at his left hip was a three-foot saber. Shoren hesitated over his bow and quiver, but left them. There would be no need for a bow tonight. Shoren did however grab his knife and slide it onto his belt. He also checked his two throwing knives, hidden in his belt. He wanted to be ready.

Shoren walked out of his tent to find Commander Ryon and Guard Master Madoc Sharon, leader of the Black Guards. Madoc was a huge man, covered in armor, with his face concealed by his helmet. Behind him stood fifty of the Black Guards, all huge and wearing the leather and chain armor that the Guards wore, each holding a large shield with the hooded skull in front of two crossed scythes, the symbol of the Guards, each carrying a seven-foot spear with a needle point. But there the similarities ended.

Each guard carried whatever weapons suited him most, and they ranged from axes to maces to morning stars to swords to weapons Shoren had never seen being carried by any except the Guards. Things like large hollow metal clubs but with a boar hide handgrip, or iron knuckles with three-inch spikes, long chains with spiked balls on the end - all weapons worn because they had proven to be brutally effective in countless battles. Madoc himself carried a hammer, a mace and one of those strange metal clubs. He had often expressed distaste for edged weapons.

Shoren motioned for Madoc and Ryon to join him at the front of the column of guards, and they both joined him with the Guards formed up around them. Shoren, Madoc and Ryon were silent. There was nothing they needed to say.

Markus was staring at the map laid out on the table trying to divine where Rekii would have gone after abandoning the meeting site. Rekii had ordered his troops to leave in small groups and head for the same site in different directions, following different routes. They should have been there. Markus had sent the messenger away to get some sleep. He wondered idly what this High Commander Shoren would do should he discover the message that he had sent to his comrades under Rekii.

He turned back to the map and glared at it for another moment. He should probably get some sleep like the rest of the camp, but that wasn't likely. Not until his friends were safe.

There was a sound outside, and Markus turned around quickly, reaching for a sword that lay in a corner of his tent. He cursed. This was bad, really bad. The door flaps were pulled open and in walked two massive Black Guards, each bristling with weapons. That wasn't good. If the Guards were present that meant Shoren knew about the message and thought it treason.

When the two Guards saw that he was alone, one stepped out of the tent for a moment but quickly walked back in, followed by Shoren, Ryon and a man who had to be the guardmaster. Markus shook his head, trying to figure out how Shoren had known about the letter. He grimaced, it had to be one of those two boys, the aides he was given. But how had they found out? Suddenly he realized that he had a sword pointed at his throat. Now was probably not the best time to consider such questions.

Shoren hefted his sword and pointed it at Markus' throat. He felt… "betrayed" wasn't really the best word, but it was all Shoren could think of. Young Charlz had warned him, but he hadn't truly imagined that Markus would betray him, especially not after his generous pardon. Markus should have been willing to do anything to avoid losing both the pardon and his new position; it was simply inconceivable that he would be so loyal to Rekii.

Shoren turned to Madoc. "Chain him. Strip him of his weapons and bring him to the command tent." Madoc nodded and began moving toward Markus, followed closely by one of the two Guards that had preceded them into the tent. The rest of the Guards waited outside. They might all be used tonight; there was no telling how far this treason spread.

Markus backed away and raised his hands. It was strange that he didn't try to run or grab a weapon. "Wait, wait. What's going on here? You've already pardoned me, you can't take that back."

"I haven't. You lost it when you kept valuable information from me. Then you lost it again when you tried to contact Rekii. Given your situation, either one could get you a rope, but both together will cost you your head, unless you can give some reason why you could possibly want to throw your pardon away."

"It's not what you think. The only message I sent was to my fellow legionmasters under Rekii. I wanted them to defect. The more men I get to switch sides the less bloodshed occurs, and we'll have more men for the Kirendad campaign. I'm sure your superiors will want that."

Shoren frowned at him. Was he telling the truth? Markus had wanted to send such a message in the beginning, but he had refused to allow it. If it was true, then maybe he didn't have to die. Even so, he had gone behind Shoren's back... "Prove it. If the message is what you claim it is, then show me."

Markus nodded. He took a moment to collect himself before reaching into his coat pocket to pull out a small, stained envelope which he handed over to Shoren. Shoren snatched it away from him and quickly read it. The letter was what he claimed, but Shoren still wasn't convinced.

"Markus, it's a very good thing that your messenger failed to deliver this letter. If he had, I can assure you that you would be dead tomorrow morning. Since he didn't, I'm willing to let you off, but only so long as you tell me everything you left out. And, Markus, if I think you're still holding back, the Guards will question you. You won't leave anything out with them."

CHAPTER EIGHT

General Rekii was sitting at a table in a large stone room, eating a dinner consisting of roasted goat, rice, and a baked potato. He lifted his cup of wine and found it empty. Rekii sighed over the incompetence of his serving women and called one girl over. She stumbled over to Rekii to receive a smack in the face for her laziness and then another for her lack of attention to his wine cup.

Without saying a word he thrust the cup beneath her nose. The girl tearfully took the cup, ran to the pitcher to fill it, and spilled wine while hurrying back to him. Rekii took the cup but glared at the puddle on the floor. The girl, no more than seventeen, ran over to the spill and cleaned it up with her own tattered dress. When she finished, Rekii motioned for her to come over. She flinched.

When she arrived, Rekii leaned over and whispered in her ear, "Girl, I'm afraid that you've been a rather poor serving maid. It appears that you need to be reassigned to another one of my men." He paused thoughtfully. "Hmm. If I recall correctly, Captain Alkof Hister was more than satisfied with your services, or maybe Lounhalt, hmm?" Rekii smiled with pleasure at seeing the girl shake with absolute fear. She still hadn't gotten over Lounhalt and his cords. "Definitely Lounhalt. Go to him and tell him that I'm trading you for Clarise and that he is to send Clarise to me immediately."

Rekii watched the girl run in terror to her fate. He took a large draught of wine and ripped off a huge chunk of the lamb with his teeth. He truly didn't understand the girl's fear. Lounhalt and his cords were decidedly more pleasant than Hister and his knives. He shook his head at the wasteful pair. There was, after all, no accounting for taste. He missed Markus. That man certainly had had no reason to stay with him beyond loyalty to his fellows, but he was a much better leader than either Lounhalt or Hister. Both of those men were with him because their pleasures would eventually have led to a noose or a sword or maybe even the impaling spike, depending on the crime, the region and the judge. For now though, with him, they were safe.

Rekii looked around. Without a doubt, the abandoned fortress they had found was a blessed find. It was strange though, in its design and layout. The outer walls and towers were made of stone, albeit stone harder than any he had ever seen. The inner buildings and walls were made of a mix of solid stone on the bottom and walls and entire buildings made of some unrecognizably strong metal. It was truly a wondrous find, and an indication that the spirits blessed his cause. The primeval stronghold was filled with a great number of such items as old broken weapons and other devices that were hardly recognizable and had no discernable purpose. It also held books. Whole libraries full of books ran throughout the fortress. It seemed so strange, a building of battle so dedicated to learning. Of course the old gods built this place and they did that kind of thing.

The old general picked up a book he had found on a large wooden desk. The book had a large seal on it – blue with an eagle. There were words around the seal, but they were in some ancient language, English maybe, or Spanish. Both classical languages, but Rekii placed no stock in such learning. He wished he knew what was in the book though; it seemed important.

The book was covered in brown leather and embossed with gold words on the cover. They said *The Personal Journal of General Hammond*. Rekii sighed. He really wished that he could read the language. In a sudden rage he threw the book into a corner as if it were rubbish and went back to his meal. Roasted goat was so good.

The old general looked over at the door through which the maid had just run. In the doorway stood a messenger, one who looked very urgent indeed. Rekii sighed and motioned him in. The messenger was young, handsome and neatly dressed, and seemed even more so in comparison to Rekii. Where the young man filled out his uniform and was relatively unscarred, Rekii had skin like boiled leather and looked like all the extra weight had been baked away, leaving nothing but bone and sinew. The young man was clean-shaven with a short military haircut. Rekii had the haircut, but his scraggly beard covered his seemingly chiseled chin. The young man had his uniform pressed and clean. Rekii slouched in his, which was covered in old wine and food stains, as well as several unidentifiable substances.

The messenger bowed. "General, Squad Leader Grizmor wants you to know that he's come back from his raids. He brought back several wagonloads of food and jewels, as well as a few new serving women, to replace the ones Hister and Lounhalt, ah, went through. He also brought back several casks of rum. He and his men are drinking through one right now. He sent the rest to the other men in the other buildings. He also wants to know if there are any further orders for him."

"Not now. Let him enjoy his time off. He can have a week. Then I want him to go west. There are villages there within a few days' ride that we have not pillaged yet. I also want him to find more rum," Rekii said with a flourish of a lamb leg. "Additionally, I want you to remind him to be careful. I don't want the Denver army to show up all of a sudden because he screwed up."

"I'll tell him, sir."

"Good."

Rekii's intense eyes followed the messenger as he bowed again and left the room. His eyes drifted over to the book in the corner. He sighed. He wished he knew English.

✧ ✧ ✧

Shoren glared over the table at Markus, who was poring over a map of the mountains in West Denver, which meant the middle of the Paradise Mountains. Despite Markus' insistence that Rekii would be somewhere west, in the mountains, they still hadn't been able to find him. They had found plenty of destroyed towns and villages, but no one seemed to know where the attacks were coming from. Markus was beginning to get very nervous that he couldn't find Rekii. Most importantly, he was very concerned about Madoc. Markus pointed at the map.

"Maybe here. This valley. It's a good place for a camp and it has many towns within a day's ride. It could be there."

"Are you sure or are you just guessing?" Shoren looked at the map where Markus pointed.

"To be honest, sir, I'm kind of guessing. Our scouts have looked at all the fallback places Rekii and I discussed. Rekii probably found another location. He doesn't want to be caught until he's sure his name will last forever. He wants to terrorize so many people that…"

"I know. You've said as much before. Maybe if we found some of his raiders they could…"

Ryon ran in, helmet in hand and out of breath. "Shoren! We captured two raiders. We were in a tiny village and who comes riding up but a whole squad of raiders. They say they're from Rekii. I handed them over to the Black Guards, but they're not talking yet. I thought you…"

"When did they get here? Why didn't you tell me first?"

Markus followed Shoren out of his seat but wisely chose not to say anything. Maybe he would avoid Madoc after all. He followed Shoren out of the tent. Ryon also wasn't saying anything at all. This should be interesting.

Guard Master Madoc Sharon looked up as Shoren strode into the tent, his anger so palpable it seemed a living thing. Madoc sighed. This would be trouble. He set the iron back in the fire and turned his full attention to the tent flap where two more people scurried in behind the commander – Lord Ryon and that traitor Markus. If only the commander hadn't found some use for the man…. But that was unimportant. The information from these two raiders, however, was important.

The commander said nothing, only removed the hot poker from the feet of the second raider. Madoc winced. It wasn't like him to forget a thing like that. It wouldn't be good for him to slip. The commander looked at him quietly for a moment. Finally, he spoke.

"What are you doing, Madoc?"

Madoc grinned a wicked grin. "I thought I'd ask these two a few questions. You know: How are you? Where have you been? Would you like some tea? That sort of thing."

"Who gave you those orders? I know I didn't."

Madoc's grin slipped. "No orders, sir. It's my prerogative as guard-master to question any and all prisoners," he said, with a pointed glance at Markus. "Besides, why waste your time with this? You have more pressing work to do than interrogate a few murderers."

"Now you're interrogating murderers? I thought you were only having a friendly chat."

"Well, sir, you see here…"

"If you ever torture someone without my order again, it will be you under those irons. Do you understand me? Your men act as a police force and protectors. Not vigilante torturers. You job is policing and fighting. Nothing else."

Black Guards liked to say that what made other men sick only made them grin, but one look at Shoren's face had Madoc blanched and not quite able to meet his commander's eyes. "Yes, sir. I understand completely."

"Good. Unchain them and bring them something for their feet. Bring some water for them as well."

Madoc scowled at the request but actually filled the order himself. When he returned he discovered that Shoren had seated the two men at a table and had ordered food brought out for them! He almost seemed to be chatting amiably with them, and was actually smiling as he apologized for the over-zealousness of his troops. The two men weren't smiling though; they suspected some trick.

"What are your names? I need to know who I'm addressing if I am to talk to you."

The first man, huge and with a topknot over a shaved head began to speak. "I am Squad Leader Grizmor and this is my second, Under Leader Karde. This is a horrible misunderstanding. What can I help you with?"

"Well, you see, I heard that you claimed to have been sent by Rekii. That means you know where he is. I need to know that. I heard about what your men did at the village where you two were captured. According to Denver law, I should just hand you over to the Black Guards, who will get the information out of you, and then kill you, but I'm prepared to be a little more lenient."

"If we cooperate, will you let us go? Write out pardons?"

"Possibly. That depends on the value of the information you give me."

Madoc sighed and carried over glasses of water for the prisoners, as well as clean cloths to wrap their feet, but he couldn't resist giving them a wide-toothed grin with a significant glance at the irons, a look that made the two men recoil. Shoren noticed and gave Madoc a look that forced him to look at the ground.

Shoren spent some more time in quiet conversation with the two men. Finally, the man with the topknot, Grizmor, leaned away and began talking inaudibly to his friend, Karde. Shoren stood up and walked over to one of the guards and ordered him to go to the command tent and bring him certain maps. Shoren himself then left in the other direction, Madoc presumed, in order to get some paper and his seal.

Madoc gripped his mace and glared at the two men. From what he had heard, Shoren was willing to give these men a pardon for their crimes in return for information. While Madoc knew that Rekii's hiding place was important, he couldn't really condone just allowing two murderers to go free. It wasn't, however, his decision to make.

Actually, the Black Guards' original purpose was to police the military and root out criminal soldiers. While no one had ever mentioned it to him, Madoc realized that, legally, the final decision was left to him. Madoc grinned and began to pull his mace out of its handle at his belt. He stopped as soon as he saw Shoren walk into the tent and raise an eyebrow at him. It would really be better to wait until after the men had given their information.

Shoren cleared the table and laid a map across it. He then set down two sheets of fine paper, the kind used for official documents, and a quill and ink jar, and then finally some green wax and a signet ring. He pointed to the map.

"I want you to show me where Rekii is, how long he's been there, how many troops he has, and how far his patrols reach."

Grizmor pointed at a small valley on the opposite side of the map from where Markus had earlier suggested. Shoren spared a brief glance at Markus who after a glance at the map shrugged apologetically. "It's right here. The general found this old, run-down fortress that could be pretty easily defended, so he had us set up in there. We've been there for about a month, living mostly off of plunder from raids. There are probably four thousand soldiers, maybe a few more in total, but at any given time the general will have about five hundred or so raiders out to get more plunder, so there will be only about three thousand five hundred men at the fortress. Sometimes fewer. Sometimes when we go out to villages and such we are to bring people back."

Shoren leaned in. "Why would you bring people back? What purpose would that serve?"

"Well, we take both men and women, but we bring them for different things. The women are for the officers' pleasure. Sometimes, if we bring back a lot of women, the soldiers get a bunch. Now we don't have to bring back so many women, because we emptied a whole village here," he said, pointing to a spot on the map. "But the general wants us to keep bringing back men, so sometimes it's difficult."

"What does Rekii want with the men? Not pleasure, I'm sure, so he must have some other reason."

"I know what they're for too. The general told Captain Lounhalt to take some of the men to build siege machines. Things like battering rams and catapults and scorpion crossbows. He's also been using some as a basic labor force, you know, heavy lifting and such."

Madoc frowned. He was no expert on siege weapons, but he knew what most of them were. Scorpion crossbows were huge crossbows that fired six-foot spears. Each spear had a massive iron head for punching right through armor. The crossbows could also fire spears with grappling hooks on them for scaling walls. They were very useful in battle and sieges. Madoc had little idea why Rekii would want catapults, although they could be used to kill soldiers as well as knock down walls, but why would he want battering rams? For that matter, wouldn't it be easier to sit in his fortress and just shoot anyone who came near?

Shoren seemed to think the same thing, since he asked the prisoner. The man's answer was surprising. "Well, I think that the general means to start destroying more than little villages on the edges of civilization. I think he wants to start attacking cities, although I'm sure that he'll need more troops for that. I've heard him say, though, that he wants people to remember and fear him so much that no child will ever again be given the name Rekii. I've even heard that he wants to lay siege to Denver itself."

Everyone just sat in stunned silence at the recitation of Rekii's plans. Madoc shook his head for a moment. Rekii was clearly insane, and this Grizmor was just as mad to follow him. Suddenly, Grizmor's friend Karde spoke up.

"I've heard the same rumors, sir. I don't know if they're true or not because in order to attack Denver we would need a lot more men then we have."

Shoren nodded. "That's fine. I want you to point out on the map the typical trails your raiding parties take."

Both Grizmor and Karde immediately began pointing out different roads and trails in and out of the old fortress. Karde even offered to draw Shoren a picture of the fortress so that he could plan his attack. Shoren agreed and had a soldier bring some more paper and some charcoal for drawing.

Once the man was finished, Shoren looked back at both of the men, and then, strangely, he looked at Madoc. Finally he asked, "Is there anything else you two think you could tell me?" Both men shook their heads "no" and stared greedily at the papers that would soon become pardons. Shoren picked up a piece of paper and a quill, only to have the paper snatched out of his hand by Madoc. "I'm sorry, commander, but when it comes to criminals, it's my decision, not yours. You have the power to grant pardons, given by the Emperor, but I am the guardmaster here, and as such I have the power to block pardons for any military criminal. These two men have admitted to treason, murder and rape. The first two get them beheaded, but the third gets them impaled, which, being a squad leader and his assistant, these two would have known."

The two men sat in stunned silence. Suddenly, Grizmor screamed "No!" and grabbed the red-hot poker that just a short while before was being applied to his feet and swung it at Shoren's head. He missed, then turned and followed Karde, who had run out of the tent. Unfortunately, they ran into two Black Guards. Black Guards don't appreciate prisoners running around their camps with red-hot metal implements.

Karde threw himself at the Guards, who simply held out their shields and allowed Karde to run himself onto their spears. Grizmor decided to run after seeing Karde eat his fill of spear, especially since the spears were now stuck. He had gotten about a hundred yards before the Guards had their spears free. The distance didn't help. Black Guards are experts at throwing their spears, and a mere three hundred feet is no difficulty for a man who has been throwing spears since he could walk. Grizmor was indeed impaled, as is the penalty for the crime of rape.

The Guards, who are known for running nearly as fast as their spears can fly, were quickly upon the quivering body of Grizmor and finished him with a quick sword thrust. The two Guards then retrieved their spears and silently watched as Shoren, Madoc, Ryon and Markus slowly walked up to the bodies. Shoren sighed finally and addressed the two guards.

"Dispose of the bodies. I don't care how." He turned to Ryon, Madoc and Markus. "Go to your tents, get whatever you need and meet me back at the command tent in half an hour." All three were silent as they walked away. "And Markus, bring your two aides. They could learn something." Markus just groaned.

Shoren walked away frowning, pausing occasionally to disperse the soldiers who had gathered to fight whatever had caused such a disturbance in the camp. When he finally reached his tent, Shoren threw his coat on his rickety camp chair and lay down on his cot. A few minutes went by, and he sat up. He shook his head with his eyes still closed, and squeezed his temples. He had another headache.

"You can't keep doing this, Shoren," he muttered to no one in particular. "If you do…" He trailed off as his hand brushed against the heart medallion that hung around his neck. To the Denver, the heart was the seat of emotion and honor. Warriors who were especially brave or honorable received heart medallions.

Had this campaign, the long chases, the horror of seeing burnt villages, the bloated and mutilated bodies of men, women and children, the frustration and sense of helplessness at never being able to catch his enemy and put a stop to the madness…. Had all that changed him? A ghost of a grim smile crept onto Shoren's face. He knew the answer.

"Yes. Yes it has."

Shoren looked over at the map and stood up. He was ice once more.

CHAPTER NINE

The young Charlz Smied sat on his pony and simply looked, first at the ruined fort that bustled with activity and then at Commander Shoren, who seemed absolutely elated to have finally caught up with his prey. The man had been becoming increasingly haggard and frustrated as the weeks had dragged on, but once those two prisoners had given him the scent he had headed straight for this spot, unerringly as an arrow. He had set a grueling pace. They had lost more than a few horses and men due to accidents, but Shoren didn't seem to care. He had cut the journey of a week and a half into only six days.

Now Shoren was ready to attack and had assembled his entire army, nearly twenty thousand soldiers, engineers and support crews all ready to descend like a mountain demon upon Rekii and his little fortress. Rekii didn't stand a chance.

Shoren sat on his horse on a small hill overlooking the road into the fortress. He smiled. For nearly a week he had been unable to get the scent of blood out of his nostrils, but now he could see his quarry and loose the full force of ten Denver legions upon it.

His force consisted of eight thousand heavy infantry and two thousand light infantry wearing no armor but their bucklers and carrying numerous javelins and short spears, tomahawks, bows, swords, whatever they were comfortable with and could carry while on a full-out cross country sprint. They were raiders and today would be used to sweep around the fortification to annihilate any survivors.

Shoren also had five thousand cavalry, divided between heavy and light. They would support the infantry right up until the final wall fell, and then they would sweep in and destroy any resistance while the infantry lay siege to the keep. Finally, he had five thousand archers.

Most were the standard crossbowmen armed with the repeating crossbows, but he had nearly a thousand longbowmen. Rekii had no chance. Shoren also had siege machines, a small assortment of catapults, a trebuchet and battering rams. He also had scorpions. It would be easy.

The fortress where Rekii had taken up residence barely deserved the name. It had been built over and expanded many times, and the locals said that the fort had been there since before the Lost Times. Shoren didn't care if the old gods had built the thing, if the spirits had built it, or if the bloody Creator had. Today he would destroy it.

The fortifications consisted of three long walls, each encircling the next smaller one. The outer wall and buildings were the most recent, built by Tyrris Plain, the legendary conqueror. They had massive round towers at each corner, which were relatively intact. But the walls were in a sorry state indeed. Most places the walls were so low that a horse could jump over them, and in some places there was no wall at all. The inner two walls were more ancient. The middle wall was covered with towers, but they were in truly deplorable shape. But the walls were still there and at least prevented his troops from just walking on through. The inner wall was in good shape and showed signs of recent repair. Inside were the massive inner keep, three barracks facilities, stables and storehouses. Outside the walls were Rekii's new slaves building all of his siege weapons. The light infantry would be dealing with them too.

Shoren lifted his sword. "The legions will proceed at a walk!" Twenty thousand soldiers immediately began to progress forward. The light infantry wheeled to the south to disrupt the siege workshops while the rest of his soldiers marched toward the walls and simply leaped over the three-foot ruins. They immediately encountered nearly a thousand of Rekii's infantry, who stood stunned, mouths agape and staring. Instantly half threw down their weapons and fell to the ground, screaming that they surrendered. The other half just charged.

"Cavalry forward, archers open fire!" The heavy infantry marched forward but still to the sides, creating a passageway through which the cavalry could charge. In the meantime, the crossbowmen and longbowmen began eliminating Rekii's soldiers. The cavalry clashed with the soldiers with a roar. The few who had surrendered began to run, only to receive arrows in the back for their troubles.

Almost as soon as it began, it was over. Apparently a thousand soldiers versus over fifteen thousand wasn't exactly an even fight. The army advanced inexorably. The thousand or so troops still inside the citadel looked up and had varying reactions, ranging from stunned rage to terror. Some fled. About a hundred charged. The rest ran inside the fort. Shoren smiled. "Set up the catapults and open fire."

Lieutenant Verzogen stared vacantly at the massive army bearing down on them. It would appear as though fate had caught up with them. Thrice-damned spirits! This was not good. Suddenly, he saw a large man sitting atop a roan stallion mustang brandishing his sword, his banded mail glistening in the sun. The horse-crest atop his helmet was green and gold. That was the commander. That man was Shoren McCarter.

Verzogen followed the troops into the keep, screaming that they needed to find bows and begin firing. No one paid any attention. The army was in chaos.

Verzogen ran up into the keep, fleeing past confused milling troops. Occasionally a man or two grabbed a crossbow and ran to a window, only to be taken down by arrows and the siege weapons that were taking their toll. Undaunted, Verzogen ran up the stairs.

The lieutenant paused at the door before going in. Rekii would not like to be disturbed. Verzogen gathered his courage and opened the door. The grizzly, rumpled old man looked up from a book he had been staring at, a book he seemed unable to read. "What do you want?"

"Sir, um, it would appear that…"

"Forgot to bow, Verzogen!" Rekii lifted his tomahawk and stood up, angrily. "Walk outside and try it again!"

Verzogen stiffened but walked outside the room, closed the door, took a deep breath, and opened the door again. This time he bowed. "Sir, there are soldiers outside. They are Denver, lead by that Shoren…"

"What! Where? How far away are they?"

"Well, sir, when I closed the gate to the keep, they were about ten feet behind me. They were setting up siege machines. They may have broken through the door by now."

"How could we not have seen them coming?"

"I don't know! They came out of nowhere!"

"I don't believe you."

"Well, why don't you just look out the window."

Rekii did, but quickly jumped out of the way as a boulder crashed through, landing in the middle of the room. Rekii leaped up and ran toward the window to watch as the battering rams crashed through the doors and thousands of troops stormed into the building. He drew his sword and gripped his tomahawk.

"Verzogen! Draw your sword! We will fight to the last man!"

Lieutenant Verzogen looked from Rekii to the hole in the wall and then back to Rekii. He shook his head. "I don't think so..." and he turned and ran. Rekii threw his tomahawk into Verzogen's back, killing him instantly. As he pulled his tomahawk from his late lieutenant's back, Rekii saw, out of the corner of his eye, troops walking down the hallway, led by Shoren. He grinned. This would be fun.

Shoren saw an old man standing over a corpse with a tomahawk in one hand and a sword in the other. Rekii. He snarled. "Get him!"

The ten soldiers following Shoren ran forward, weapons out. Rekii hurled his tomahawk into one man's face, grabbed the corpse's sword and backed into the room and shut the door. Shoren could hear a bar slide into place. He growled and ordered the two largest men to ram the door.

It took a few tries, but the old door finally gave way, opening to three shots from a repeater crossbow. The first bolt took a man in the face, the second slammed into a shield, and the third went wild, clanging off the stone wall. A knife spun out from a shadowy corner to thud into one man's shield. The troops spread out and Rekii emerged, wielding a vicious curved blade in each hand.

"Wait! Commander Shoren! I challenge you! One-on-one, man to man! Don't be a coward!"

He leaped forward, but slammed into a shield and fell to the ground with an "oomph." The five soldiers immediately began to pummel him with their shields until Rekii lay groaning in a half-conscious fetal position.

Shoren smiled and walked forward. "General Rekii Ubel, I charge you with high treason, murder, rape, assisting the escape of known criminals, and inducing half a legion into treason, the penalty for which is death. You will be sent to Denver where you will be beheaded. Do you understand?"

"Screw you!"

"No, thank you."

The soldiers chained Rekii, lifted him up, and began to drag him away, leaving Shoren alone to examine the room. He slowly walked around, looking at all the books and the desk. He sat down and looked at one of the books in particular. It said *Seal of the United States Army*. It was blue and had an eagle on it. He shrugged.

He stood up and began scanning the volumes on the bookshelves behind the desk. There were numerous books, some in English, Spanish and even Aramainian. There were books scattered around on the floor. On the desk were several books and a half-finished plate of mutton. Shoren sighed. There wasn't anything important. Wait. His eyes caught something.

A book. Shoren walked over to it and picked it up. The cover proclaimed it *The Personal Journal of General Hammond*. This could be important.

Shoren sat at the massive wooden desk with the great blue eagle seal on it, trying to translate the journal. After working on it for several hours he had managed to translate only four pages. The journal had proven to be extremely stubborn; for one thing it was written in a form of English that Shoren wasn't familiar with. He vaguely remembered his classical languages instructor had taught him about cursive. In Denver, the cursive style was never used since it couldn't be applied to Denver letters, and in addition, most of the books that remained from the Lost Age were written in standardized angular letters.

Shoren growled. He had spent most of the evening translating the damn thing and he had learned almost nothing. He had looked through the other books in the library only to discover that he was having trouble reading them as well. Others were in several languages that Shoren didn't know, languages that had died when the Aramainian Empire of Tyrris Plain had fallen. He took another look at the journal.

This is an account of my time as the acting commander of the weapons and supply cache of Fort Resistance as a part of Operation Dragon's Hoard. This isn't my official log, merely a tool I use for myself to record things I couldn't record in the log, or merely to collect and organize my thoughts. It will also help me remember things. I suppose this is a fitting place for the exile of an aging general who's losing his memory.

Shoren set the book down. The translation was tricky. English was a very complex language, especially in the cursive script. There were also several letters that he didn't quite know, but he thought he had figured them out for the most part. The only thing he needed now was time. Time and a few reference books to crosscheck his knowledge of the language. He would have to check and see if there were any books here that had both English and Denver copies. That would have to wait though. He shrugged and picked up the book to read some more when he heard a knock on the door.

"Come in!"

A young messenger in a blue uniform walked through the door. He walked over to Shoren and handed him a small, tightly rolled scroll. "Sir, a message from Captain Verdad."

Shoren took the scroll and set it down on the desk. "Thank you. Wait outside for a moment and I'll give you a message to send back to the captain. It was only after the messenger left that Shoren split the seal and unrolled the scroll.

General Commander Shoren,

My troops have eliminated all major enemy activity. Our information tells us that approximately one hundred and fifty rogue troops must have escaped, but they were headed in the direction of the Plains. The raiders there will most likely kill them. We slew more than five hundred enemy soldiers. All the captured villagers

surrendered immediately, nearly a thousand of them. Thirty-two of the rogues surrendered, and I followed your orders in that I will bring them here in order to incorporate them into your larger force.
Captain Jorge Verdad

Shoren leaned back and sighed. He had absolutely no idea what to do with the thousand-plus refugees, some of whom had seen their entire villages destroyed. Really, he had no idea where to put them. He shrugged. Maybe Josef would know what to do.

Shoren stood up and walked to the window to stare at the troops drilling in the courtyard below. Many of them were former supporters of Rekii. His orders were to incorporate any rogue troops who surrendered and wanted to receive a pardon into his own army. He walked over to the table and drafted orders for Verdad to bring in all the new soldiers as well as all the refugees.

He handed the message to the young messenger to take away and returned to the book.

Operation Dragon's Hoard was recently implemented as a security measure in the event of a continental, conventional invasion. The plan is to have secret, hidden stockpiles of fuel, weapons, planes, trucks and tanks, as well as supplies. Those include preserved food, water and medicine.

Fort Resistance, just like every other part of Operation Dragon's Hoard is hidden deep in the mountains, close to the west coast; a place that is believed to be a possible point of invasion. And while it is easily accessible by aircraft, it is difficult to find and equally difficult to reach by foot or land vehicle. One more thing. Every single part of Operation Dragon's Hoard is a secret. There are no official records in the Pentagon, White House or Congress. In fact, Congress and the President don't even know the operation exists.

I believe that the only people who do know are the ones involved. Even I don't know where the other bases are, or how many there may be. The only ones who would are the top brass, likely hidden away in Cheyenne Mountain.

At this Shoren stopped. He remembered the Sacred Mountain, Del Sheyenne Gebirgskain in the Denver language, but that was a holy place where it was said the demons dwelled. The demons were not said to be evil, but they were not good either.

The word Sheyenne and the word Cheyenne were very similar, but that didn't mean they meant the same thing, especially since the English word for Sheyenne was sacred or holy. Shoren shrugged. *Worry about that later,* he thought to himself.

He stood up. Soon it would be time to leave. Soon.

CHAPTER TEN

Major General Josef Nixon sat on his huge red horse at the edge of Denver territory. He was on the main road, near a town called Ausblienik. Ausblienik was built shortly after the Lost Times, near the site of a much older town called Fairview, Montana. Today was the day Rekii Ubel, traitor to the Denver nation, would be officially handed over to Josef to be brought back to Denver, where he would likely be executed.

Josef wasn't wearing his armor, even though it had begun to fit better. Today he needed to be in his full dress uniform, a tradition harking back to the days of Tyrris Plain. According to tradition, a high-ranking prisoner had to be able to face his jailer. In the days of Tyrris Plain the armor was the uniform, but now was different. The theory now was that the armor prevented the accused from seeing the face of his accuser. It was ridiculous. But it was what it was. If he knew Shoren at all, Rekii would be very secure. Very, very secure.

Then he saw Shoren, with his officers and one hundred of his men to serve as a bodyguard, ride into the center of the town with Rekii and several other men covered in chains and in a wagon together. The wagon had troops marching in a square formation around it, and then more soldiers riding in a square around them. Shoren wasn't taking any chances. Well, it was time to move.

Josef adjusted his red surcoat and jerked his head at his assistant, Over-Major Artur Campo, to bring the hundred men he had brought into formation behind him, all ready to take command of Rekii from Shoren.

As Josef rode into the town square with his men, he saw that perhaps the entire town was out and watching what Josef sincerely hoped would be the most exciting thing they ever saw, involving soldiers at least. When Shoren saw him, Josef could see the younger man visibly relax. He rode up to Josef.

"Well, major general, here are the traitors. Do we really need to go through the ceremony?"

Josef frowned. "You know as well as I do dat de defense lawyers could get Rekii off on a technicality should we be lacking on de ceremony. Not that such is likely to occur o' course; it's just better to be prepared."

"Yes, well, I suppose you're right." Shoren rode back up to Rekii and addressed him directly. "Rekii Ubel, on this day, the seventh day of the month of Abril, in the year 2207 After the Collapse, I, General Commander Shoren Torro McCarter, hereby relinquish my right as an Imperial Monitor against treason. Do you understand?"

Rekii glared at Shoren, cocked his head and finally spat at him. Shoren opened his mouth angrily but closed it again, knowing that any breach of ceremony could be catastrophic to their case. He didn't have to say anything anyway; one of the Black Guards smacked Rekii in the gut with a club.

Rekii glowered at the Guard but muttered a low "Yes."

Josef then eased back in his saddle before adjusting his red beret, making sure that the white plume was in place. But after a moment he did speak the formal words. "I, Josef Bairzich Nixon, on dis day, de seventh day o' de month o' Abril in the year 2207 After de Collapse, do take upon me-self de duty o' de Imperial Monitor against treason and as such I take command o' de traitor Rekii Ubel."

After those words, Shoren's own troops fell away from the wagon with the traitors and Josef's troops surrounded it. The Black Guards Josef had brought with him then surrounded the wagon, allowing Shoren's Guards to go back to their lines.

As the two sets of Guards passed one another they shot challenging looks at each other that at any other time would likely have resulted in bloodshed. It was because the two groups were from different clans. Josef's Guards were of the Golothzen Clan, meaning the Skulls, whereas Shoren's were from the Slychon, the Scythes. The clans were fiercely competitive and the Golothzen and the Slychon had been rivals for a century and a half. Bringing the two rival groups together was probably not the best of ideas.

The adversarial nature of the Black Guard clans never – well, not often – led to open violence, but with the Guards it was best not to test that. The temperaments of the different clans weren't so much those of differing gangs at war as of sports teams that sought to outdo each other. The rivalry between these particular clans started one hundred and fifty-three years prior in the Fifth Aztlan War, where an army of fanatics had marched up into Tejanos and Navajo lands in a bloody war of racial genocide. The Golothzen had only a double-fist, just over four hundred men against nearly three and a half thousand Aztlani marauders. The Double-Fist of Golothzen Black Guards destroyed the much larger force with less than a score of dead Guards.

The Slychon Clan was given the assignment of assassinating the High Sacrificial Priest of Aztlan in retaliation for another Aztlani attack just fifteen years later. The assassination provided the spark for the Sixth Aztlan War. The Fuegen Slichen brought the skull back to Denver where they placed it in a prominent place in their clan headquarters. The Golothzen hadn't yet surpassed that feat, and now that the Slychon had participated in the capture of one of the worst traitors in Denver's four hundred year history, it seemed as though the Golothzen would never surpass them. At least they would have the honor of escorting the traitor to Denver, a mild honor as the honor of the Guards went, but an honor nonetheless.

Josef nodded brusquely to himself. Now that his own Guards and troops had taken control of the wagon he continued. "Rekii Ubel, you are now under my control. I will be escort'n you to de Imperial Palace. Do ye understand?"

Rekii switched his glare to Josef now but did say, "Yes."

Josef grinned and motioned with his sword. The wind picked up all of a sudden and blew his red and white surcoat. Unlike his tight and rigid dress uniform, which was covered in insignia, awards, knots of rank and shoulder cords, the surcoat was plain, mostly red and reaching to his mid calves. The buttons were white, as was the jerkin that covered his shoulders. The collar that stood over the jerkin was red.

Josef raised his sword over his head once again and made a circle-like motion and shouted a command, "Into formation! We needs to get de prisoners back to de main army!" All of Josef's troops quickly moved back into a column formation and promptly marched out of the town. Josef looked back at Shoren. This night there would be a meeting between his officers and Shoren's.

✵ ✵ ✵

Shoren handed the reins of his horse to the horse handler to take away to one of the stalls in Ausblienik and walked to the small town's main inn. The owner of the inn, a Mistress Annel Luvek offered Shoren a mug of ale, which he declined. He wasn't interested in ale. Shoren didn't often drink, but when he did, he could drink with the best of them. He never drank ale though. Either wine or brandy.

Josef was sitting at one of the tables, a bottle of whiskey in front of him with a tumbler full of ice. He had already been drinking for a couple of hours before Shoren arrived. He grinned. That was Josef for you.

Shoren sat down and called one of the serving girls over. A pretty, young red-haired maiden made her way across the room.

"Captain, we have red and white wines, brandy, ale and various juices, although I'd guess those drinks couldn't interest you. We also have whiskey, which the major general there is drinking. So what would you like, sir?" she finished with a giggle.

"Whiskey! Whiskey and ale all around!" Josef shouted, waving his glass.

Shoren shook his head, but directed a calm smile toward the girl. "I would enjoy a glass of brandy actually."

The maid nodded and quickly sashayed back to the kitchen. Shoren turned around to look at Josef.

"Who's paying for all this? This party could cost thousands of golds."

"Shoren, de Palace be paying for de party, you know? Ye don't hafta' worry 'bout a ting."

Shoren came immediately to the point. "Well, actually, I wanted to talk to you about what happens next. I need to know what I'm going to be riding into."

"Yes, yes, about de Kirendadi. Jest so ye know, it's important to keep dis quiet, you know? Any leak o' dis, and de morale o' de men could drop like a hot stone. I tink dat if ye want to hear what I got to say bout it, we needs to go somewhere private."

Shoren nodded. "All right, but I want to get my brandy first. I do need a drink."

"Sir? I have your brandy right here. If you want or need anything else just let me know," the red-haired serving girl said, with a giggle and a smile and a very deep breath.

Shoren grunted at her, took his brandy, and followed Josef to a private booth.

"Well, Josef, I want to know what's going on. Why can't I let the others know? It could be important."

"We can't be telling de orders because de news from de front is very bad. We sent troops up north, but discovered dat de Kirendadi don't be fighting in de open land. No de be liking to fight in de mountains. Our heavy infantry cannot fight dem dere. We have suffered too many losses to continue, but it gets worse."

"It can get worse?"

"Oh, yes, it be much worse. Now de Kirendadi is coming after us, trying to take us out. Why, even me own unit has been seeing some fighting. Dat's what's worse."

"Josef, what are you even doing out here? I mean, you're in charge of the entire Denver army. Normally you wouldn't even leave Denver."

Josef laughed, then groaned and pressed a hand to his head. He looked up. "Shoren, de fact dat I'm out here at all should be telling you how bad it is. When a major general must be out on active field duty, den ye know how bad it be. Too many commanders have died, way back in Denver we don't know who's alive or dead, let alone be finding new ones. Dat's why I'm out here. Now we has de new classes trained up and I can take Rekii back and set on me fat rump like I supposed to do. I be hating dis shit."

Shoren winced at the expletive. He hated it all too, but he wouldn't have put it quite like that. He looked at Josef. "I can see that you're very interested in returning to your drink. I'll leave you to it. Thanks for the warning."

"No problem! Shoren, ye haven't barely touched yer own drink!"

Shoren lifted the glass with a sigh. He took a few sips for Josef's sake, and began walking away, sipping his brandy. Finally he finished it and walked over to the main bar, set the glass down, and walked out of the tavern.

CHAPTER ELEVEN

Josef stood before the aging Emperor in the Imperial Throne Room in the Imperial Palace in the city sheltered by the Peaks of Paradise, Denver. He was wearing his full dress uniform and he was buttoned to the collar and had ironed his coat. He had even gotten a haircut and had trimmed his salt-and-pepper beard. Behind him stood two Black Guards holding a chained Rekii. Rekii was merely standing there covered in chains. The two Guards were not dressed up at all, for a Guard the armor and weapons that he used in the field was all the uniform he needed. The four Protectors standing at the edge of the Emperor's dais looked almost ineffectual when compared to the brutal competence of the Black Guards.

Richerd took in the entire scene, the Guards, Josef and finally Rekii Ubel. Josef and the Emperor. Richerd smiled as his father, Emperor Otto, began to speak the endless ritual words and Josef replied, as was ritual. Those rituals were yet another custom that he would do away with as soon as he was emperor, which if Richerd had anything to say about it would be a lot sooner than anyone thought.

A great number of people were going to have to go, especially that Josef. He was far too honorable and honest to do what needed to be done in order to ensure that Denver not only remained strong but grew ever stronger.

CHAPTER TWELVE

Another arrow hissed past Shoren's ear, causing him to lean low against his horse. Kirendadi arrows sped out of nowhere to strike Shoren's heavy infantry. The light infantry hurried up the hill on both sides to engage with the raiders. Up ahead armed men from the city of Koro were standing on the road.

Shoren swore as an arrow became lodged in the eyehole of his helmet. He was unharmed because the helmet was currently situated in his right hand, since this gathering was supposed to be neutral. He slipped the helmet on.

Shoren's legion, a column of ten thousand soldiers, was marching through a pass to crush a small army of Koro troops that had gathered much too close to the border. When they found the troops on the road heading in the direction of the Denver troops, Shoren had been able to see that he outnumbered them nearly five to one. He had also been able to see that they were flying a white flag, a common symbol for negotiation. Shoren found this to be an excellent excuse to bring his troops much closer to the Koro troops. He had also ordered his archers to be ready and his cavalry to ride up around the hills near the road, and that's when thousands of arrows began raining down seemingly out of nowhere. From the numbers, either there were multiple ten thousand archers up in the trees, unlikely, given that the army of Koro, even with their Kirendadi allies, could not come up with thousands of archers. That left only one other possibility – that Kirendadi raiders had stolen some of the Denver crossbows, horrible though that thought was. Shoren hissed as another arrow lanced by him. He needed to get his troops forward. If his legion could charge the enemy, the archers would stop firing for fear of hitting their own troops. If he couldn't get his troops forward, then what was now a highly disruptive situation could easily become a full rout.

"Charge! At them! May the bloody black spirits take you! Charge!"

Shoren could see that his orders were falling on ears deafened by panic. In fact, he could already see some of his cavalry turning to flee – those who weren't trying to charge up the hills. The infantry had mostly begun setting up the tortoise formations with their shields, crouching low together with interlocking tower shields on each side and others held over top of the heads of the formation – an excellent defensive position that was in theory completely impervious to arrows.

Theory and practice were not the same however, as hundreds of bandits with repeating crossbows proved. The bolts continued to chew up any troops that it caught, and once a tortoise opened up, a few well aimed shots could tear the formation apart.

Shoren caught sight of a bugler. "Bugler! Sound the charge!"

The young man remained still. "Bugler! Sound the charge now!"

The young man, more a boy really, continued to sit on his horse, seemingly frozen. Shoren, having been a bugler himself once, understood the boy's problem, but that understanding did nothing to get the bugle sounded.

Shoren rode over to the boy to awaken him to his job, or at the very least to take the bugle and sound the charge himself. But just as he reached the boy, his own horse simply seemed to fall away and the ground rose up to meet him. Instead of the friendly embrace Shoren would have preferred, the ground gave him several hard knocks before allowing him to roll away. Once he stopped, Shoren sat up but discovered that he couldn't see at all. *What?* he thought. *Am I blind?* But a reflexive check of his helmet revealed that in his haste to don it, he had failed to strap it on, allowing it to rotate during his tumble.

A few seconds of struggle had the helmet off and at his side, allowing Shoren to see. He quickly reclaimed his sword but failed to find the bugle boy, although he did in fact find the bugle. Still crouching low, Shoren raised it to his lips and set off the six-note sequence for "Charge straight ahead of the main force." He was pleased to see that the cavalry began to turn around and charge at the small army of Koro troops, but less than thrilled to see that the infantry for the most part remained where they were. Shoren sounded the charge again before sending out the seven-note sequence for "Break formation and attack." The heavy infantry broke rank, began at a jog and finally at a run to reach the enemy. The cavalry quickly caught up, passed them, and hit the Koro troops with destructive force. The infantry also caught up quickly and eagerly waded into the fray, not only for vengeance on the trick the Kirendadi played on them from above, but also because they noticed more troops fleeing behind those of Koro.

The Denver infantry could see not only the dragon banners of the Koro, but also the hammer of the Kildenhain, the red leaf over the white star of the Brentarians and the three silver stags of the Saldenese disappearing over the horizon. How could their scouts have missed that?

It took Shoren only a few minutes to find his horse. From the arrows in its left shoulder and the way it was hobbling, it looked as though Guerrero had been hit a few times before falling over from the pain. Shoren looked over and saw the last dragon banner fall before he turned his attention back to Guerrero.

Shoren stopped in the middle of pulling off his gauntlets. The arrows had stopped. It quickly became clear why when the light infantry began pouring back down into the pass, carrying a surprising number of Denver crossbows, but also numerous Kirendadi raven banners. The small flags were not actually banners at all, but small, solid shield-flags stuck into the ground to indicate rally points as well as the identity and location of the chief. There was also a kind of language based on the movements of the flags. These all had the typical raven on the round shield, but also the many yellow strips tied around the flag, indication that the group was fighting under a mercenary status. They also showed the tribe of the group and the personal symbol of the leader, this time an evergreen tree for the tribe and a stylized red flame for the leader.

Shoren nodded before pulling his gauntlets off and beginning to stroke Guerrero's uninjured shoulder. Guerrero screamed in pain as he began to pull the first arrow out, but Shoren's hold on the reins kept the horse from knocking him over. The second and third arrows were easy to remove, and Shoren used a cape from a fallen officer to soak up the blood before bandaging the wound. Shoren motioned for a soldier to bring him another horse and sounded the bugle call for "Into formation." The legion's other buglers picked up on the call, and Shoren began to look for surviving officers, which he quickly discovered was a rarity up here. He sighed. They would have to set up camp and look after the wounded soon enough.

✢ ✢ ✢

Shoren was standing in General Mekal's command tent, staring at a map of the lands of the Kirendadi and also the city-states beyond. He saw the numerous markers indicating troop locations and movements, and also the markers for battles. While several were green, battles ending in success, all too many were colored red for failure, or black, indicating a force almost completely wiped out. There were more black markers than green or red, and Shoren was distressed to see that the battle he had fought the week before that had ended in his horse being wounded was marked red even though he had succeeded in destroying the Koro troops.

Shoren had ordered his troops forward to get them out of the pass and had sent his remaining cavalry at a heavy pace and his infantry at a walk with wagons to carry the wounded back. Two days into the chase however, his scouts had returned to report that they had been unable to find the enemy troops, so Shoren had stopped to rest and resupply while letting the main body of troops catch up with him. Shoren and his troops were now just a day's march from the city of Kildenhain. Shoren had been able to see the red sculptor's hammer on a field of gold. Of course, the Kildenhain had said that the hammer was a sculptor's hammer, but to Shoren's eye it looked like any other hammer.

General Mekal was going to try to storm the city in the hope of capturing it before the winter snows came. The general estimated they had only about two more months of decent weather, unlike in Denver, far to the south, where they would normally have had double that amount. The situation was delicate. The Denver forces needed to capture Kildenhain or they would be forced to lay the city under siege while blanketed in a winter that would be a lot harsher on them than it would be on the city. Kildenhain, Koro, the Kirendadi and whoever else happened to be up here would be able to strike at the Denver while Mekal's army, being unfamiliar with the terrain and the harsher winter, would be stuck. Denver's mighty siege machines would be useless; in fact it was very possible that all of the explosive bombs might even freeze. And through it all, Shoren had no doubt that the Kirendadi would be spreading out skirmishers to strike at his own troops.

He could see it, every day, a small group shoots some arrows at his troops, maybe hitting them, maybe not. Men sneaking in to kill the Denver livestock, burn their food, destroy their siege weapons, or kill their horses. He could see legionnaires getting shot at while looking for food, looking for fun, looking for a place to crap. Every day just a few losses, but over an entire Kirendadi winter, even a few daily losses would soon add up to significant attrition. To combine that with deserters, lack of food, and diseases that come from staying in one camp the whole time... the casualties would be enormous. Shoren grimaced. They needed to take the city now. Shoren brought his attention back to General Mekal.

"If we can surround the city and prevent nothing from getting in or out, at the very least we can starve them out. Commander Potriken, how go your efforts to build more catapults and scorpions?"

"Not as well as expected, sir. We have built three new catapults and four new scorpions, but that still does not bring us back to full strength. Kirendadi raiders have been attacking our engineers. We need more guards."

"Raiders have our foragers too. We simply don't have the men to spare. I say that we start the siege now, and try to destroy the walls with what we already have. If we concentrate our attacks on certain weak points, we should be able to break through rather quickly." That came from Commander Mekoth, in charge of the third legion.

"Commander Shoren? What are your thoughts about this?"

"Well, general, I was actually thinking about where Kildenhain gets its supplies. If we can choke off those sources, we wouldn't even need to surround the city."

General Mekal looked thoughtful for a moment. "That is a good idea. Our scouts indicate that Kildenhain operates like most Denver cities. Numerous farming towns are in place around the city, with roads leading to each other and to Kildenhain. This allows the city, much as Denver, to be self-sufficient and not rely on food from far off in the event of some emergency. Cut that off, and the city will starve, or at least be thrown into a panic."

"Do they have anything like the Harvest Guilds?"

According to Denver law since time immemorial, each Denver city needed to be able to grow at least seventy-five to eighty percent of its own food. Some cities took the law literally and were quite capable of feeding themselves entirely, also to trade food to other cities. Denver itself was one of those cities.

The Harvest Guilds were a social phenomenon unique to the Denver. Guilds were in charge of specific crafts, and they kept a great deal of knowledge and skill within their ranks. An individual merely needed to pay an annual due and the guild would teach him professional techniques that he couldn't learn anywhere else.

The guilds' other purpose was quality control. The guilds were self-regulating and they checked every member every year to ensure that his product was to the guild's standards. When the product wasn't, the guild would require a small fine and insist that the craftsman relearn the techniques of his trade. Guilds also published lists of those whose work was not satisfactory. When a craftsman's work was incompetent to a dangerous level, he faced strict fines, censures, or even removal from the guild. As a result, there were few people who would buy from anyone not in a guild.

The Harvest Guilds were an extension of that concept, and each guild applied all its accumulated skill and knowledge to a single farming product, be it wheat or maize or beans or beef or fish. This meant that all land and water was put to the best use possible and that no farmland was wasted for want of proper techniques, and also ensured that all food sold was clean and free of disease or contamination. Farming without the knowledge acquired by the Harvest Guilds seemed very strange to all the Denver gathered there.

"No, they don't. That should make it easier for us to disrupt their harvest. Shoren, before you went after the traitor Rekii Ubel, you served in the light cavalry, yes?"

"Yes, sir, that is so."

"Good. I want you to take a battalion and wreck those farms. Take the grain and livestock for our troops, and then burn the buildings, and destroy the carts, wagons and tools of the farmers.

"I want you all to prepare your respective forces and prepare to begin the siege as soon as we are in position around the city, which should be in four days. This meeting is at an end. Shoren, stay here."

"Yes, sir." None of the other officers even wanted to look at Shoren, except for Ryon, who nodded to him as a gesture of support. After all the officers had left the tent, General Mekal looked at the map for a moment.

"Do you know, Shoren, why your command has been reduced from a full legion, ten thousand soldiers, to a mere battalion of five hundred raiders? Do you?"

"Sir, I assume it's because I lost nearly a fourth of my command in an ambush not all that long ago. Two thousand soldiers dead, all of the cavalry grounded, and I destroyed only two thousand Koro troopers and an unknown number of Kirendadi raiders. I then failed to catch another group of enemy soldiers that had escaped, no doubt using the time the Koro troops bought in order to flee, so now we have two thousand dead men and six thousand enemies off frolicking the spirits know where, and all because I walked into an ambush I should have seen coming. Sir."

"Well, well. Now is not exactly the time for self-recrimination, Commander Shoren. You should have seen it coming. It's a textbook trap and you walked right into it. However, you did do a better job than most would have in rallying your troops and defeating the enemy. You also gave chase to the enemy right away, something many other officers wouldn't have done. Initiative in the Denver army is no longer what it used to be, especially compared to the days of Tyrris Plain."

Tyrris Plain was an ancient warlord who had conquered a vast empire that had extended from the coastline to the Plains, from far north of the Kirendad to the borders of Aztlan. Though the empire had never actually seized the nation of Tejas, the only nation to remain independent and largely the same since the Lost Times, the empire had once touched on Tejas' western and northern borders.

Much of Denver culture came from the empire of Tyrris Plain and its predecessor, the nation of Colorado. Colorado had been a quasi-independent nation-state, tied up in a loose confederation that history said harkened back to before the Lost Times. But after Tyrris Plain rose to power, Colorado quickly became the most powerful nation of the confederation. Afterwards, it came to conquer its neighbors and Tyrris Plain did his best to bring about a world-spanning empire. His descendants carried on with his tradition, and pushed the Aztlani as far south as the Rio Grande and allowed the Navajo to settle – for the first time in centuries – where the Aztlani had been.

Tyrris Plain's empire finally collapsed though, and one of the results of that was the development of Denver as an independent nation. Many pieces of Denver culture remained the same. The guilds, for example, were in place long before the Denver came into its own power.

Another example was the organization of the military. Before Tyrris Plain, armies were loosely organized in squads and fists as the smaller units, and then divisions and brigades as the larger units. Tyrris Plain, and later the Denver who copied him, divided everything up into units of ten and five. Military organization started out as ten troopers to a squad, five squads to a platoon, two fifty-man platoons to a company, five companies to a battalion and so on, with sub-legions of one thousand men, brigades with five thousand, and finally legions and divisions with fifty thousand men.

Since then Denver had come to dominate much of Tyrris Plain's fallen empire, and many Denver saw themselves as its natural heirs. This caused some conflict, given that few of the Denver were skilled enough to fight such a large scale war anymore. The current situation was proof enough of that. Had any of the Denver commanders here possessed even half of Tyrris Plain's skill or daring, the war with the Kirendadi would have been over by now and Koro would effectively lie beneath Denver's thumb.

As it was, it was not outside the realm of possibility that the Denver military might be thrown back and it was even possible that the Kirendadi could actually push the Denver back into their own territory.

Shoren brought himself back to the moment at hand. He saluted. "Sir, may I withdraw to select a battalion of cavalry?"

General Mekal looked him over and refrained from replying for a moment. "Yes you may, Shoren. I want you on the road by tonight."

Shoren nodded. "Thank you, sir. May I have a list of the light cavalry units, sir?"

"Yes, take it. It's on the table."

"Thank you, sir."

Shoren left the tent holding the list in his left hand. Before anything else, he needed to requisition another horse and see about getting Guerrero home. It might be a good idea to give that assignment to Charlz, especially since it was simply getting more and more dangerous. The boy and a few of the nobles who were anxious to leave should have no difficulty in getting back to Denver safely.

He walked over to one of the impromptu stables, right up to the stable master, a bald-headed fellow with the once powerful frame of a soldier who had gone to seed. Shoren sniffed. There was no smell of manure or anything else. The hay was fresh and clean. This man took care of his horses. *As well he should,* Shoren thought, noticing the pin on the man's collar indicating a former cavalry trooper.

"Stable master, I am Commander Shoren McCarter. I find myself in need of a new horse. I need a fast and strong horse, preferably a Comanche mustang, although any type of mustang raiding horse will do."

"Well, sir, I do have a few Comanche mustangs in reserve, mostly horses whose riders were killed. I see that you have the proper authorization to request a single horse, so if you would follow me?"

The stable master led Shoren deeper into the stable to show him several stalls with Comanche mustangs. Comanche mustangs were a kind of horse that was raised by the Comanche Nation that lived in the Paradise Mountains of the Denver Empire. The Comanche produced fast and hardy horses that were perfect for the rugged mountains and open plains that Denver light cavalry had to travel through.

Shoren looked at a few of the first horses and nodded almost imperceptibly to himself. The horses were good enough, but there was nothing that set them apart from other hussaria horses. Shoren continued down the line and noticed a roan mustang stallion. He motioned for the stable master to lead the horse out so that he could see him walk.

The stallion had a good long stride and no perceptible lameness, and Shoren ran his hand over the horse's legs and belly, feeling for any other problems. He opened the stallion's mouth and checked his teeth and gums. Both were clean and free of disease. The stallion's eyes were bright and clear. The creature was perfect.

"I'll take this one. What's his name?"

"Hister, after one of the black spirits, true, because of his own black spirit. He's a strong fast horse yes, but he's also got the wildness of a true killer horse. If you want him you can have him."

"Well, I'll take him. He's the best of the stallions here."

"Let me have your papers and I'll mark your name down on my records and you can be on your way."

Shoren thanked the man and followed him. There were only a few minutes of paperwork that needed to be done, mostly a promise to care for the horse until his duty was over and a new application for the military to provide feed and medicine for the horse even though Hister was going to be using Shoren's own equipment.

Shoren gripped the horse's reins and led him away from the stable and over to one of the cavalry sections of the camp, reviewing his list as he went. Most of the heavy cavalry had been destroyed, but they weren't a choice anyway. As he examined the list of active cavalry battalions with their recent action, Shoren noticed that one of them, the Alpha Battalion of the Seventh Legion had more recent combat experience than the others and was also at near full strength. As such, it was ideally suited to Shoren's needs. Nodding to himself, Shoren turned and led his horse to the site of the Alpha Battalion.

As Shoren reached the light cavalry, a captain walked out of his green striped tent and straight up to Shoren. He saluted.

"Sir, I am Captain Gorge Tomsen. Is there anything I can do for you?"

"Yes, captain, there is. I'm Commander Shoren. I'm taking command of your battalion and we're going to be raiding enemy farms and taking as much as we can in order to supply our own troops for the siege of Kildenhain."

"Sir, when do we leave?"

"As soon as possible. If we can be ready to leave immediately, it would be best."

"Yes, sir. I'll muster the troops and we'll be ready to leave within the hour."

"You have all your equipment ready?"

"Yes, sir. We'll leave the heavy tents and anything else a horse can't carry."

CHAPTER THIRTEEN

Shoren sat up on his saddle, looking over yet another tiny farming village. Behind him sat one hundred men on horseback, ready to descend upon the village and then disperse to go after the farms further out in the countryside. Shoren had split his battalion into five groups of about one hundred men each. Each group would attack a small village, overrun any resistance, quickly capture whatever stores of food and livestock they could, and then burn and destroy the rest.

Shoren turned his horse to continue down the small wooded path that led up to the tiny hamlet. Once they were close but still unseen, Shoren drew his sword, swung it horizontally, and stabbed it up toward the heavens and then straight down to point at the village.

The men quickly moved to a skirmish line and charged toward the village, at first loosing a few arrows and then drawing their own swords. Before, they had been silent. Now they seemed to be trying to make up for their earlier quiet with loud yelling and shouting, all intended to intimidate the villagers into fleeing. As usual, most fled, but the town militia, mostly young men who were poorly trained and poorly armed, gathered in the square while everyone else fled. Shoren made a circling gesture with his sword and the skirmish line became an entrapping two-deep circle, the first row wielding swords while the second row drew their bows and simply but surely fired upon the militia.

The militiamen, mostly wearing either a helmet or a breastplate but rarely both and never more, and mostly armed with hunting spears and ancient swords, now dispersed from the square, charging at the cavalry in an attempt to escape, all the while continuing to be shot at. They very quickly reached the edge of the circle and tried to fight, but farmers on foot do not last long when pitted against a larger force of highly trained and well-armed and armored cavalry. Though they put up a valiant fight, each and every one of them was summarily cut down. There was no glory in it and even less honor. It was simply duty.

Now the soldiers dismounted, every fifth man holding the reins of the four horses next to him. They moved in pairs to search through houses and shops, granaries and stables. Everything. Shoren himself paired off with a soldier after giving orders to leave the bodies where they lay and began a house-to-house sweep. In the town hall Shoren encountered two men, desperately gathering food and other supplies. Once Shoren stepped into the pantry, the two men jumped away and drew knives. Shoren drew his sword and immediately thrust it forward at the nearest man. The other man leaped toward him in a rage but was quickly run through by Shoren's sword. The first man, taking advantage of Shoren's distraction, ran away.

The other Denver soldier returned from another room of the town hall and shook his head. "There's nothing in here, sir."

Shoren nodded. "Let's see what else there is in the other buildings. We need to be gone quickly though."

Shoren stepped out of the house to see that the Denver had taken much of the stored grain and other foodstuffs as well as many goods from the small village market and piled it all high into several stolen wagons. The wagons would be sent back to the main army, but first the hussaria needed to ride to the surrounding farms and repeat the process.

Shoren called for each squad leader to come to him as he rolled out a map he had taken from the town hall. He pointed out different farms to each squad and sent them on their way.

Shoren himself would be traveling with the squad that captured the herds of sheep and goats that had been driven up to pasture by the sheepherders. He turned his horse on the road toward the meadows. There shouldn't be any guards worthy of the name, just a few teenagers with slingshots and wooden staves. Shoren intended to let them go, the way he had been letting all the other villagers except the militia escape, and the way his troops had orders to let the villagers and farmers escape.

Shoren knew that once his troops left, most of the farmers would head for the relative safety of the city. Those who returned would probably gather what they could, bury the militiamen, and then flee terrified to the city. This influx of farmers and villagers into the city would fill the residents with fear at the stories they told of Denver raiders tearing through the farms, stealing and destroying all they could. They would also add more mouths that needed to eat, shortening the life of the city's already dwindling food supply. Also, and this was as important as any other reason, once the Denver captured the city, they would need people to work the surrounding farms in order to feed the city, and they didn't want to have to bring up Denver farmers.

Shoren pulled out his horse bow as he neared the end of the trail that led him and his ten hussaria to the meadows. He saw several teenagers surrounding a large flock of sheep. Shoren rode up to the tallest boy with his bow drawn.

"You, boy. These sheep are now the property of the Denver Empire. Get the other boys together and have them gather up the sheep and follow us. Once the sheep are safely in Denver hands, you will be permitted to leave. Do you understand?"

The boy nodded, terrified, and immediately hurried away to obey. Shoren unnocked the arrow and eased back in his saddle, pleased that it would be so easy. He looked over at the sheep once more, only to see one of his soldiers tumble from his saddle. Shoren saw where the trouble was coming from and quickly raised his bow. One of the sheepherders had taken it into his mind to fight off the Denver with a sling.

The boy picked up another rock and placed it into the leather strap from which the weapon hurled the small stone. He lifted the sling over his head and circled it, or at least it began to circle when three arrows suddenly sprouted from his neck, torso and thigh. Shoren hurriedly stuffed his bow back in its case before drawing his sword. As he did that though, he squeezed his knees together. Hister, a well-trained horse, began advancing on the boys.

They were terrified, and their faces showed it. They cowered and quivered and one made water all over himself. Shoren didn't waste a minute. "Hand over your slings!" The boys complied. "Now, I want you to gather these sheep up, and if you don't…." Shoren thrust with his sword, holding the point just an inch away from the nearest sheep-herder's nose, making glaringly obvious the penalty for disobedience. That taken care of, Shoren rode back to his fallen man, who apparently had not been wearing his helmet when the stone had struck him. He was dead. He was not the first of the raiders who had died, and he probably wouldn't be the last, although he did have the dubious honor of being the only raider to die at the hands of a mere boy.

One of the other men dismounted, picked up both bodies, strapped them to the horse of the fallen raider, and then tied the reins to his saddle. Hister, true to the dark spirit he was named for, snorted and snapped at the five remaining sheepherders as they gathered up the village's sheep. Once they had gathered up all the sheep they could, the nine surviving hussaria rode in a kind of circle around the sheep and herding boys, trying to make sure no sheep escaped while simul-taneously keeping an eye on the boys and on the road in the event that some Kirendadi or some Kildenhain soldiers showed up. It would be a bad business to have gone to the work of gathering all these sheep only to get ambushed part way back to the rally point.

Shoren sheathed his sword. While he did keep an eye on the road, it would be several hours back to the village, and after an uneventful hour, he began to be wrapped up in his own thoughts. First about this new assignment, one he didn't relish, but one that he had to do. He knew that he had been given this job not because he had experience with light cavalry, but because he had been ambushed and a fourth of his legion now lay dead. The battalion commander could have done this job as well as Shoren. All this was nothing more than a punishment.

Shoren knew however that a lower command did not last forever, and while he had been afraid that his prospects for being a general had gone, he knew that he still had a chance. There was still a chance.

Just do this, he told himself, this and whatever else Mekal gives you, this nothing. Mekal needs experienced commanders, and he'll give you another chance. Yeah. Maybe not a legion, but at least a sub legion.

With that boosting his confidence, Shoren smiled. The smile vanished when he began to think about the war in general. He didn't know if it had been given a name yet, whether the Kirendadi War, or the Koro War, or Emperor Otto IV's War, or something else he hadn't thought of. He did know from both his mother and Elina that Richerd had alternated between pushing for the war and expressing doubt. In public he either did not acknowledge the war or was very derisive of it, but in assembly with his father and his father's advisors he was supportive, at least in the beginning. This Shoren remembered from before he left Denver, and he did not trust Richerd then. Letters from both his mother and Elina made Shoren trust him even less now.

According to those letters, Richerd had a hand in everything to do with the war, from reinforcements to supplies to overall strategy. Shoren's mother had told him that Richerd was up to something. She didn't know what it was, but he was up to something. She was mostly fixated on how the progress of the war affected her family's position, but she had told him that corruption seemed rampant in the Assembly. Elina was mostly concerned with Shoren himself and would likely be greatly distressed to hear about what had happened to his command just two weeks earlier.

On Shoren's end, he knew that supply trains came irregularly, if at all, and reinforcements the same way. It was more than likely that they would have to finish with what they had, no matter how much they needed the reinforcements. Mekal spoke constantly about how much those troops were needed, because they could occupy the already captured territory and free up more troops to fight further north. Also, as General Mekal constantly pointed out, Denver had the troops. There were, probably, all in all, nearly a million soldiers spread throughout Denver and all along the various borders. Denver could easily spare additional troops for the Kirendadi campaign.

Shoren looked up and noticed that they were almost to the rally point, and he could see in the distance the other riders as well, coming down to just outside the now empty village. Once the riders were gathered together, Shoren glanced around to see that each squad had arrived. He stood up in his saddle.

"Squad leaders, report!"

Each squad leader rode forward and detailed the food, livestock, tools, medicines and other supplies that had been taken from the farms prior to burning them to the ground. Once they were finished, Shoren ordered almost everyone into formation around the captured goods and supplies, mostly carried in wagons. Some of those wagons were driven by soldiers, but only a few; the rest were driven by terrified farm folk. The remaining soldiers were left behind to burn the village.

Now that his troops were on their way back to the main army with their prize, Shoren allowed himself to relax and a small smile to creep onto his face. This raid was the last one Shoren had planned; all the villages had been looted and destroyed. His entire command would be back at the main army camp with their own prizes.

It wasn't long until he arrived back at the camp, turned over the supplies, and went to find himself someplace to wash up. Once he was finished, he lay down to get some rest. He had done what he could. Now all they had to do was take the city and hold out for the winter.

CHAPTER FOURTEEN

Shoren stared at the letter lying on his writing desk. While he had been receiving mail throughout the campaign, this letter was special because it was the only letter that had arrived in three months, as a part of the only supply caravan to have gotten past the Kirendadi "counter-siege" in nearly three months. It was nearly three months since Shoren had brought in the stolen food and while it had proven to be very useful, it was in no way sufficient to feed a hundred thousand soldiers over an entire winter.

Shoren had been sure that Kildenhain would fall when he saw the four massive trebuchets that began pounding on its walls. He had been sure when the wall towers collapsed that he would be spending the winter in a warm mansion behind the massive stone walls. Sadly, that was not to be. Kirendadi raiders had wrecked two trebuchets and a much larger number of other catapults and siege machines. Since then, every day had seen more casualties – not in battles or skirmishes, but men dead while foraging, men dead while scouting, men dead where they sat, where they slept, where they squatted.

The few scouts who had returned had reported finding massacred caravans, all the soldiers dead and the supplies vanished. Even the carts were burned or stolen. Entire columns of reinforcements were dead on the road or had simply vanished entirely, as if they never were. At the same time, the Denver hadn't been able to find the Kirendadi or the other raiders that seemed to have made a hobby of killing starving soldiers in their sleep. Every time the infantry went out, the men were killed. When the cavalry went out, the horsemen found nothing but bodies.

Shoren laughed to himself. He had managed to get a higher command now, even greater than what he had before. He was in charge of his old legion, now at half strength, and then another legion at near full strength. The reason? The other commanders had died. One had been killed trying to chase down the raiders, and the other had fallen off his horse and broken his neck. Compared to the screw-ups of some of the other commanders, his own wasn't that bad. One sub legion commander had actually taken his troops out to chase down what he thought was a large force of Koro soldiers. The entire group froze to death, right down to the mounts. The enemy soldiers were never found.

Shoren turned back to the letter sitting on the desk. It was from Elina. The letter detailed more on the political climate back in Denver. It spoke of how Richerd had taken most of the power of the Emperor for himself. Emperor Otto was very ill, and Richerd had been going through the government and firing and replacing many politicians in key positions. The Assembly had had many changes in its leadership and members. The major general was even rumored to be taking an early retirement, due to some very nasty rumors of his being involved in the disappearances of a few high-ranking nobles and wealthy and influential merchants. It was, or so went the rumor, only the royal magistrate's consideration for Josef's many years of loyal service that prevented the disgrace of an investigation. That the nobles were connected to the illegal slave trade seemed to be of no consequence.

It also spoke of rumors of Tejas trying to expand its influence in Denver, even trying to break the ancient treaty that formed the boundary between the two nations, of an Aztlan army massing in their deserts and jungles that could rip through the Navajo, completely bypass the Tejanos, and strike the "unprotected belly of the Denver" as Richerd was reported to have said. "It is," Richard is reported to have continued, "past the time that we allow our enemies to gather while we waste our resources in the northern war of our fathers. We must be strong enough to destroy the plagues of the empires to the south. Anything less is treason. The weakness of our fathers is why Otto's War is lost."

Elina had then mentioned that the shipments of reinforcements were being slowed down. The political unrest in Denver was coming to a boiling point. She admitted that she was actually afraid and that she was leaving Denver to live on her family's mountain manor. She also said that she missed him and that she hoped he would return soon. Shoren sank onto his cot. He actually missed her too. The past year had caused him to think a great deal about what he wanted to do with his life. The constant death had made him wish more than once for a simpler life, one without all the struggle and viciousness of war. He also realized that he missed his home more than anything. He missed his country ranch, his family's herds of horses that they raised and sold, the dogs and small ponies that they raised as pets for the nobility. He missed the open fields, the mountains, his mother and brothers and sisters. He missed the city and he missed... Elina. Shadows of the damned, he missed Elina.

One of the two guards stationed outside of Shoren's tent poked his head in.

"Sir? A runner had just arrived from General Mekal. He wants all of the legion commanders to appear in the command tent immediately, sir."

"Thanks. I'll be there in a moment."

The guard nodded and resumed keeping watch. Shoren himself bent over to pick up his boots and green coat. Once he had put those on, he buckled on his sword belt and stepped out of the tent. On his way to the command tent, he thought more about the corruption and how this war was simply too political. He didn't care; there was nothing that he could do about it now.

When he reached the command tent, Shoren found that it was already full. All the remaining decalegion commanders and General Mekal were standing around a table with a map on it. Mekal looked up.

"Ah, Shoren, glad you're here. Come on, come on," he said, pushing the other commanders out of the way so Shoren could see the table.

"First things first. I'm lifting the siege."

"What!" "Why?" and other similar cries rose from the throats of the gathered commanders.

General Mekal raised his hands in a calming gesture in an attempt to get everyone to be quiet. "Please, everyone, trust me. I have good reasons." He put up a hand to cut off the protests.

"The first reason is that meadow to the south where twenty thousand brave Denver lie dead. The second is that I have received a report of a Koro noble doing what was previously thought impossible: the unification of all the northern city-states and the combining of their armies. Our scouts report that they'll be ready to move by spring. We need to lift the siege of Kildenhain and move back into already pacified territory. I've already sent some riders down to get reinforcements.

"The first thing that we need to do is select a city or fortification that we can turn into a stronghold and make a stand at. Any suggestions?"

"How about Garriton?" one of the commanders asked. "It's a reasonably large city with enough storehouses to feed the army as well as its own large garrison, and it has numerous strong fortifications."

Another replied with a negative. "Garriton is too exposed. There are at least four roads traveling into it and the enemy can just cut it off. I think our best chance is actually to try to fight them in a battle once we have received our reinforcements."

Shoren glared at him. "We haven't had any reinforcements in three months. We haven't had any supplies or orders or anything in three months. We're going to have to assume that we won't get any, and that we have to beat them with what we have. I think we should strip the city garrisons to supplement our forces and try to get them to attack a stronghold of our choosing. Personally, I'd have to say Garriton as well."

The arguing continued on for another few hours before the plan was set to pull back to Garriton. The Commanders all went forth to brief their troops and to get them ready to move. Kildenhain had gained a reprieve.

✣ ✣ ✣

Morken Luviecell grinned as he looked at the map in front of him. He had been terrified when the seemingly invulnerable army of the Denver had ridden up into Kirendadi territory just a year before. Denver was a massive empire, bent on the reclamation of the empire of Tyrris Plain, of which they already controlled the majority. Denver was huge and powerful, but inwardly focused, an unfortunate viewpoint for an imperialist power.

Due to its long inward focus, Denver had become vulnerable, weak. The hollow façade of power was proven to be just that, thanks to its foolish invasion of the north. Morken smiled. He was not weak, and neither were his people. The invasion had proven this. It shouldn't be hard at all to crush the Denver's imperialist army and then march down into the unprotected northern frontier of the empire and cut out its heart. Or maybe not. A better idea would be to take its heart and control it, to rule it, to claim the largest empire in the known world for a tiny city in the north. Lord Morken Luviecell would disappear in time, overshadowed by another name – Emperor Morken Luviecell.

CHAPTER FIFTEEN

Shoren looked over at the ramparts being constructed around the city of Garriton. Runners had gone back to try to get reinforcements but they had not yet arrived. Wooden hoardings were being built around the walls to protect the archers and crossbowmen who would be defending the city. Some larger towers were being fitted for catapults and spear throwers, and in the open places behind the walls the much larger trebuchets were being constructed.

General Mekal had also gathered all the Denver troops from the surrounding cities in an attempt to supplement his numbers. Sadly, the forces he had been able to collect raised the size of the army by only a few thousand, but that few thousand was rested, strong and well-fed, and they had high morale.

Shoren turned away from the defenses under construction and walked toward the stairway. He stood on the top level of one of the city's inner towers, a keep, in order to gain a better view of the construction of the defenses and determine weak spots. So far, the only one he had seen was that there was simply not enough. Too many enemies and too few Denver were around for any commander to be comfortable.

The other thought that continually nagged at him, and he was sure nagged at the other commanders and General Mekal as well, was: What if they had misunderstood the Koros' intentions? While it was believed that the goal of the Koro up north was to destroy the army here and push the Denver out of Koro territory entirely, it was just as possible that the Koro might decide to simply skirt around their army and strike at the interior of Denver itself. Shoren knew very well that if the enemy decided to strike at Buffalo or Greybull or Shoshoni it could. Not only could it, but it could cause a lot of damage doing so.

Shoren knew that if he was in the Koros' situation that was what he might very well do.

He paused for one more look around the city and saw a rider coming over the hills to the south. A rider! That had to be one of the messengers that General Mekal had sent to the divisions along either the western border or the eastern frontier. None of the others would have had time to make it back yet. This one surely brought news of relief.

Shoren turned and ran down the stairs, his aides and legion commanders trailing behind him. Once he had reached the main floor, he stopped for a second to catch his breath and let his aides catch up with him. Once they had, he continued at a much slower pace. It wasn't appropriate for a decalegion commander to be seen running through the halls like a small child, and now that he could be seen by others, Shoren stopped such behavior despite his eagerness to hear what the messenger had to say. By his officers' looks of impatience, they were of the same mind. Once Shoren reached the outside, he ran to the hitching post where the horses were tied, untied his horse, mounted, and rode toward the general's headquarters. His officers followed him.

General Mekal had taken over the government buildings in the center of the city as his headquarters. That's where the messenger would be heading. The old columned buildings that dated back hundreds of years had been taken over and built over, not only to withstand a brutal siege but also to command any street fighting from a safe and secure position.

Shoren quickly hurried up the steps to the main meeting room in the headquarters. He was not surprised to find that he was the first officer there, having had the best view. An aide looked up.

"Sir?"

Shoren was excited now, and began to push the aide toward General Mekal's office. "Go tell the general that the first messenger he sent out has returned. While you're at it, tell him Decalegion Commander Shoren is here as well."

"Uh, um, yes, sir. Right away, sir. Um, all right." The aide nodded to himself and hurried to the impressive oak doors that led to the office that General Mekal had appropriated for himself. After a few minutes the aide returned with a harried expression. He passed by

Shoren without looking at him and walked toward the doors. Once he reached them, he turned around.

"Oh! Sir! The general wants to see you right away."

Shoren nodded his thanks and walked inside. General Mekal was seated at his desk, poring over maps of the city. Mekal looked up.

"Commander Shoren, sit down. I sent my aide out to get the others. They'll be here soon enough."

As predicted, the other ten legion commanders did in fact arrive at Mekal's office in a very short period of time. With them was the messenger, who strode up to General Mekal's desk and stood at attention. Shoren could see a corporal's insignia on his green uniform.

The corporal saluted. Mekal returned the salute.

"Well, corporal, where are you coming from?"

"Sir, I just returned from General Walsh's Division along the eastern frontier. His fifty-thousand men are guarding against possible depredations by the Sioux and their allies."

"I'm sure he is. How many troops will he be sending?"

Here the messenger hesitated. "None, sir."

"I'm sorry?"

"None, sir. He explained to me he has orders not to send any troops anywhere. He had them copied for me to show you."

At this the messenger reached into his bag and pulled out a scroll tube. He popped the top off the tube, pulled out the sealed scroll, and handed it to Mekal.

"Sir, General Walsh seemed to indicate that they have been having some problems down south. I don't know what they are, and he didn't either. He seemed very frustrated. He did say he would send an appeal to the major general to change the orders in light of the new situation, but he didn't seem very hopeful."

Mekal sighed. "All right, corporal. You've earned some rest. My aide will show you a place where you can stay."

"Thank you, sir." The corporal, sounding relieved, saluted and walked out of the room.

General Mekal broke open the red seal on the scroll, opened the scroll, and read it silently to himself. When he was finished, he let it drop to the desk in front of him. He looked very angry. Shoren decided to risk a question.

"Sir, what are we going to do? I mean, what if the others have the same orders General Walsh has and we don't get any reinforcements?"

Several of the other commanders looked at him in alarm. Commander Striver, a much older officer, made a motion as if to brush away such doubts.

"I don't think everyone would get such orders. I mean, the whole point of having troops spread out along the border is that they can move from place to place to defend the empire. It would be foolish in the extreme to forbid the movement of troops."

"A good deal about this campaign has been foolish in the extreme," Shoren said. "We've been without supplies for months and reinforcements are slow in coming. None of this makes any sense."

Shoren looked over at General Mekal. "What idiot signed those orders anyway?"

Mekal looked at him for a moment. Finally he said in a quiet voice, "The Emperor himself."

"Why in bloody, cursed hell would Emperor Otto sign such orders?"

Mekal looked directly at Shoren. "Emperor Otto? No, these were signed by Emperor Richerd III."

CHAPTER SIXTEEN

aptain Frank Miller observed the carnage from his position in
the Comanche transport helicopter before checking the ammo
in his M-class assault rifle with grenade attachment. He looked at the
men in the chopper with him, all heavy armor and helmeted faces. His
armor, the latest version of the U.S. Marine's Self-Contained Assault
Battle Armor, had an onboard computer system that linked with all the
other suits of armor and gave him a readout of the physical well-being
of his entire company. The system also issued orders that always got
to the soldiers and did any number of other amazing things.

Frank, while grateful for the more advanced computer system
and the new composite plate armor, a new-old mix of steel, lead and
depleted uranium, was largely unimpressed. He had been ten years old
when the army began mass-producing powered armor, but SpecOps
troops had been wearing prototype versions since before he was born.

As the Comanche began its descent, he shouted orders to be ready.
Once it landed, he leaped out, followed by thirty marines. He looked
around. The rest of his company was all landing nearby. The lieutenants and sergeants whipped their respective platoons and squads
into shape and Frank sent them into various alleyways of the nameless
Chinese city he was attacking this week.

The entire attack had begun only a few hours before, a massive
bombardment of missiles, lasers, bombs and rockets that tore up the
city's defenses and infrastructure. Civilians were dying, that was true,
in fact they were dying by the thousands, but it was the same thing
that the Chinese had done to the Russians when the Russians had
discovered the Chinese smuggling tanks and troops to Mexico to be
in place for a quick KO strike against the United States.

Things had looked pretty bad there for a bit. Iran had built itself a substantial empire very quickly. After Iraq and Afghanistan fell, Syria hadn't been far behind and Kuwait had fallen in 2052, ten years ago now. That had resulted in an empire that stretched from Palestine to Pakistan and controlled massive amounts of the world's oil.

The United States had, thank God, switched from foreign to domestic oil supplies years ago and was working on the cutting edge of alternative fuels to replace oil entirely. China had not, and neither had many other nations, which led to the current situation. Iran had tried to gouge China by charging oil at over three thousand dollars a barrel and no one else would sell. The United States sold its own oil much more cheaply, but only to its allies, and if one of those nations didn't toe the American line, then the price jumped up or the oil disappeared, ensuring that most of the world bent over backwards to keep the Americas happy. Naturally, America used oil as a bargaining chip to get greater rights for oppressed peoples, like the Cubans or the Guatemalans.

The final result was a Chinese war against Iran. The Russians, always happy to kill Chinese, invaded China with the excuse of saving the United States. This drew the United States into the war when the Chinese invaded anyway. At first it was everyone against China but when Iran began massacring Israelis, Saudi Arabia attacked Iran, since the Saudis feared Iran more than they hated Israel. The United States had to declare war on Iran a few days later and Tehran disappeared in atomic fire, just like Beijing and Hong Kong. And Washington, D.C. And Philadelphia. And Moscow. And St. Petersburg and Paris and a great many other cities, until the United States had taken out the majority of China's nuclear launch sites.

That was the goal here today, to destroy a temporary launch pad from which China could launch a short range nuclear missile.

Once his marines were in order, Miller uploaded the situation map and a yellow objective marker into each soldier's Heads-Up Display, so everyone knew where to go and what to do once there. He was already moving before the confirmation lights winked on from each platoon leader.

The first thing he saw was a group of Chinese troopers with AKs and other rifles, but no heavy weapons. Frank shot the leader in the head and shot off a few more rounds but only one connected. The little bastard took it in the shoulder and kept coming but another round from a different marine stopped him dead – literally. A round from a PN-48 Jackhammer Automatic Shotgun tore a hole in his chest the size of a car tire. The gun fired either lead slugs or shot and carried a hundred round clip that could be emptied it in about a minute. It could also be set to semi-auto.

The Red Guards quickly fell back to a more fortified position: an apartment building complete with sandbags, reinforced walls, man traps, mines and heavy machine guns. Frank sighed. Those machine guns were liable to be shooting armor-piercing rounds and if the bastards weren't hiding a few RPGs on that rooftop, then Frank would be damn surprised.

As soon as the Chinese saw his troops, they opened fire with the machine gun. It tore through two of his men before they found cover. A few rockets hammered at the building, but the Chinese fought back with rockets of their own. Since the Americans were stuck, Frank called in air support and an Apache helicopter demolished the building in short order.

With that obstacle gone, Frank had his men spread out by platoons to surround the launcher. Frank's group didn't have any more trouble, but a few other units radioed for help and the helicopter was right there. The launcher was only lightly guarded and it was easy enough to rig with the C4 Frank had brought with him before calling for an evac.

Once back at the carrier, his company didn't even have time to rest before being re-armed and sent back out. It was going to be a long day.

CHAPTER SEVENTEEN

Shoren was poring over maps in his quarters, desperately looking for some place to lay an ambush or a trap or anything that would slow the enemy down and weaken his forces. Finding nothing, Shoren threw the maps off the table and reached for the bottle of whiskey sitting on a shelf. He tried to pour himself a glass, but found the bottle empty. He had drunk more than he thought. He looked pensively at the bottle. With a scream of rage he chucked it at the open door, and it shattered on the hallway wall.

Shoren began looking through his room for another bottle but found them all empty. Desperately now, Shoren went off to find himself something, anything, to drink.

Over the past few weeks, messengers continued to return, each with the same story. No troops were coming. None. They all either had orders to sit in place or weren't where they were supposed to be or had disappeared entirely. It was incredible. Some of the messengers, those sent to the capital and further south, hadn't yet returned. At this point it didn't matter if troops were brought up, they wouldn't make it in time.

The Koros' army, led by that ambitious maniac Morken Luviecell, was not only a week away but had actually swollen in size. There was no way that the Denver here in Garriton could possibly hope to resist; they could only slow the Koro army down.

As if that weren't enough, Shoren still didn't know how the citizens of Garriton would react when the Koro got there. Garriton had been Koro's mercantile rival until the Denver had taken it over a year and a half ago. The Denver would not be able to protect the city, that was certain, but what wasn't certain was whether the Koro would destroy it. It made sense. After all, they could crush an invading foe and their chief rival in one blow. The city reeked of fear.

Shoren growled. If he could find some kind of mind-numbing potency, he could forget all about this for a bit. In short, he intended to get drunk. Yes, he was going to get very drunk, and damn what anyone else thought.

As Shoren weaved to and fro across the hall, something decided to jump in front of him, causing him to go stumbling across the hall until he finally fell down. Falling head over heels he scrambled to his feet.

"Bloody, frozen, thrice-damned, donkey-loving, black, black, bloody spirits!"

Shoren began punching and kicking whatever it was that had decided to trip him. He drew his sword and swung, only to have it get stuck in the frame of what had once been a very ornate and very expensive table. Shoren looked around. People were staring. Muttering to himself, he decided he'd just get drunk in his room. Besides, his servant Jon could always get him more whiskey.

✲ ✲ ✲

General Mekal sighed as he stared at the map. They were three days away. He had done everything that he knew to prepare for the coming storm. He had ordered pits dug and flammable pitch poured inside, more pits with stakes that were covered up so that a marching soldier wouldn't see the trap. He had even ordered all of the large animals from the city zoo to be gathered outside the city so that they could be stampeded at the incoming army during the battle.

One order he had given that he hoped would solve two problems was that all the city's alcohol be taken and poured into large barrels that would later be set aflame and thrown at the enemy. The decision to do that came after he had learned that Shoren, his youngest commander, and one who had never been on this side of a siege before, had gotten drunk and ended up destroying an ancient table in a conference room terrifying numerous servants as he weaved through the halls. The young man seemed to think he was on his way to the pantry to find more whiskey or something; he hadn't been very coherent. Mekal sighed. The young man was stressed. They all were.

✣ ✣ ✣

Morken Luviecell stood on a hill overlooking the city of Garriton. He had been there once, as a boy, and the city had struck him as being impervious to most assaults. Now looking at it, even keeping in mind the massive army he commanded, the city looked completely impenetrable. It was only a façade. He knew his army could and would overwhelm the city's defenses, crack open the walls to squelch the weak and soft people within. He smiled. Yes, people, not soldiers. This was the perfect excuse to crush Koro's greatest rival. Even if his other plans came to naught, his glorious city-state would come out ahead.

His smile turned sour. Whatever else you said about them, the Denver were clever soldiers. They had displayed an altogether unexpected knack for laying traps and ambushes. It seemed that spending centuries consumed in intrigue and backbiting had given the Denver something good after all. His troops had suffered some pretty brutal traps, avalanches, rock slides, logs rolling down a hill, arrows from the underbrush, and every other little trick that surprised even the Kirendadi, a people commonly believed to be the best ambushers in the world.

Morken turned around and walked toward the horn blowers. They looked at him. He nodded. The young men put their lips to the hollowed out rams' horns and blew with all their might. All over the camp, horns rose up in a raucous call to battle and a draconian warning.

✣ ✣ ✣

Shoren hunched down as the Koro trebuchet launched yet another missile toward the city. He squinted his eyes in an attempt to see whether it was a simple chunk of stone or if it was something else. *It had uniform shape,* he thought. *It was probably something else, probably filled with something nasty, like lime or burning pitch. The Koro engineers had some nasty turns of thought. They were almost as bad as…Denver's.* Worse, Shoren decided. No Denver would have thought to hurl diseased cows over the city's walls, or the severed heads of captives. On second thought, the Denver probably would have too.

Shoren laughed ruefully. At least now he knew which side the citizens of Garriton would decide to fight for. The Koro had dressed the heads in Denver helmets and other wrappings, but most of them were actually local farmers, or the wives of farmers, or the children of farmers. More than a few were the infants of farmers.

Shoren watched as the missile hit the wall. Once it did it burst into flame. Shoren stood up again.

"Keep shooting! Keep shooting! Hold your positions!" Shoren took up his own bow but sighed. The enemy troops were still out of range. They seemed to have decided that they wanted to pound the walls until they collapsed before moving in. A Denver trebuchet launched a massive stone in return that pounded in the center of one of the advancing columns. The stone failed to strike the ladder the column was carrying, but it did succeed in scattering most of the troops. If only there weren't so many.

Shoren ducked and was showered by a great many sharp rocks. He stood up. Off a bit to his right, to the west, a trebuchet had hit a weak spot in the wall and cracked it open. Men on both sides swarmed, the Koro to exploit the opening, the Denver to plug it. They clashed right in the middle to the sounds of cries, breaking bones and the wet slap of rivers of blood.

Most of the Denver had abandoned their heavy shields in a desperate bid to block the Koro from coming through, and now they were paying for it. Armed only with their short swords or long swords, they moved quickly, but the Denver simply couldn't hold back the tide of Koro. Some few soldiers didn't even know how to fight without a shield and soon lost their shield arms while attempting to guard from enemy blades.

The crush of men was so great that men died standing up, their life's blood draining from them where they stood, or they were unable to fall as their entrails slopped on the ground out of bellies now sliced open. The broken wall became so slick that men began to fall in the viscera of friend and foe alike.

An arrow whizzed by Shoren's head, narrowly missing his ear. He ducked. A scorpion fired a large javelin that impaled the soldier immediately to the left of Shoren. That's when Shoren noticed the ladders. All along the remainder of the wall were Koro ladders. Shoren dropped his bow and pushed one ladder backward. He heard screams and then a crunch.

An enemy stuck his head up past the crenellations of the wall and began clambering over, but Shoren lashed out with his scimitar in an overhead, arcing strike that cleaved the man's head from his brow to his nose. Shoren used the dead man's shoulder as a brace to pull out his sword. He slashed another man across the neck, right through the throat. The spray of blood blinded him, and that's when he felt the arrow pierce his left shoulder. Another struck his right thigh, and just as he cleared the blood from his eyes he witnessed another arrow push its way through his left forearm.

Shoren reached out, grabbed a crenel and tried to pull himself up, but his knees buckled and he fell over. He felt two pairs of hands lifting him up as he heard the retreat sound and felt the world descend into darkness.

✵ ✵ ✵

Shoren woke up in a house filled with screaming and groaning men. The floor and tables were slick with blood. He was lying on a mattress of piled rags and was almost completely undressed. He looked around in a panic and saw his armor in a pile behind his head and his sword next to him. He sighed. He hadn't been captured. A man in a blood-soaked doctor's coat ran up to him.

"Ah, good. You're awake. How are you feeling?"

Shoren sat up. "All right I guess. What's going on? Did we hold? Has the enemy fallen back?"

The doctor laughed. "I wish. Instead we've merely stopped them. They've taken the southern walls and the gate sections, but we've held onto the rest. The so-called keep has held, and the general is still running things from there." He fixed Shoren with a critical eye. "You've lost a lot of blood but you should be all right. You've been here a little more than a day. When you feel up to it, we need you back at the front."

"Just give me a minute. Do you have anything to eat?"

The doctor nodded and handed Shoren a bowl of some kind of meat and vegetable soup and some stale bread. He shrugged. "Don't ask what's in it. You really don't want to know. The bread may not be fresh, but it's the best we have. Good luck."

Shoren nodded, trying to hold back his revulsion as he realized the most likely source of meat at the current moment.

He looked at the doctor. "This isn't…"

The other man smiled grimly. "Yeah, it's horse all right. Didn't you notice the empty stables on your way in?"

Shoren just grimaced and started shoveling soup down his throat.

When he was finished, he checked his bandages before putting on his armor. Some parts were missing, like the left-hand gauntlet that he had removed to wipe away the blood from his eyes. His helmet was intact, though dented, and the green-feathered crest was mostly gone. He bashed out the puncture holes in the armor with a nearby soldier's war hammer, and walked over to several barrels filled with various discarded pieces of armor. After sorting through some of it he found a left training gauntlet that fit. It was made of stiffened leather and while it wasn't as good as steel, it was better than exposing his bare flesh to the enemy. He buckled on his sword and some knives and walked outside.

Once outside he realized he was on the north side of the city, backed up against the mountains. The situation was worse than the doctor had said; the enemy held fully half of the city and was besieging the keep on three sides. Shoren scanned the city for the banners of his command. Spotting them, he set out on foot but quickly sighted an unattended, saddled horse just milling around. The horse snorted when Shoren approached but let him climb on. Shoren was pleased to notice his leg protested only slightly as he galloped to the front.

Once he was there one of his subordinates ran up. "Commander Shoren! Thank the spirits you're here. We thought you were dead."

Shoren laughed. "Somehow I just can't seem to manage it. I almost died up on the wall, but someone had to go and carry me to a hospital; not that I'm complaining or anything."

The nearby men laughed. Shoren grinned too. "What's going on? How many men are left?"

The soldier grimaced. "Not many, sir. We've lost a lot of men, and many more have been picked up by other legions. A full third of our own force, and we're only at half-strength here, is made up of men from other legions. Everything is just chaos."

"That's fine. We need to push back. I think it would be best to reinforce the keep."

The soldier nodded. Shoren issued orders and very quickly the troops were gathered together and began running and galloping toward the keep. Shoren's men were just passing by a Denver trebuchet whose crew was still trying to take out enemy troops when the whole machine suddenly burst into flame, an exploding jar having found its mark. Unfortunately, the explosion also killed many of Shoren's troops and scattered many more.

It was then that Shoren saw the Denver flag lowered from the flagpole over the keep, and the Koro flag rise. At the same time, the line broke. Denver imperial troops began scattering and falling, cut down from behind as they ran. Shoren charged his cavalry at the Koro, determined to rescue the general or at least do his best to restore the balance. As he passed the keep, he saw dead piled higher than a man on horseback, the drains rushing with blood. He also saw that the Koro made no distinction between the Denver and the Garriton, and more than once saw women, some older than his mother and some barely out of girlhood, dragged away by men who slavered over them like hungry wolves. Shoren did his best to help, but he simply couldn't save them all. The whole city was being set aflame, and there, on top of a pike mounted on the keep, sat a severed head Shoren recognized - that of General Mekal.

Shoren and a large force of cavalry fought their way through until they reached the southernmost point of the city. The huge fissure in the wall was still teeming with enemy troops, but the gate sat open and unguarded. It had been greatly damaged by enemy catapult fire and had been largely forgotten in the rush to capture the center of the city. Shoren and his troops rode through an open gate.

✡ ✡ ✡

Shoren rode along in a column of fewer than a hundred men. Though they had escaped, Shoren and his fellows had lingered until the Koro left. The Koro had remained in the city for two days and before moving on, the enemy general had ordered the heads of the entire Denver command staff mounted on the spikes sticking above their banners. The Koro had dragged away their own dead to be buried in a single mass grave. The rest they left to rot. Once the Koro had abandoned the city, Shoren and his troops had ridden in to gather what supplies they could – there were almost none – and to look for survivors – there were none. Only then had they ridden on.

In an effort to skirt the southward bound enemy, Shoren had ordered his small detachment to head east, into Sioux and Lakota territory, but now they were lost. Dear spirits, they were lost.

CHAPTER EIGHTEEN

S horen looked at the sun as he rode ever onward. It was hot today. It was hot every day – hot enough to drive a man mad. There was little shade, little water and less food. His people were starving; many were already dead. Shoren had long since lost count of the days spent in the Great Plains, but he was sure they had been heading east for a few days, and then south. Then they had gotten caught in a dust storm and had lost all sense of direction.

Shoren reached for the canteen stuck in his packsaddle, opened it and tipped it so the water could pour into his mouth. It would by no means be a proper temperature, but at least it was wet. When he discovered it empty, he swore. Shoren hefted the canteen, swore at it again, and when that failed to fill the bloody thing with water he stuffed it back into his saddle bags. Shoren began looking for another canteen of water when a rider galloped up beside him.

"Sir, that band of Sioux that's been shadowing us has picked up the pace again. I think I spotted another. What should we do?"

Shoren looked the man over. He had abandoned most of his armor to the ever-increasing heat, as had most every other soldier, including Shoren. After all, who would they fight all the way out here?

Shoren looked over at the cloud of dust indicating the Sioux's position. He shrugged. Maybe they were friendly. He laughed. When the nearby troops looked at him as though he were mad, he laughed even harder. He wondered whether he was mad or whether they were. Either way it was reason to laugh. He laughed until they made camp that night.

✦ ✦ ✦

Shoren sat up in his blankets, having heard a noise in the night. He looked over at the scruffy camp. No tents, no food, no supplies, no nothing. As he looked around, he heard the noise again. It sounded familiar, but not. Others throughout the camp began to wake up too. There, he heard it again! It was some sort of ... whooping sound. Then he heard the thunder of horse hooves and the whistle of arrows. It was an attack!

✳ ✳ ✳

Early Dawn was a Sioux battle chief. This was a rank similar to a captain or lieutenant and existed in a much more hierarchical structure than that of his ancient ancestors. As it happened, Early Dawn's band had been accompanying its tribal clan in its more western nomadic route when their scouts had discovered a large army of invading Denver cavalry. The Sioux chief had never expected anything good to come from interaction with the Denver and so had begun following them to determine their goals. The force had continued to move east and then finally south, almost perfectly matching his clan's movements. It was then that he decided to strike at the Denver and drive them from his home.

Early Dawn had gathered all of the elite Dog Soldiers and every other warrior not only from his clan but also from some clans who were traveling nearby. When the Denver had stopped for the night, the Sioux had stealthily approached on horseback before making the attack.

Early Dawn let out a whooping battle cry and let loose his arrow from his horse bow. He rode from the south, but warriors were attacking from every direction so that no Denver would escape. One man stood up and screamed at him in his clipped but guttural language. Early Dawn buried a hatchet in the man's head. Early Dawn noticed with an ever-increasing curiosity that these Denver did not behave like an invading force. Most of the men tried to flee, to escape instead of standing and fighting, and the ones who stood and fought attacked like wild men, typically alone and with only their swords or bows with none of the precision or meticulous, cold efficiency that had conquered half the western world.

It wasn't really so much a battle as it was a slaughter, and it wasn't very long before most of the enemy lay dead. With pleasure he began rounding up the enemies' horses when a curious sight caught his eye – a tall man atop a horse doing battle with other horsemen. Early Dawn continued watching and was rewarded with the unmistakable flash of a Denver curved sword, a saber slicing through the night sky. He grinned a feral grin and rode forward.

Early Dawn was not a holy man, nor was he an exceedingly religious one, but when he saw the fire in the man's green eyes he was sure he was in the presence of a spirit. In fact, the man's eyes seemed familiar. Why?

"Ver di agler del gebirskain! Anik! Anik!"

The man was screaming at his fellows, without realizing that they were dead. Early Dawn rode forward to do battle with this spiritual man who had killed at least five of the Sioux. The man rode forward and lashed out with his sword at Early Dawn's neck, but Early Dawn avoided the blow and tried to strike with his tomahawk. The man was simply too far away and so Early Dawn tried again with his spear. The sword deflected the spear, but a quick jab to the man's shoulder fed his spear the first blood. Early Dawn pulled back his spear to exalt in his victory and to shame the Denver man, but the Denver paid no attention to this and thrust his sword into Early Dawn's exposed chest. Early Dawn slid from his horse, dead, an expression of triumph still written across his face.

Confused Shoren pulled his sword free of the dead man's chest. If the warrior hadn't been too busy gloating to actually follow up on his attack, Shoren might be dead. He didn't understand how a soldier could allow himself to be given over to such arrogance and such a feeling of invulnerability. The man had clearly gloried in the fight and actually took pleasure from it. Shoren had been taught to stomp on emotions that could cloud his judgment, and therefore had struck when an opening presented itself. The phrase "honorable warfare" didn't exist in Shoren's mind. As the Sioux began to back off, Shoren risked another cry to his men.

"Defend yourselves! Fight!"

Shoren stopped yelling and turned to face another warrior who approached with a spear, Shoren gauged the man's strength and judged that the best place to strike would be at his left side. He spurred his horse, taken from another dead Sioux, and raised his sword when an immense weight fell on him and knocked him to the ground.

Shoren rolled forward and stood up, gripping his sword in both hands. It seemed another warrior had leaped on his back. He faced this new threat with ruthless detachment but inside his mind appeared a voice.

~Stop! Wait! You do not know what you are, what you could be! Do not die a wasted death this night!

Shoren looked around in confusion. He lowered his sword for a moment but brought it back up. He never saw the much older and revered rider behind him who unceremoniously knocked him out with a large wooden stick.

CHAPTER NINETEEN

Shoren sat up and threw off the animal hide blanket that covered his body. He looked around. It seemed as though he was in some sort of tent. His clothing and weapons were nowhere to be found. Well, this was an alarming situation. He stood up carefully, trying to determine the cause of the pain in his head. Shoren growled as he remembered the voice in his head. Something very strange was going on here and he meant to find out what.

As he stepped outside the tent, he stared in wonderment at a Sioux nomadic camp. Once he was more than a few feet away from the tent though, two large and rather unfriendly looking individuals approached him and gestured toward the tent. Shoren shook his head and tried to step around the two men. One muttered something and grabbed his arm and whirled him around to face the tent. Swearing, Shoren broke away from the man.

"Look, sir, I don't know who you are or where I am, but I want to leave. Give me a horse. Now." The two men continued to look on impassively. "Give me horse now. Black spirits take you, give me a thrice-damned horse now!" Shoren raised a fist.

"I wouldn't do that if I were you."

Shoren turned around angrily. "Just who are you to tell me what to do? I want to leave this place and these two louts are blocking my way!"

"If I were you I would be very glad that those two 'louts' don't speak the Denver language. Smiles at Dawn and Talks a Lot tend to be temperamental and if they could understand you they might do something... drastic."

Shoren sighed and looked at the man. He was an older man with a creased face and a gray Mohawk, an imitation horse mane just like the one that adorned Shoren's now missing helmet. He wore simply decorated buckskin trousers and tunic. Both were red in a pattern that reminded Shoren of either flames or the sun. The tunic's shoulders and upper torso were solid red with swirling rays extending toward the ground. His belt was decorated with some kind of teeth, buffalo teeth probably and a small variety of beads. He wore a well-made iron tomahawk and a small round buckler hung over his back on a strap.

Shoren looked at him thoughtfully before opening his mouth. "All right. I have a few questions for you then." The man nodded. "Which one of these is Talks a Lot? Both seem practically mute."

The man laughed. "The taller one is Talks a Lot. He really is very chatty most of the time. He just doesn't like you."

"Oh."

"Well, young man, let's go back to your tent. There are some things we need to discuss. By the way, these two are for your protection as much as to keep you from escaping. It may shock you to know that we don't like foreigners and we don't like Denver in particular. Many people don't."

Shoren shrugged. People could think what they wanted. The Denver were the heirs to Tyrris Plain's Empire and everyone else could just get used to it. One day the ancient dream would be realized. The Eagle would fly again.

✳ ✳ ✳

None of this was vital to the present though, so Shoren turned his attention back to the path to his tent. If he remembered correctly, the actual word for the specialized tent was tepee. Once Shoren and the old man reached the tepee, Shoren did his best to sit comfortably on the ground, but it wasn't until he simply stretched out on the floor that he could relax. The old man simply sat down.

Shoren looked at him. "You said you wanted to talk to me about something?"

The old man didn't answer immediately. Instead he looked out of the tent flap to see that one of the two guards was standing at the front of the tent, and the other was patrolling to make sure that no one wandered nearby, just in case a warrior who could understand the Denver language walked close. Once he was satisfied, the old man turned and looked at Shoren.

"My name is Red Wolf. I am what you might call the leader of the Horsemen of this tribe. The Horsemen are a very special and sacred group of warriors. As our name suggests, we are an army of mounted cavalry. However, unlike every other army in the world, we ride Horses."

Shoren could hear the capital letter in that word. "I take it these 'Horses' are somehow special or unique, right? I know that Plains mustangs are among the best in the world. In fact, I ride a Comanche mustang stallion myself."

"No, no, that's not what I meant. These Horses are intelligent. Wait, hear me out. I can see you're getting confused. In our own language, the two words are the same, but they have different meanings. Everyone knows which kind of horse you're talking about though. How can I make this simpler?"

Red Wolf frowned as he struggled to find a way to explain to Shoren something even the Sioux didn't fully understand, something Shoren's own language had no concept of and thus wasn't equipped to articulate.

"We'll call them big brothers. That's what they call themselves, you know."

"Wait. These horses 'call themselves' big brothers? How? Who are they big brothers to?"

"The other horses; the ones that don't talk. They…"

Red Wolf's next words were drowned out by peals of laughter from Shoren. He was laughing so hard his ribs started to hurt and tears to come to his eyes.

"Stop laughing! This is serious! I mean it!"

Shoren finally stopped laughing but had difficulty keeping a straight face when he again looked at Red Wolf.

Once Shoren was finished, Red Wolf began again.

"This ability we have, we Horsemen, is to communicate through our minds to the big brothers. The big brothers have been with us since before the Great Void, what you call the Lost Times. The big brothers were once with us, but then they disappeared. After the chaos of the Great Void they reappeared, as did the ability of the Horsemen.

These big brothers live almost as long as we do, which is good because most Horsemen will find a big brother that matches their personality and with whom they form a deep friendship. Once this friendship is formed, it is very rare for the big brother to allow anyone else to ride him."

"Stop. Before you continue, I have a question. You keep referring to 'Horsemen' and big brothers. Is it only stallions and men, or are there talking mares and horsewomen?"

"There are. The term Horsemen can mean either someone who talks to the Horses or someone who is a member of our order of soldiers.

"Now I have a question for you. During the battle when we captured you, my horse spoke to you and you reacted. Have you ever heard any voices like that before?"

"I didn't hear any voices. This is all insane. I don't want you imposing your silly superstitions on me and I don't want to talk to you anymore! Get out!"

Red Wolf sighed with regret. "I wish that I didn't have to do it this way. Come with me."

With that Red Wolf stood up and walked out of the tepee. Shoren sighed and followed him. Once he was outside, he heard a voice say to him, *~You are a fool, Denver.*

Shoren turned around. "You listen to me, my name is Shoren and I…"

Shoren broke off as he found himself face to face with a rather large and impressive looking roan mustang stallion. It looked him right in the eyes and Shoren was arrested by the complex intelligence he saw. He felt a prickling, more like an itch in the back of his mind, and realized that the horse and Red Wolf were now looking at one another.

"Damn…"

~Now do you understand, Shoren of Denver? Now do you see what you are?

"Who, what are you?"

~I would have thought that Red Wolf would have told you all about that. My true name is not for humans to know, but you may call me Fire in the Wind.

"This is insane, absolutely insane. I don't believe it. I won't."

~Only a fool remains purposely blind when others try to show him the truth. You are a Horseman, and there is nothing you can do about it. Come, I will show you the fields.

"The fields?"

~Yes, the fields where we rest and play. They are also where the Horses who are not bonded stay. You will also meet the shaman there. He is in charge of all of you Horsemen, and is very curious about whether you are truly what you seem. Tell me, Shoren, about your dreams.

At the words "dreams," Red Wolf's head jerked up in surprise, a look of alarm on his face. Shoren felt that itching sensation again, and assumed it must be mean that Red Wolf could "talk" to his Horse in the same manner that Fire in the Wind spoke to him. Finally, Red Wolf looked back at Shoren.

"Have you had any strange dreams recently? Dreams that seemed real, where you aren't yourself, where you know things that you couldn't possibly know. Anything like that?"

Shoren looked from Fire in the Wind to Red Wolf and back again. "Yes."

"How many and what were they about?"

"I've had three such dreams in the past year and a half. The first one was very strange. I was in the body of an Aztlani man, although that wasn't where the dream-me came from. In the dream I was in some sort of camp in Tejas. That's all I remember.

"During the second dream, I was in the bodies of two different men. They carried weapons that seemed very strange, but in the dream I was very skilled with them. At first I was an old soldier from the Lost Times called Frank Miller. Later, I became John McCarter. I remember that because, well, he's very important.

"I had another dream about John McCarter, but this time he was much older and I saw the beginning of what may have been the foundations of Denver. Of course, that would have been before the first part of the name was dropped. It would have been Neo-Denver back then."

~Why is this John McCarter important?

"He is a part of our history, though some believe he is only a myth. He founded the city of Denver and was its first leader. According to the myth, he brought order from chaos."

Shoren barely noticed the itching this time, partly because he was getting used to it, but also because he was stunned at the sight of all the horses. They were magnificent and represented every breed Shoren knew about, as well as some he didn't.

He also barely noticed the elderly man who approached them. He had an aura of knowledge and wisdom about him. Red Wolf and Fire in the Wind both greeted him respectfully. Shoren didn't. He was tired of fools who thought they knew everything. Red Wolf glared at him until the old man put a hand on his arm. After that, the two were deep in conversation.

Shoren started to walk into the middle of the Horses. If this was true and these animals could really talk, it would take more than one to convince him. He wanted to speak to them all.

~Shoren, I don't think that's a very good idea…

Shoren shook his head. The Horse wouldn't. He kept walking. Finally, he could hear.

~Wow, a foreigner…looks strange, I wonder…~Look! It's Fire in the Wind! Hi, Fire in the Wind…~and so then I said, oh no you didn't and he was all like…~Who's that? What a strange looking human…~He looks scared, maybe a Horseman…~No, he's not Sioux, he's probably just some lost idiot…~know foreigners, lower than dirt…

Shoren stopped, stunned. There were too many voices. Dear Spirits, so much noise! He couldn't take it.

~Told you he's an idiot…~Come on, let's have another race…~Not now, Pony…~I'm napping…~I wonder if Fire in the Wind will get mad if I kick the foreigner…~Who cares, do it anyway…~The shaman ought to separate you two…~Come on, I want to race…~you never let us have any fun…~Stupid foals…~Stupid stallions…~What! Why you little…~Sorry…

Through gritted teeth, Shoren whispered, "Shut up!"

~I want a race…~I'm going get you…~Mommy, he called me a donkey… ~Be nice to your brother…

"Shut up!"

~Donkey, donkey, donkey…~mommy…~race…~idiot foreigner…

"Shut up!"

~I hurt my hoof…~You know, the grass is greener over…~The grass is good here…~donkey…~I warned you…~race…

~SHUT UP!

The entire field went quiet. Fire in the Wind, Red Wolf and the shaman all ran up to Shoren, who was on his knees, holding his hands over his ears and shaking.

"What was that?"

"You know what that was, Red Wolf. It was a Command. He commanded them to be quiet."

"I've never seen anything like that before! By the Great Spirit, I can't Command at all! Not that I would, it's wrong and immoral, but the whole herd! Who is this man?"

"I don't know, but three dreams in less than two years? That's unheard of.

"That's if he's telling the truth."

"He doesn't know enough to lie. Each of those dreams sounded true to me, and he has no idea what they are. A normal Horseman might have three dreams in five years, not two."

"Actually, he told me the first dream was a year and a half ago. They all came in a six month period."

"Amazing."

"Let's get him back to the tepee."

As they lifted him onto the back of the now-mute Fire in the Wind, Shoren slipped into blissful unconsciousness.

✻ ✻ ✻

Shoren awoke sometime later to hear the same two men talking. He first heard Red Wolf, and then the shaman speaking.

"What should we do with him?"

"I don't know," the shaman turned to look at Shoren. "Ah, I see you've awakened."

Shoren sat up and shook his head. "Yeah, I think I'm all right. What happened?"

The shaman looked at him strangely, as though at a curiosity in a zoo or museum. Red Wolf seemed to think he was a rabid beast.

"You Commanded the Horses, Shoren. That's where a Horseman expresses his dominance over his Horse and makes him do things that he would normally not want to do. Morally, it's akin to coercing someone at knifepoint. You are not going to do it again." The shaman's eyes held absolutely no question.

"This... Commanding.... Why is it taboo? I would imagine that in an emergency that kind of ability would be useful."

The shaman looked at him for a moment, again curious. Shoren's seemingly innocent question, a question that made sense to a Denver military mind, made Red Wolf shiver. To even think of some things; to question their prohibition... Red Wolf shivered again.

"The bond between a Horse and its rider is sacred. Ideally, it is a friendship or a partnership in which the Horse and the rider work together to achieve a shared goal. They are equals in this partnership.

"When a Horseman forces his will upon his Horse, or any Horse in fact, it makes such a partnership difficult. If he continues to use his power to Command, the bond can become almost unbearable. Although I have no experience with it, nor do I believe does anyone in living memory, the old lore tells us that as the relationship between Horseman and Horse deteriorates, it can become fatal. Horsemen are so rare that it is a tragedy to lose even one. Even you. Especially one with such a power as you."

Shoren leaned back. Although he had begun to accept his new power, he didn't fully understand the implications of what the shaman had just said. It was all too much at once.

"What happens now?"

Red Wolf looked up. "Now we take you back to the fields so that you can get used to being around the Horses. It often takes years after discovering one's abilities before bonding with a horse. It's uncommon to find an untrained adult, but it happens often enough that we know what it's like. It should only be a few years before you can bond with a..."

"A few years! Bloody black spirits! Isn't there some way to shorten the time? Some way to cheat?"

"Cheat? Why cheat? The process is a wonderful and exciting journey of knowledge. To skip any part of it, well, you would just be limiting yourself."

Shoren frowned. "Well, I had hoped to be able to return to my own people soon. I haven't been home in so long it hurts."

"That's too bad. You see, you aren't going anywhere until we get to the bottom of this. The ramifications of your discovery are very important."

"My discovery? I haven't discovered anything."

"Oh no, I was referring to our discovery of you."

"You didn't 'discover' me. I've been here the whole time. I've just recently learned about my powers, although you could say that I've discovered you and I'll bring my 'discovery' back to my own people."

Red Wolf snorted. The shaman just sighed at Shoren's comment but rolled his eyes when Red Wolf snapped at Shoren, "The knowledge of lesser nations is of no concern to us." At Shoren's sudden glare he added, "In fact, compared to you and me, some of those people are truly subhuman."

Shoren's eyes nearly bulged out of his head. His hand slid toward the hilt of his sword and began to close round it but grabbed only air. Shoren grimaced, but began covertly looking for another weapon. He wasn't covert enough however, because even though Red Wolf didn't notice, the shaman did, and chided Red Wolf, hoping to avoid losing either his war leader or this strangely valuable foreigner. Shoren was valuable all right, but he was also dangerous. Oh, he could be very dangerous, and not only for the obvious reasons.

"Red Wolf, that was cruel. You should remember that you are talking about another man's family and friends. He alone among his tribe is unique, so everyone he loves and cares about you just called 'subhuman.' Think how you would feel if you or your family was considered subhuman or inferior."

Red Wolf scoffed. "No one would dare call a Sioux subhuman, but I see your point. Shoren, I'm sorry."

Shoren nodded, even though he still wished he had a weapon. He had heard about the Sioux before, but that had mostly been dry histories and the whispered murmurs of border troops. The arrogance of these people was truly insufferable. Shoren growled at the irony that occurred to him. Red Wolf just rolled his eyes and muttered something incomprehensible under his breath.

The shaman turned to Red Wolf. "As we walked, I believe you were going to tell Shoren a little bit about the history of the Horsemen. If you would, please, as I am sure our friend does not have the time he would normally have."

Red Wolf nodded. "The power originated long ago, in long distant memory. At one time, a time even more ancient, there were no horses. They did not exist in this world. When the horses came, we saw them for what they were, the most sacred of all animals because, you see, we understood them and understand them in a way that no others do. This is evidenced in that only Sioux are Horsemen."

Shoren arched an eyebrow but said nothing.

"You see, we were blessed, and when the spirits saw that we understood the horses in a way that no others did, they saw fit to send us the Horses, and later the Horsemen. It was as though the Great Spirit himself resided on Mother Earth. There were many great prophets, and it was a time of peace and prosperity. Then, the time of darkness. Foreign demons, ancestors of your own people, stole away our sacred lands and our Horses. They killed all the Horsemen. All seemed lost. All was lost. We call this time the Great Void, or the Time of No Voices. Then came what you call the Lost Times, and then chaos reigned. In the fires of chaos we were granted back our lands, and the sacred Horses and Horsemen returned to us. The Great Spirit had set things right once more."

Shoren rolled his eyes. "How is being a Horseman passed on?"

Red Wolf looked at him blankly.

"Breeding? How is it passed? Mother to daughter, father to son, or is it some other pattern? Is there a pattern that you are able to discern at all?"

"Well of course. The trait is passed down from one's parents. Obviously, the more Horsemen in your past, the greater chance it is that you will be a Horseman."

"What about me? Where do I fit into this whole thing?"

"Well, I have discussed it with the shaman, and we both think you must be a descendant of a Sioux. I believe one of your parents was a Sioux, or grandparents. At least great-grandparents, but no further back than that. Why are you laughing?"

"Because you think I have a Sioux ancestor." Shoren continued to chortle, despite drawing curious glances from passersby.

"Well obviously, but I don't see why it's…"

"Heh. Red Wolf, I can name you my heritage for the last five generations. I have a book at home with my heritage for the last thirty. There isn't a single Sioux in the whole list."

"Why would you have that…oh, never mind. We're here."

Shoren walked up to the edge of the field. He wondered absently if they would remember him. The horses were all frolicking like the day before, but as they gradually began to notice him, they began to settle down. At first everything was just a dull roar, a kind of indistinct rumbling "sound" that gradually dimmed until he heard nothing and felt only an itching in the back of his mind. Well, that answered that question.

Shoren began scanning the herd, but stiffened abruptly in alarm as he realized what he was doing. He was looking for familiar faces! Well, familiar muzzles anyway, but it was muzzle. Singular, not plural. He was looking for Fire in the Wind.

The Horse approached Shoren cautiously. *~Hello, Shoren. You seem better than you were yesterday.*

"Thank you. I think that as I get used to the mental noise, it will be easier and easier to bear. I…am sorry about yesterday. I didn't realize what I was doing."

~I understand. He motioned to the rest of the herd. *~They fear you now. They think you are a spirit in human form, come to torment them. They don't know what to expect from you. Neither do I.*

"I don't know what to expect either. This is all still very strange to me."

~Why don't you try to talk to me with your mind? It's very easy to learn. Just will your thoughts to me. Project them out at me. It sometimes helps to envision your thoughts and put them in little handkerchief. Ball them up and then throw them to me. Try it.

Shoren did his best to send "Can you hear me?" but gave up. "Did I do it? Were you able to hear me?"

Fire in the Wind snorted and tossed his head. Shoren frowned with mental effort.

~Can you hear me?

Fire in the Wind neighed loudly, reared up on his hind legs and nodded encouragingly. *~Good! Good!*

~I was able to do it? I can't believe this! I'm actually talking with my thoughts! This is amazing!

~Good, good. I want to introduce you to a very special Horse. Ah, here he comes.

Up came a large painted mustang stallion. At his side trotted a tiny gray pony who was just chattering at a mile a minute. Shoren couldn't hear the paint talking, but he got a very distinct impression of annoyance and faint irritation. For some reason, Shoren felt as though this Horse was as alone as he was.

Fire in the Wind motioned for the other Horse to step forward. *~This is…Little Knife, or if he prefers, He Who Has No Name. The gray pony is Yakman.*

~Yakman?

~Yes. He's called that because…

Another, more high-pitched voice entered Shoren's mind. *~I'm called Yakman because the other Horses think I talk too much, yes they do.They say I wouldn't shut up if a stallion kicked my jaw.Interestinglyenough, onestalliontrieditonetimebuthegotin troubleitwasfunnytowatch.Alotofthe otherHorsesaremeanthoughbutnotFireintheWindhe'sso niceespeciallytom yfriendLittleKnifeorifhe'stryingtosoundawesomeTHENAMELESSONE soundsimpressivedoesn'tit?*

"Wha- What?"

Another deeper, more reserved and quiet voice entered Shoren's mind. *~Yakman, this is the Horseman who Commanded us all to be silent yesterday. I would prefer if he didn't Command your mouth shut permanently. On the other hand, keep talking.*

~LittleKnife,youneedtobealittlemoreappreciativeofmyfriendship. WhatifIstoppedtalkingtoyou?

~Oh happy days!

~AnywayShoren,huh.Youreallyaresoamazing.Ionceheardofsomeonelikeyou hekilledlotsofpeopleareyougoingtokillanyonehaveyoustabbedanyonewithy- oursword?

It took some effort, but Shoren managed to send a message. *~Have you seen my sword?*

Wowamazingyoucantalkwithyourmindandafteronlyonedaytoo!OfcourseI' veseenyourswordtheshamanguyhasitinhistepeeit'swaycoolitlookslikethepatchon LittleKnife'sbutt.

~YAKMAN! I'LL KILL YOU!

~Catchmeifyoucandemonbutt!

~DIE!

~Yakman, Little Knife. Stop! I wanted to introduce you to Shoren precisely because of the symbol on your flank.

The painted horse suddenly looked wary. *~What do you mean?*

~What I mean is that Shoren is a foreigner. He is alone here in the Sioux tribe, just as you are largely alone in the herd. I thought you might be able to find purpose away from the Horses who mocked and derided you.

~You're no better than they are. You all want to be rid of me, and all because of some stupid patch on my rump!

~That's not true and you know it. I've always tried to help when I could. I've never called you…any of those awful names the others do. I've tried to be your friend.

~I'm sorry. So, Shoren is it?

"Yeah. Oh, wait." *~Yes. I am Shoren. Shoren McCarter. Pleased to meet you.*

~Does Shoren McCarter mean something in your language?

~Yes…no. It's an old name whose meaning has been lost to the pages of history.

~Why do you still use it?

~It's an old traditional name. Predates the Lost Times, or at least some version of it did.

~Right. Anyway, do you want to know what Yakman and I were fighting over?

~You mean what you wanted to kill him for?

~Well, I didn't mean it. Shoren could feel a subtle change in the way Little Knife's voice "sounded." Instinctively he knew that only he could hear the Horse's next words. *~I always say that to Yakman, but I've never meant it. Well, I've usually never meant it. There are times though… but anyway, other than Fire in the Wind, Yakman's my only friend. Plus, Fire in the Wind is too stuffy and traditional. He also has a rider whose duties take him off for trips that last months at a time.*

~Anyway, the Horse continued, this time out loud, *~I have on my rump a very peculiar symbol. Some think it's a portent of doom or an omen of evil. It's a sword. Go over and take a look.*

Shoren walked over to the Horse's right. There, on one side, was a perfect image of a Denver military saber. The blade was one shade of brown, the hilt another, and finally the hand guard and pommel yet one more. Spirits, Shoren could even see the designs on the hand guard through a variety of browns.

He reached out and touched the "sword." "So this is why…sorry." *~This is why you are not accepted by the other Horses? Because you have a patch on your flank that looks like a sword?*

~Yes. That patch has kept me on the edges of the herd for my entire life.

~What about Yakman? Why is he on the fringes?

~Can you not guess? Little Knife snorted. *~In truth, he remains by choice. He's my friend and he's as loyal as they come.*

~That's right, I'm as loyal as only the most annoying pony on earth can be.

~Of course. This time, Shoren heard amusement. *~About the annoying part that is.*

~Hey!

Shoren rolled his eyes at the interplay. *~I think the name Little Knife just doesn't do you justice. You need a new name, a better name.* Shoren frowned for a moment. *~You are Fury Fidelis, the Sword of Loyalty. Fury for short.*

The Horse cocked his head. *~Fury Fidelis? Sounds intimidating. What does it mean?*

~Fury Fidelis is, according to legend, the sword the original leaders of Denver carried. It was supposedly lost after Denver was conquered by Tyrris Plain. All Denver officers wear the words 'Semper Fidelis' on their swords. They come from an ancient language meaning 'always faithful.' Fury Fidelis essentially means Fury of the Faithful, or Fury of the Loyal. It was supposed to remind the leaders that even though they commanded the loyalty of the people of Denver, they themselves needed to stay loyal to the people. It was a reminder to be uncorrupt. Legend holds that only someone who is uncorrupted and pure can carry the sword. It supposedly will reappear in the hands of Denver's savior in its hour of darkest need.

~You want me to carry this name? Wouldn't people dislike me once again?

~No. Actually you would be honored. As for the legend, the sword was real, but as for the rest it may just be myth. The meaning however, doesn't change.

The painted mustang stallion pawed at the ground. He lifted his head to look at the sky. He looked at Fire in the Wind. Fire in the

Wind looked thoughtful, an emotion Shoren was unused to seeing on a horse. Yakman on the other hand, was staring at the nameless paint, his pony eyes wide with awe. He looked back at Shoren, clearly sensing something momentous was about to happen. Something earth shattering. The next few moments would decide the course of history, and the only one who knew was the chatty little pony who never shut up. He was silent now.

The painted stallion looked up at Shoren. He looked him right in the eyes. *~Shoren McCarter, son of Denver, I accept your name. I am no longer Little Knife. I am no longer the Nameless. I am no longer…well, I am no longer anything else. I am Fury Fidelis, Sword of the Loyal. I am Fury.*

Shoren stood dazed. What happened? The Horse, Little Knife, no…Fury had accepted his name. Instantly, a wave of mental pain had overtaken him, a sense of being ripped in twain. He felt himself ripped apart and then put back together again. His legs buckled beneath him. Before he could fall, Fury caught him.

"Wha…What happened?"

~That was the bonding experience, Shoren. I had not expected it to be so… unpleasant.

Shoren flinched when Fury's voice appeared inside his mind. He shook his head. He tried to speak with his mind but seemed unable to. He grimaced.

"So, we're bonded to each other now? As in you're my Horse for all time, and I'm your Rider for all time?"

~Basically. I can feel your emotions, your physical state, how tired, hungry or sick you are. It's a very useful ability actually. That's one reason you'll live longer than a non-Horseman. You should be able to feel these things about me.

~Will you live longer than an ordinary horse?

~Yes. You and I will both live to be about the same age.

Shoren shook his head. As the dizziness wore off, he was able to "feel" Fury's emotional and physical state. The Horse was slightly worried and felt apprehensive. Shoren nodded. So it was all true after all.

~Perhaps we should go back to the others and see what comes next.

~Jump up on my back. You are my Rider now, after all.

Shoren nodded and jumped on Fury's back. He shifted uncomfortably; he wasn't used to riding bareback. He'd have to see whether Fury would accept a saddle or not. As Fire in the Wind and Fury turned to leave, Yakman followed. Shoren turned a questioning glance his way.

~*I go where my friend goes. No matter what.*

Shoren allowed a smile to creep onto his face. It seemed as though the pony was made of iron beneath that carefree demeanor.

✼ ✼ ✼

Shoren rode up to the shaman and Red Wolf. The shaman raised an eyebrow when he saw Shoren astride a Horse, worse yet, a painted Horse! When he turned around to take a look at Red Wolf he saw the older warrior's eyes were wide with awe. They were also filled with fear.

Though he had not told Shoren or Red Wolf, the shaman had been in communication with the shamans of some of the nearby sister tribes. Another commonly used power among the Horses was that they could communicate mind to mind over long distances, sometimes upwards of one hundred miles. These Horses had relayed his message all the way back to the only really permanent settlement the Sioux had.

It was a massive, sprawling city in the middle of the Plains. It didn't even have a name; it was simply called "the City." In it lived a central council that ran the affairs of the entire Sioux nation. The city itself was divided into numerous sections that each tribe owned. The various clans of the tribes passed through the city annually to resupply and to plot out their route for the following year. They did their best so that they spent a full season there each year and rotated the routes so that they came at different seasons each year. Some clans traveled together, becoming sister clans. There were so many Sioux and so many routes that it was uncommon to not encounter another clan every week or so. Some places where clans continually met became permanent or semi-permanent settlements; especially in areas where the soil was good for farming.

The central leadership of the shamans also rested in the City. It was they the shaman had been trying to reach. His message must have arrived quickly, for the previous night he received an order to abandon his tribe's predetermined course and to travel directly toward the

City. The shaman sighed. That he must obey was without question, but he didn't know how to change course without throwing everyone into a panic.

The other item that worried him was the fact that he had lied when he said he had never heard of a Horseman as strong as Shoren. The story was almost the same. A Sioux man whose whole tribe had been destroyed, an unknown Horseman. At least until he was an adult. This man too had bonded to a painted mustang in an amazingly short amount of time and had once stampeded a whole herd of Horses with a simple Command. The Horses slew the westerners who had killed his tribe. While whole areas of his life were shrouded in mystery, it was known that the empire of the western emperor Tyrris Plain had fallen as a direct result of his actions. The shaman had heard of another who had plunged the eastern nations in a war that lasted nearly one hundred years. He shuddered to think what was to become of the man now riding before him.

✵ ✵ ✵

Shoren frowned. Fire in the Wind stared at him, his face full of undisguised shock and fear. The shaman was harder to read. He looked as though he needed to say something that he didn't relish saying. Something he was almost afraid to say.

No one spoke. Shoren rolled his eyes.

"This Horse and I have bonded. His name is Fury Fidelis, Sword of the Loyal, named for the most famous blade in Denver history.

~As Shoren has said, I am no longer Little Knife. I am no longer without a real name. In truth, I am no longer Sioux.

"So what happens now? Can I…we go back to Denver?"

The shaman sighed. Life was so unfair. "No."

"Excuse me?"

The shaman swallowed. Red Wolf stiffened. The nearby warriors began drawing weapons. They didn't need to understand Denver to hear the blade hidden within Shoren's voice.

"I'm sorry. I truly am. However, we must go straight to the center of Sioux life, the Great City."

"The 'Great City'? I thought you were nomads. You don't have any cities."

The shaman laughed. "We have a city. One. Singular. There are many permanent settlements, you'd call them towns, but we have but one city."

"Where is this city? Why should I go there?"

"It is a month to the east. You will be examined, simply to try to determine what you are and how you fit into our beliefs."

"You mean you and your kin are going to learn all about me so you can accurately re-invent your religion?"

"No! No." He calmed down the warriors who again drew weapons. "Our beliefs are truth. We simply wish to discover where you exist in the framework of our truths. You will see. Our beliefs are truth."

Fortunately for Shoren, the shaman took his sarcastic nod for acceptance and never heard the muttered, "So are everyone's. Your truth and my truth and his truth. Two of them aren't truth. Maybe three." Of course, Shoren muttered in classical English just in case.

The shaman sighed with relief. "Trust me, Shoren, you will be able to return to your home. It will just be awhile."

Shoren looked him in the eyes and nodded. "I want my sword and armor back."

The shaman was genuinely surprised. How did he know? He saw the small gray pony and nodded. Yakman. The best friend of the demon-Horse.

"You do understand why all of this is shocking to us, right? You are a foreigner, you have abilities no Sioux has had in millennia, if ever, and you bonded with a painted mustang after only a few days. A few days! Plus, a painted mustang, the most sacred of all the Horses. In addition to all of this, you bond the one mustang with a sword-shaped patch. You realize how this strains credulity. The one Horse that would accept an outsider, the one Rider who would accept a Horse with a sword-shaped patch all together. We only rode to where you were because we needed the water. We only attacked because you seemed to be following us. There has to be some reason for it all. We hope to find it out in the city."

"I still want my weapons and armor back."

"Well…"

"What am I going to do? Where would I go? Do you expect me to attempt to slaughter all of you and escape? I'd die."

"Well all right. You can have them back. Just don't wear them in public. At least, not often."

"If you insist."

"I do. Well, I must speak to the chief…" The shaman took a deep breath and headed off in a different direction, clearly eager to get away from Shoren and the questions his very existence raised.

CHAPTER TWENTY

Shoren stood once more on a hill, his steed once more grazing nearby as he looked yet again over a foreign city. Today was different however in that he had no army at his back, no elite troops under his direct command. Tonight this city would not be steeped in fire and blood. Even his clothing was different today. The last time he looked over a city like this, he had been wearing the steel armor unique to Denver. It was made of steel strips formed into a scale-like second skin that was extremely flexible and protective. Shoren's armor had been made in a secret Denver factory using ancient techniques that gave the armor its distinctive bluish-blackish hue. His green cape had hung over his back, and he had held his helmet at his side, its green imitation mane, unique to the cavalry and unique to officers, ruffled in the wind. His saber had hung at his hip, and a short sword had been strapped to his back. He had also worn a variety of knives.

Today he wore only a knife strapped to his belt, but the rest of his armor and weapons were easily within reach, strapped to the saddle as they were. Most Sioux Horses wore no saddles, just a blanket, but Fury seemed to take pride in the leather contraption that marked him as different, special. He wore no reins. Shoren wore comfortable Denver riding pants, gray today, but wore a buckskin shirt given to him by Red Wolf. As if to make up for it, he also wore the green hooded cape. Finally, he gazed upon the city simply to take in its magnificence, not to determine how best to destroy it.

Even so, his military mind could not help but notice that the city would be difficult to capture, though that seemed accidental rather than by design. First of all, the city was surrounded by vast plains and could spy out any approaching army days before it arrived. It was also split into numerous mini-cities, each with its own walls and gates and fortifications. Each mini-city also had its own soldiers and each was independent of the others; an attacker would literally have to besiege each and every one. The final difficulty Shoren could see was the building materials. Lacking a major source of wood, the city was built from a mixture of imported stone, sod and mud bricks, making it almost impossible to set aflame. Shoren could see no tepees, likely due to the novelty of a solid roof over one's head when staying in the capital.

He heard a whistle and turned around. Red Wolf gestured impatiently as he mounted Fire in the Wind. The Sioux had stopped here only for a moment to take in the city. It would still be another few hours before they arrived. Shoren slipped back onto Fury and joined the rest of the group. He patted Fury's neck.

~Have you ever been to the City before?

Fury snorted, probably in amusement. ~Of course I have. We travel to the city each year.

~Why?

~Well, our travels all revolve around the city. It's a trading center unlike anywhere else in the Plains. When we arrive, we not only bring goods acquired from our travels of the previous year, but we also plot out our routes for the next.

~Really? I had kind of thought that you just sort of wandered from place to place, following the herds of buffalo or something.

~No, no. We follow predetermined routes. The buffalo follow general patterns and so do we. The planners in charge also ask that when we return we tell them about the condition of the route that we followed. If a waterhole were to dry up, or if a buffalo herd were to change direction, that affects everyone who next follows that route. So we tell the people in charge so that they can plan accordingly.

~Interesting.

~I think so. We travel all over the east and west and the north and the south. We see the whole plains.

Shoren nodded and returned to his own thoughts. Already he was more than impressed with the riding abilities of the Sioux. The tribe's entire camp could be broken down in about fifteen to twenty minutes, a feat unrivaled even by Denver light cavalry. They were better riders and trackers and hunters than the Denver, and Shoren did not want to think about heavy infantry out in this endless heat, marching for days on end. It would be rough. Clearly not impossible, but rough.

Before Shoren knew it he was at the front gates of the city. Once he was close he amended his opinion on how hard the city would be to capture. Even though fire would not be an effective tool, he believed Denver siege machines could batter down the gates and walls without any real difficulty. Trebuchets could probably reach almost anywhere in the whole city, and if the buildings were anything like the gates and wall they would collapse quickly. In fact, Shoren wondered why the Sioux even bothered to build defenses at all.

He had a thought. The Sioux probably hadn't faced a major invasion within the last few centuries, if ever. Actually, Tyrris Plain had tried to add the Plains to his empire but failed. The Sioux had simply known the terrain better and had been able to use that knowledge to harass the Aramainian troops up and down the entire frontier. They also had been consistently giving ground to the Aramainians who promptly overextended themselves. Cut off from their supply lines, they had been relatively easy to destroy.

~Fury, do you know the story about the Aramainians. About how they invaded?

~Of course. Almost everyone knows about them. Why?

~I just wanted to know how far they reached. Did they attack the City itself?

~Yes. They actually destroyed a great deal of the city. That's why the walls were built. Aren't they impressive?

"Hmmmm."

Once the tribe was inside the city, it broke apart into its various sections. The shaman rode up to Shoren.

"All right, Shoren. While the tribe gets settled we're going to go over to the main Shaman's Council building for the first session with the team set up to investigate you. Let's go."

Shoren nodded. Fury looked up and turned to follow the shaman's own horse. They rode past buildings built in a variety of styles but all of the same sod bricks. They rode down an assortment of twisting and curving roads. After some time, they came to a large circular building. Shoren looked at it in bemused curiosity. It had a series of circular steps that rose up like a conical pyramid. Each step had windows and was covered in surreal drawings, as well as statues in a great variety of sizes and forms.

Shoren turned to the shaman. "Where did those statues come from? They look too different to all have come from the same source."

"They are all trophies of war and battle. Each statue represents a different victory over a foreign culture."

Shoren didn't say anything, his eyes drawn to the elderly men and women gathered in front of the pyramid. Each wore buckskin pants and shirt, but each outfit was dyed in a different color. Shoren saw blue, green, orange and purple, as well as different shades of different colors. They also wore eagle feather headdresses, animal bones and skulls, as well as capes made from some kind of hide Shoren didn't recognize.

The shaman he knew leaned in and whispered to him, "Once we are right in front of them, our Horses will bow, and then we bow while on our Horses. Then we dismount and bow again. Do not rise until given permission. Do not speak."

"How do Horses bow?"

"Never mind."

Shoren looked on in amazement as both horses stood straight up in front of the gathered shamans, stuck their right legs out straight and curled their left legs beneath their torsos and bent low, so low their muzzles almost touched the ground. The shaman shot a significant glance at Shoren who was beginning to bend at the waist. When the shaman touched the fingertips of his right hand to his forehead, Shoren copied him.

They both then dismounted, with Shoren reaching to grip reins that did not exist. He instantly pulled his hand down, embarrassed. Much to the collective horror of everyone watching, he stood straight upright, stiff as a post, heels together, before bending at the waist. Fury kicked his foot.

~Stick your foot out! Do what I did!

Shoren glanced over at the shaman, a look of abject horror on his face. The shaman had stuck his right leg out in imitation of the Horses and bent his left leg beneath him. Shoren quickly copied him. The shamans looked imperiously at Shoren. After a stretch of time that seemed to last forever, one of them nodded and tapped Shoren and the shaman with a fan made of eagle feathers. The shaman straightened. So did Shoren.

The shaman in green spoke up. *~You Horses are free to go for now. Since this will likely take a long time we will not ask that you stay. We will call for you when you need to return.*

~Someone needs to remove my saddle. I don't exactly fancy traveling about the city with it on my back.

The shaman in blue looked up, his eyes flashing with anger. "A saddle! No Horse wears a saddle! This is barbarism!"

The green shaman frowned at him. "The Horse is bonded to a Denver. Their horses wear saddles. It only makes sense for this Horse to wear one, if for no other reason than for the Denver's own comfort."

"There is no excuse for a saddle! How can any nation expect to harmonize with its horses if…"

"Where do I put this?"

The green shaman looked at Shoren. "What?"

Shoren held up the saddle. "Where do I put this? I don't want to leave it out in the street."

The blue shaman smiled unpleasantly. "Unlike in your cities, no Sioux would take something that does not belong to him. In Sioux territory a man can leave his door unlocked for months without fear of theft."

"You'll pardon me if I don't take that for granted. I'll find someplace inside." He headed off toward the building.

The purple shaman stopped him. "You'll need to take it to that building over there," she told him, "the only weapons allowed inside are the spiritual ones."

Shoren shrugged. That was typical. He hefted the saddle and weapons and hauled them over to one of the outbuildings. He set everything down and took a little while to make sure that everything was safe and secure before closing the door, shaking his head when he noticed the lock on the door. When the door was locked and his gear secure, Shoren finally turned to the shamans.

"All right, everything's secure. Shall we go inside?"

The shamans nodded and motioned for Shoren to join them before they went inside. The shaman that Shoren had come to know was not allowed inside. He gave Shoren an expression of encouragement. The others escorted Shoren inside.

When Shoren first walked inside he saw that the building was decorated as garishly and discordantly to his eyes inside as it was outside. Light poured in through the open windows. Shoren also saw brackets where torches could be placed at night.

The purple shaman looked at him. "We will go to the lower chambers. It will be cooler for you underground."

Shoren nodded his thanks as he wiped sweat off his brow. It was hot here, and Shoren, being used to a cooler climate, was still having trouble adjusting.

"What do the different colors signify? Do they tell what tribe you are from?"

The blue shaman sneered at that. "Of course not. They signify nature spirits with whom we are associated. I have blue clothing, meaning that I represent the Eternal Sky. The violet lady over there represents the mountain tops of which you Denver are so fond. The green…"

"I represent the flowing grass of the Plains, and as such I have the highest seat."

Shoren nodded, his military mind filing everything away. "Are there more of you?"

This time the mountain shaman answered. "There are eight in total. Eight spirits, eight directions."

Shoren nodded. He grinned. It was cooler already down here. They finally reached a door flanked by torches. He stepped inside. Inside sat five more individuals, each wearing buckskin of a different color than the others. He nodded. All eight accounted for.

A woman in red got up from her cushion. "Please, sit down. I represent the Eternal Fire of the Light-Giving Sun. How are you called?"

Shoren didn't answer her right away. Instead he continued examining the room. There was only one door, and his back was to it. The eight shamans reclined on cushions in a semi-circle around his lone cushion in the middle. Not the best tactical situation perhaps, but it would do. He looked at the sun lady.

"My name is Shoren. As you may know, I am from Denver. I am also a Horseman."

"We know this. If it were not true, you would not be here. If it were not true, you would likely be dead."

Shoren laughed. "Considering the thrice-damned bloody circles you seem to be running me through to make sure I am who I say I am, I might consider death a better bargain."

The curses were necessarily in Denver, since Shoren was unable to reproduce them in the Sioux language. The red shaman looked at him in confusion. "'Thrice-damned'? 'Bloody'? What do these words mean in your language?"

"They are curses, lady. I do not know how to reproduce them in your language."

Another shaman spoke, this one in a blue that was lighter than the buckskin that adorned the oh-so pleasant individual who had escorted Shoren down into this...this...cellar. "I believe they mean 'thrice-damned' and 'bloody'. Is this not right, Shoren of the Empire of the Setting Sun?"

Shoren thought for a moment. "Thrice-Damned. Bloody. It seems to lose a bit of the flavor in your language." He looked around. "Do you have any questions or not?"

The red shaman sighed. "Yes we do. I personally am interested in your family history. I am curious how a Sioux Horseman could have been accepted into your society. I also want to know which of your ancestors was Sioux. It must be either your father or your grandfather, yes?"

"Why couldn't the Sioux be my mother or grandmother? There is no reason that it couldn't be a Horsewoman instead of a Horseman. And what do you mean by how was a Sioux accepted into my society?"

"Well, I just meant that your society tends to be less tolerant than our own," the Shaman of the Sun stated, not realizing the irony of her statement, "and was your Sioux ancestor a woman? That would be interesting in its own right, given what we know about Denver. What was his or her name?"

Unlike the Shaman of the Eternal Fire of the Light-Giving Sun and her brethren, Shoren did catch the irony behind her words. She claimed Denver to be an intolerant nation, yet her people destroyed a weak and starving group of travelers for the crime of entering their land. He had proven to be a powerful Horseman, yet here he was, a virtual prisoner until his fate was decided by these arrogant intolerant priests! He did have to respond though.

"I don't have any Sioux ancestors. I've already told the tribal shaman this several times."

A younger man in light blue leaned in. "We know that the Spirit's Gift, the ability of the Horseman, is passed on from father to son, mother to daughter, mother to son and father to daughter. Do you understand?"

Shoren shrugged. "Look, I don't know about that, but I can tell you for sure that no one in my recorded family history is a Sioux. Think about it. I'm taller than all of you. I have blond hair and green eyes. My skin is a much lighter color. You are all burgundy, with black hair and brown eyes. There is nothing to indicate I am of anything but Denver descent. If you still don't believe me, send me back to Denver. In the family records is my family tree, recording my familial history for four hundred years."

The blue shaman stood up and addressed the others. "This is pointless. It's obvious the foreigner is lying. He must have a Sioux ancestor, or else he wouldn't have the Spirit's Gift. I want to know what he intends to do with these powers."

The green shaman of the bloody waving grass or something said that was a good question. "Well, what do you intend to do with these powers, Shoren?"

Shoren shrugged. "I want to go back home, rejoin the military, marry Elina, and live in my manor." He stopped. He did want to marry Elina, not because it would be advantageous but because he wanted to. Perhaps the time away had changed him more than he thought. He wasn't sure how healthy that was but it seemed unavoidable.

He looked up. The blue shaman had said something about his rejoining the military when he wasn't paying attention. He shook his head and tried to pay attention, but the man sat down and was replaced by the shaman in green.

The shaman in green turned to Shoren. "Shoren, I think it's time for us to confer privately about our meeting. You will be escorted back to the tribal area to pre-prepared quarters that are used for foreign visitors. It will be set up in a manner that a Denver would find comfortable."

The mountain lady immediately stood up. "I'll escort him."

The leader looked surprised. "All right. But hurry back. We would not wish your voice of wisdom to be absent from this council." The lady nodded.

As Shoren and the mountain lady left the building she stopped him. Shoren felt a now-familiar itching sensation in the back of his mind. Very quickly, a long-legged mustang mare trotted up. Shoren sent out a similar call to Fury and after a few moments, Yakman. Both arrived not long after but as was usual, they were bickering. Shoren shook his head and mounted Fury. Some things just couldn't be helped. After a few moments of silence, the purple lady of the mountains looked at Shoren.

"I need to tell you something."

Shoren hadn't really heard her. He had slipped into a daydream of the sort he hadn't had since he was a boy. He was thinking about Elina, and he hadn't even realized what he was doing until Fury bucked a bit and jerked his head at the woman atop the Horse next to him. He looked over at the woman.

"I'm sorry, could you repeat that?"

She sighed. "I need you to pay attention. This is very important. You need to be very careful about what you say. Tomorrow when we meet with you again, do not mention that you intend to rejoin your military. Do not say you will be involved with politics. Actually, it might be best if you simply said that you intend to live on your manor with your wife and do whatever it is that you do there. Understand?"

Shoren looked at her. That whole little speech had been spoken in fluent Denver. Not only did she have the grammatical structure and vocabulary perfect, she spoke without a noticeable accent, saying even the most guttural of sounds with ease. "You speak Denver?" he asked somewhat hesitantly. She frowned.

"Of course I do. I am the Shaman of the Mountains after all. Your people are of the mountains. It makes sense for me to know your language."

Shoren took another look at her. She was older than he was, maybe twice his age and then half again. Despite that, she remained a surprisingly attractive woman. He took another look. She was Sioux all right, with Sioux coloring. No…slightly lighter. Her hair was black as midnight, but almost bounced and curled at the ends. Her green eyes glittered in the firelight. Her green eyes…

"Your people too. Your people and your language too. You're half Denver."

She laughed. "My father was Denver. He was wounded in the invasion of your people's…our people's nation. He was brought back as a captive and decided to stay with the tribe. Some of our men, including my uncle and grandfather, decided they didn't approve of his union with my mother and put an end to him. They got him too late though. He left my mother with a child and a courtship-bracelet. They couldn't do anything about the first, but they sure ended the second. My mother never forgave them, and both my uncle and grandfather died in a 'trail accident' not long after." She looked down.

"I made a mistake when I spoke about the military," Shoren said. "I expect that it will only give the shamen who are hostile to me an excuse to end me. That blue one especially, the one who represents the bloody sky or some stupid thing."

"It's not stupid. He represents the Guardian Spirit of the Eternal Blue Sky, just as I represent the Guardian Spirit of the Mountains." She fixed him in a piercing glare. "You would be wise not to mention the military again."

Shoren nodded. They shortly arrived at the building where Shoren was staying. The lady shaman in the purple shirt bid him good-bye before returning to what Shoren considered the Shaman's Headquarters, even though it probably had a much fancier name.

Shoren leaped off of Fury's back and removed the saddle and blanket in silence.

~What are you going to do? the Horse asked. He tilted his head. *~The Shaman of the Mountains made it sound dangerous to go back to the Sacred Circle. Do you intend to?*

~Well, for now I think I ought to. I don't think I'm in any immediate danger so I'll go back and see what they say. They might let me go.

Fury nodded his head but snorted his displeasure. *~I hope you are right. I think Yakman and I will see if we can find the grass-circle, although I think the one here is a square.*

Shoren nodded and headed up to his room for a while. After lighting a few lamps he discovered that the room was decorated and furnished in an approximation of what the Sioux must have assumed was the Denver style. He shook his head. The alabaster statues next to clay pots with some truly horrendous and gaudy paintings on the wall struck Shoren as not only tacky but simply in overwhelmingly poor taste. He continued to search the room and found some cloth wall hangings with images and words stitched into them – tapestries. The characters stitched into the tapestries were unfamiliar though the images were typical: soldiers, monsters, soldiers fighting monsters, monsters fighting women and children. There were a few that pictured castles, forts and other buildings but those were few and far between.

He continued to look around and discovered a strange flag. It was like a pennant with a triangle cut out of it. It had red and white stripes and a blue triangle filled with stars that formed a circle. Shoren also saw a battle standard that was a blue square with a red X in the middle. Stars ran up and down the X. The X was also trimmed in white. The staff was made of wood but was capped in a bronze fist. Beneath the fist but above the flag was a bronze rectangle containing letters that Shoren once again couldn't read. He compared them to the letters on the tapestries and discovered that the letters were not from the same language. This seemed true of many of the tapestries.

Shoren examined the books arranged on the bookshelf but quickly swore in frustration when he discovered that all of the books were in a variety of foreign languages. He tried to match the languages of the books with the languages on the tapestries and flag before finding a book in a language he recognized…but couldn't read; a book in High Texican, one of the two Texican languages, High Texican and Low

Texican. They were essentially the same language save some differences in sentence structure and vocabulary. High Texican was closer to the ancient language of English and Low Texican was closer to Spanish, although Texican contained elements of both.

Shoren walked over to his bags and began searching through them. Once he had found General Hammond's journal he set it down on a carved pine desk, the only item in the room that looked like it had actually come from Denver. He lit the lamp on the desk and began to read.

Several areas he couldn't read, because they were smudged or smeared or otherwise unreadable, but he still managed to glean a lot of information. After only a few pages, he learned more about the Lost Times than did most scholars in a lifetime.

March 15, 2057

> *Today over the news we learned about another democratic uprising in China. More protesters had joined this one than had joined any of the others and so many hoped that it might accomplish something. No such luck however. The Chinese told the protesters to disperse once and when they refused, the soldiers began to fire into the crowd. This has sparked a wave of similar protests all over the world, and a sanction from the United Nations although that seems to be nothing more than finger-wagging.*
>
> *The United Nations did threaten to remove the Islamic Caliphate from the Security Council if they refused to stop their genocidal programs against the so-called "heretics." France for some reason seems to be on the side of the Caliphate.*

Shoren frowned. What in the world was the Islamic Caliphate? Or the United Nations? Or France or China? He assumed that they must be countries of some sort that existed before the Lost Times. He had never heard of any of them, so he assumed that they didn't exist anymore. He did wonder though where China was and whether it would be possible to visit it, or at least whatever was there now.

The damn dragon-boys are trying to push the Russians around again too; it's a good thing the Ivans are on our side instead of the other way around. For a while they looked like they were going to fall right back into the Soviet stage. They came dangerously close, but now they're even more capitalist than the United States.

I probably shouldn't call the Chinese "dragon-boys," but they've been known as that since they changed the flag in 2013. The old Chinese flag had been a scarlet rectangle with a large golden five-pointed star in the top left corner. The star had four smaller golden stars in an arc next to it. After the last of the original Communist Party leaders died, the younger leaders moved the large star close to the center and had replaced the other four stars with a large gold and black dragon that encircles and grips the star. The supposed reason is an upswing in Chinese nationalist and historical pride, and a desire to blend the old Chinese culture into the era of Communist China.

March 18, 2057

Some Mexican who's been running around calling himself the "Prophet of Aztlan" is holding a huge rally in Mexico City this week. He's been preaching against what he calls the "oppressive Christian regime" and has been calling for a universal Hispanic revolt against the "European Tyrants." According to the CIA's dossier he spent a long time in the Middle East and seems to be promoting a new faith that's a blend between fundamentalist Islam and the old polytheistic Aztec religion. So far he hasn't made a lot of friends, although plenty of poor farmers and such seem to love him.

Shoren set the journal down. The language was more difficult than he had expected, in part because of the difficulty in learning the language itself and in part because of the unique way in which General Hammond used it. Shoren shook his head. He didn't know why that surprised him. In Denver, English was only used in special ceremonies and in translating old books. Sometimes scholars wrote in English, though mostly to show everyone how educated they were. General Hammond would have actually spoken English as his own, and written it all the time.

Shoren shook his head and put the book away. He pulled off his boots and lay down on the bed, which wasn't too uncomfortable. He closed his eyes. Then opened them again. He couldn't sleep. Black spirits. Bloody, thrice-damned, flying, flaming spirits! This wasn't working. He couldn't sleep.

With a curse and a growl, Shoren heaved himself out of bed. He was tired certainly, but he was more nervous, more afraid, and even had an itching in the back of his...

"Damn." He shook his head. He tried to stretch his mind, even cocking his head to point an ear at the source of the itching. It was useless. He pulled on his boots and walked toward the door. "Who is that and why can't I understand you?"

Shoren assumed that it had to be one of the Horses trying to talk to him. What he didn't understand was why he couldn't... well, "hear" wasn't exactly the right word, but it would do, Denver not having that concept in its language. Sioux did though, their word for it was "ointa." He practically ran down the stairs before stumbling into the darkness of night. He looked around.

He could see the path that led to the green-circle and he could sense that Fury was just a little bit along that path. Shoren stopped. He was coming to associate the feelings he got from Fury as being a little ball or box that sat literally in the corner of his mind the way a box would have sat in the corner of a room. When he examined that emotional bundle now he felt the passive, restful feelings he had come to associate with sleep. Was Fury dreaming? Shoren quickly shook his head, he knew the feelings that came when Fury dreamed. What then, could the feeling be?

~Hello, Shoren.

Shoren jumped nearly a foot in the air while trying to reach for the sword that he had left in his room. The motion spun him around and cost him his balance, his left foot off the ground, his arms reeling and spinning. He fell down.

~Nice landing.

Shoren glared at the little pony that had emerged from the darkness. *~Thank you,* he mentally whispered back.

~Afraid of eavesdroppers, Shoren? Don't worry, I've inspected all around, the whole block is asleep.

~If you say so.

The pony snorted and tossed his head from side to side. Shoren had come to recognize that as a sign of amusement, almost like a silent laugh. *~I do say so, but by all means speak like this. It will help keep our conversation a secret. Just so you know, that itching in your mind was me. I wanted to make sure you came out here. Come on, you'll want to hurry when I finish talking, but it will take awhile and so you will want to be comfortable.*

Yakman indicated a bench with his head and stamped a hoof, kind of a silent exclamation mark. Shoren walked over and sat down on the bench. He motioned for Yakman to continue.

~All right. Down to business. Shoren, you're in danger.

Shoren lifted an eyebrow. *~Thanks. I know.*

~No, you don't know that you're in danger. You think the Great Shamans don't like you. You think the Sioux wish you weren't around, showing them that they're not as superior as they think. You think you might be in trouble, that this is unpleasant, that the situation may be dangerous in an abstract, distant future. I, on the other side of the fence, know that you are going to meet the Great Shamans tomorrow. I know that you will leave your weapons behind and enter unarmed because the only weapon in the Sacred Circle is the "spiritual kind." I also know that the shamans intend to assassinate you tomorrow, using knives and axes and spears. They can do this because any weapon wielded by a shaman is by definition of the "spiritual kind." Or at least that's what they just decided. I'm sure many would disagree, including the past shamans. I know at least one of the current shamans does, the Lady of the Mountains, since they tied her up and put her in a cell. I know that if you value your life you will flee tonight.

~What about the lady shaman? She's on my side! We have to do something!

Yakman shook his head. ~ *No. She is not in any physical danger, and any delay will definitely put you in danger of any number of lethal, physical things. If you leave now, you can return to your home. I will accompany you and Fury.*

Shoren glared at the pony. *~This is all very strange. You've never spoken with such authority before. I've never heard you like this.*

Yakman stomped his hoof. *~We have no time! Let's go!*

Shoren nodded and ran back up into the room he had been given. He took another look at the bizarre tapestries and battle standards before picking up his armor and weapons and gear. Once finished, he carried it all to the bench. Yakman wasn't there. Shoren looked around and saw him chivying Fury along. By the way he weaved back and forth and tripped over his own hooves every couple of steps, the stallion seemed in no condition to run away from the city.

~Fury, you need to hurry. We need to leave the city. The shamans want to kill me.

The stallion looked balefully at both Shoren and Yakman. He snorted. Then he turned to Yakman. *~You woke me up for this! What have you been telling him to make Shoren think that? Shoren, nobody wants to kill you. Go back to sleep. I know I am.* Being as good as his word, Fury turned away to walk back toward the grass-circle.

Yakman hustled around Fury to stand in his path. *~They are going to kill him, Fury, and you too. I heard them say it. They arrested the Lady of the Mountains to keep her from talking.*

Fury snorted. *~ They can't do that! It's against all our laws!*

Yakman shook his head and stomped his hoof. *~Our laws, Fury! Our laws! They can and will do as they please in this case, there's no law against it or against their authority in this matter. We have to flee now!*

~In that case we do need to hurry. Let's...oomph! Fury turned around to glare at Shoren who had just finished strapping the saddle onto his back. He had kneed the stallion in the stomach to push out all the loose air so as to strap the girth tightly. Fury turned his head around and made as if to kick Shoren, but instead refrained. Yakman started laughing at him, his lips curled back away from his teeth with his head rocking back and forth. He even made a kind of chortling noise. Mental laughter ccompanied it.

Shoren swore under his breath when Fury tried to nip at Yakman. He picked up the rest of the supplies and began strapping them to Yakman's back, despite his protests. *~What do you think you are doing! Get those off of me!*

Shoren just shook his head. *~If you want to be useful, you'll carry this gear; otherwise I'll leave you behind.* Fury began laughing this time, with a stamp of a hoof for emphasis. *~Of course, if you stay behind, Fury will have to carry all of the gear.* The stallion quickly quieted down.

Shoren shook his head. "Dear spirits, one might think you two are married." The two equines didn't notice, as Shoren had the wisdom to mutter the comment below his breath.

Once the two horses were settled down, Shoren made his way to the gate that led outside the city. No one questioned him; no one stopped him until one man stepped forward just a few blocks away from the gate. "Hey, foreigner! What are you doing?"

"I'm just going out for a ride. I think it might be good for me and my horse."

The guard pointed at Yakman with his spear. "Will it be good for the pony too?"

"Yes. It'll be good for him too."

The guard walked closer toward Shoren, Fury and Yakman, the latter of whom stayed very still. "I should say it would be good for him. He's very round in the belly area, probably the fattest pony I've seen all...wait. He's not fat! Those are saddlebags! Guards! Hey, guar... oomph!"

After ramming the man in the stomach with his head, Yakman stood over him with his hoof to the man's throat. *~I am not fat. I'm just very circular.* He shook his head. *~And round.* He snorted in the man's face. Shoren jumped off Fury's back, picked the man up and dumped him in an alley.

Fury nudged his back. *~Aren't you going to make sure he doesn't go anywhere?* The stallion placed a sharp, heavy hoof right over the jugular in the Sioux's throat.

Shoren sighed. *~Don't, Fury.* He kicked the man in the head. The man groaned, but did not wake up. "He's not going anywhere."

Shoren turned around to receive a snort from Fury right in the face. He shook his head and realized that the gravity of the situation had finally hit Fury. The stallion, having heard his life and the life of his friends threatened, especially his rider, had been brought to the very edge of bloodlust. Shoren mounted Fury very slowly. Fury set off at a fast pace even before Shoren told him to. Fury trotted right past the gate guards, not stopping when they walked amiably toward him, not stopping when they stepped right in his path, and not even when they let loose with their arrows, although he did kick one. Yakman rammed the other.

Once free, Fury took off at breakneck speed, and Yakman had difficulty keeping up. It was only after Shoren smacked him in the head that he slowed down and allowed Yakman to catch up.

As Yakman came trotting up, Shoren looked at him. *~Well?*

The pony stared right back. *~Well what?*

~You know damn well what! What was that back there?

~Oh that? I'm just a little sensitive about my weight, that's all. Nothing to be concerned about. In fact I'm pretty healthy, I just am, to quote a small child, "the cutest fat little roly-poly pony" that the little girl had ever seen. I was proud for a while until I discovered why the other ponies were snickering at me.

Fury snorted. *~That's not what he was talking about and you know it. And just so you know, you were sensitive way before you met that little girl. Isn't that right Roly-Poly Pony?*

Yakman looked at Fury with something approaching rage. Then, with all the dignity a short, fat pony named Yakman can muster he said: *~Screw you.*

Shoren laughed aloud. *~You two really are married.* Yakman snorted his displeasure. Fury bucked, and would have sent Shoren flying off his back if he hadn't grabbed hold of the stallion's neck.

Shoren shook his head. *~No Yakman. I meant why are you suddenly so different? When I first met you, you were fast talking, chatty, and to be honest, just this side of annoying. Now you're not.* Fury turned his head to look back at Shoren before looking at Yakman. The Pony remained silent. Fury snorted. Yakman snorted back. Shoren pinched the bridge of his nose in irritation.

~Well, what did you expect? Did you really think a typical pony would be able to stand Fury's company for an extended period of time? Mustang stallions

are supposed to be serious and competitive, but Fury's a little extreme. Plus, he's too dour for any sane pony to spend any amount of time with.

Fury snorted again and tried to nip at Yakman.

Yakman shook his head. *~The Sioux are an extremely traditional people. They love stereotypes and become distressed whenever their traditional stereotypes are broken. A normal pony is chatty, excitable and frivolous. A mustang stallion who is a loner with a patch like a sword and is also friends with an annoying pony is one thing. But a stallion being the friend of a different type of pony, one who is intelligent, serious, and able to eavesdrop on private mental conversations, that's something else entirely. Do you understand?*

Shoren nodded. *~That explains it then, I guess.* He looked forward to the road and back toward the Sioux. *~We need to hurry. It won't be long until they give chase.*

CHAPTER TWENTY-ONE

Shoren sat atop Fury's back. He was constantly watching for any movement that might indicate that his pursuers had caught up with him. The Sioux had been chasing him and the two horses across the Plains for nearly two months now, forcing him to move at night and rest during the day. They had nearly caught him several times, and escape was more difficult each time they found him.

There it was! Movement! Shoren squinted. There were four or five Sioux warriors on horseback, traveling in the same direction he was. Shoren didn't think they had spotted him yet, but he definitely preferred escaping undetected to having to fight them.

~Fury. The Horse's ears perked up. *~There are warriors traveling the same direction we are, about a half-mile or so to the east. I want you to walk over to that clump of trees. I think we can hide there until they are gone.*

Fury's only response was a toss of the head, but he turned toward the trees. Fury must have been talking to Yakman because Shoren felt that itching in the back of his mind that indicated the Horses were talking for a few moments. It was only for a few moments but there was no way to tell if the warriors were Horsemen or just regular warriors, or if they were Horsemen, how sensitive they were.

The little group had just reached its would-be hiding spot when they all heard the five warriors give voice to a whooping battle cry. Shoren winced and swore and drew his sword. The warriors thundered toward him, three carrying thin, barbed lances, and the other two brandishing tomahawks. Not a one had drawn his bow. Shoren galloped Fury away before drawing his own bow. He let loose with a few arrows, hoping to distract them as he maneuvered around.

For the five warriors, the goal was simple. Kill Shoren. If they failed, they would bring word back to their war leaders that they had found him. Those leaders would mobilize the much larger war bands to comb the area for Shoren, sending riders as far as possible in every direction in order to catch him. Shoren had to kill these five now so that they wouldn't get a chance to do that. They were probably forward scouts and wouldn't be missed for days – longer if he could hide the bodies.

Yakman ran in the opposite direction from Shoren, whinnying and making a noisy ruckus in order to make the warriors think that Shoren wasn't where he was. It worked some of the time, but didn't always. This was one of those times when it didn't. One of the men had put away his lance, pulled out his bow, and begun loosing arrows at Shoren. He missed horribly. Shoren released an arrow right at him but missed. He swore.

Struck by sudden inspiration, Shoren leaped off Fury with hurried instructions to keep circling. Shoren ran toward the clump of trees. He climbed up the tallest one for a vantage point before shooting off arrows. He grinned when he struck one in the shoulder. The warrior reeled back in his saddle but didn't fall off. Yakman rushed forward to snap at the wounded man's horse. The horse reared back and the warrior fell. Yakman put a hoof to the side of his head, killing him. One of the warriors tried to stab Yakman with his lance, but the pony fled out of sight.

Shoren took aim once more and loosed another arrow. This one hit its target in the neck. Shoren exultantly sought another target but saw with more than a little alarm that the only remaining targets had their backs to him, out of bow range.

Fury and Yakman ran up to him as he climbed out of the tree. *~The others escaped!* Fury cried in some alarm. *~We need to get out of here!*

~Yes we do. They fled east and south. That's probably where the war bands are. We need to head north for a while, and then west.

~Maybe we ought to try to flank them, Yakman suggested thoughtfully. *~We go east and south around them to get to Denver. They'd never expect it. Although, it would be very unfortunate to run into them by accident.*

~I don't think it's worth the risk, Shoren said. *~We head north."*

They rode until daybreak. Shoren decided to keep going, hoping to move as fast as possible. He didn't see any signs of the war band, and didn't for three days. When he did, he saw them heading east again, back toward the City.

~Why are they going back?

~I don't know, Fury. I... Shoren trailed off as he saw a large dust cloud moving toward him. He leaned forward. *~That's no cloud. It's an army!*

Shoren franticly searched the saddlebags for the looking-glass. After raising it to his eyes, he swore. "Bloody black spirits! It's a Denver army!"

~What! What are the Denver doing here? Yakman yelled in considerable stress. *~We're in the middle of the Plains!*

~Maybe that's why the war band was going back east, Fury mused. *~They probably want to warn the City, considering that that army is much larger than the war band chasing us. Do you think we ought to approach them?*

~Yes, I think so, Shoren said. *~They'll probably get us safe passage out of here.*

~I doubt that they're more than a few hours away. If we run quickly, we could catch them.

~Let's go then.

The little group galloped across the open plains to the army, but it was farther away than it seemed, so much farther that they didn't reach the army until late in the day. When they did, the army had already set up camp. The sentries stationed around pointed their pikes at Shoren, demanding that he dismount.

One sentry, dressed in the half-plate and chain of the Denver legions, stepped forward. "Do you speak Denver, Sioux? What about Texican, High or Low?"

Shoren growled. "I speak Denver, soldier. I am Commander Shoren McCarter. I was part of the invasion force attacking Koro. My army was defeated by a joint Koro-Kirendad attack in the city of Garriton. I led about a hundred survivors to the Plains in order to escape, but we were massacred by the Sioux. I've pretty much been a prisoner since."

The sentry had lowered his pike. "That so, eh?"

Shoren nodded.

"Well, in that case, we'll bring you to the major-general. He'll know what to do with you."

Josef is here? Shoren thought to himself. *That doesn't make any sense.*

"What's the Denver army doing here anyway? I mean, what's going on?"

The sentry looked fishily at him. "Commander Shoren, I don' rightly know what all we're doing out here. If you're who you say you are, then I bet it's got something to do with you and yer surviving troops."

"What?"

"I don' really wanna talk about it wit' some parson 'at just come up outa no-where's in Sioux garb. You're browner then most Denver also. But ye speaks like ye're from the west Denver, maybe the capital, which squares wi' what I've 'eard o' you."

The soldier stopped in front of a large green-stripped three-peak tent. A Denver flag waved in the breeze from the middle, tallest peak.

"Well, here ya're. Wait a sec, and I'll tell the major-general you're here."

The soldier stepped inside the tent after handing his halberd to one of the door guards. Well, actually more like flap guards since the tent didn't have a door. The two guards outside glared at Shoren as if he was going to try to steal a weapon and kill everyone, despite his nonchalant manner. They did stare when he started whispering to Fury and Yakman. He tried to imagine what he looked like to the Denver. A sun-tanned soldier who spoke perfect Denver but dressed like a Sioux, talking to a mustang stallion and a fat little pony. He shook his head.

The first soldier walked out again. "The major general will see you now. I just want you to know, if you try anything, you're going to die right quick. Lemme jes' tell you, I'll be jolly as a grouper fish killin' you as not. The same goes fer these fellows and even the major general. Good luck." The man smiled an unpleasant smile, took his halberd, and walked away. Shoren told Fury and Yakman to stay put, and walked into the tent.

The first thing he noticed was the multitude of maps. There were maps all over the place, in a variety of languages and conditions. Some were Denver military maps, while others were traders' maps. A few seemed to be maps copied from the personal logs of some adventurer or other.

There were only a few men inside. One was a portly balding man Shoren didn't recognize. There were two middle-aged men, a redhead with a big nose and a scraggly beard, and a blond with no real distinguishing features at all. Next to the redhead stood Ryon, Shoren's best friend. Next to Ryon stood a strangely familiar older man with short-cut, graying hair. He was clean-shaven, trim and almost dapper looking. Shoren looked around again. Where was Josef?

The huge man was nowhere to be found. Shoren knew that he couldn't have missed him, since he over-topped the familiar looking man by almost a foot, with shoulders almost half-again as broad. It seemed strange that he wasn't there.

"Well, well. You're not what I remember," the strange man said. "You seem to have fallen rather a long way, whereas in the same span of time I've risen to my highest peak yet." The man's voice was smooth and silky, and it was recognizable. So were his eyes.

"Rekii!" Shoren drew his sword. "What are you doing here? You should have been executed!"

"Legally, that's true. I committed too many crimes to be allowed to live. I guess it's just lucky for me that another committed even greater crimes, and unlike myself, he required more than a talented youngster to defeat him. His defeat required a man of great skill and ingenuity, a man of experience. This man's numerous atrocities were great enough to threaten the fabric of civilization and were true and great sins against heaven itself."

Shoren rolled his eyes. "What are you talking about?"

Ryon stepped forward. "Your friend, Shoren. Josef Nixon. When Emperor Otto died, his son Richerd took over. I don't know what was going on in Josef's head, but he split the army and tried to take over Denver. He revolted against the proper authority, Shoren."

Shoren frowned, sheathed his sword and crossed his arms. "So… what happened?"

Rekii stepped forward. "Emperor Richerd gave me a full pardon and the new rank of major general if I could defeat Josef's army." He smiled. "I did. It wasn't easy, especially not with the invasion by the Koro, but I did it."

Shoren looked at the two men. After a few moments of silence he sighed and waved his arms in a "Go on!" gesture.

"The Koro were crushed completely. Some of the prisoners and some survivors from your own army said that a large number of soldiers escaped the massacre at Garriton. Since recent events have largely depleted the Denver armed forces, we decided to kill two birds with one stone and come out here looking for them." Rekii held up his hand. "I'm sorry, forgive me. The Sioux have been raiding border villages without mercy recently. We're here to rescue the survivors and to punish what Sioux we can find."

"Well, if you're looking for survivors, I think I'm it. After the battle, I managed to lead something like a hundred men away. We wheeled east, trying to avoid the Koro, but we got lost. We traveled for a long time, starving and thirsty, before the Sioux attacked and annihilated us in the night. They seemed to think we were invading."

Rekii nodded. "They have done similar cowardly night attacks against several of our towns. They have no honor. Courage? Yes. Resolve? Yes. Skill? Yes. Honor? Compassion? Honesty? No. They have none of those."

Shoren shook his head. "During my time with them I got a different impression. What Sioux have you come into contact with? Maybe it's a different group?"

Shoren angled his head for a look at the maps all of the men had been crowded around, but the redheaded man stepped in front of him. The portly fellow slapped him on the back, which had the double effect of turning his eyes and his thoughts away from the maps.

"Let's get this man a bath, a bed and some proper clothes." He leered in a disturbing manner, or at least in a manner disturbing to Shoren, who was used to nothing but business while on campaign, not the guffaws that burst from the others at the man's next, equally disturbing, statement. "Maybe some of those wenches that've been trailing the army can give him something else he hasn't seen in a while! I doubt a Denver'd be likely to find too much friendly company way out here!"

The only person Shoren noticed who saw his cold glare was Ryon, who simply smiled in a sickly manner and shrugged. Shoren, who was used to professionalism in the military, did not like the informal manner with which these new, unfamiliar men operated.

The other person who saw the glare was Rekii, who nodded to himself and smiled a tiny, personal smile. Yes, Shoren McCarter was exactly as Rekii remembered him. Rekii shook his head. No, not exactly. The young commander had his own secrets, secrets that he wasn't likely to share. Soon enough, the smile was back. The young whelp may have changed, but his attitudes had not, and that meant he could be manipulated. For Shoren was not the only one who had been busy this year, and Rekii had spent a great deal of time coming up with ways he could pay back this audacious young pup who had the nerve to lead an army, this youngling who hadn't worked his way through the ranks, who had been given his command because of his mother's influence and his father's name, who had the nerve to capture himself, Rekii, and then to prove, by walking into a trap a two-year-old could have seen coming and losing nearly two thousand men, that he was in fact not a prodigy, just a headstrong, lucky fool. Well, Rekii was sure of his path now. Oh, yes. He knew what he was going to do. Yes. He knew.

CHAPTER TWENTY-TWO

Shoren stood in the stall, rubbing down Fury. The stallion was displeased at being in a stable and stall. When Fury and Yakman reached the small border town of Stadton, the two horses were sure they had reached some great city. When Shoren explained that this was nothing more than a small trading and farming town, they didn't believe him. Fury insisted that he had never seen such a place and absolutely refused to believe Shoren. Yakman was a little more open to the idea, but just a little.

~Honestly, Shoren, do you really expect us to believe that your people have towns that are bigger than this? The City is only a little bit bigger than this place, and most people there only live there a few months out of the year. Where do they get the food to feed them all?

"I told you; we farm it. We grow maize and wheat, beans and rice, and we raise livestock. Things like cattle, sheep and pigs. Some places raise chickens. Towns near a lake or river will actually raise fish and some towns will maintain a herd of deer or two for venison.

~I think you're just yanking my tail. You are from around here though, so I guess I have to believe you. Fury looked around, shook his whole body, and stomped his hoof, the equine equivalent of a shudder. *~This place is crowded, really crowded. You said Denver is even bigger than this?* Fury stomped his hoof at Shoren's nod. *~How much bigger?*

"This town holds about four and a half thousand people. Denver holds over two million."

~I don't believe that. Yakman came walking up. *~It's just too big. There aren't a million people in the whole Sioux nation, but you say there's that many in one city? I don't believe it.*

Shoren frowned at the pony but didn't say anything. Instead, seeing a few stable boys enter the building to clean some stalls, he reverted to mental conversation. *~Yakman, in Denver we don't have Horses like you do. All we have are regular horses, and even they aren't smart enough to undo the knot keeping them in their stalls.* Remembering a few incidents from childhood, Shoren added, *well, most of the time they aren't.*

~Wouldn't a horse, even a Little Brother, try to get out of this cramped little place? I don't like it, that's for sure.

~They do. That's how they're raised. Come on, I'll put you back in your stall.

As Shoren led the pony back to his assigned stall, he felt an itching in the back of his mind. Fury and Yakman were having some sort of conversation, it seemed. After he finished brushing down Fury and had carried his saddle to another room in the stable, one of the teenage stable boys looked up in confusion. He looked around, scratched the back of his neck – the closest physical place to the mental itching Shoren felt – frowned, shook his head and continued in his work. Shoren noticed the confusion and remembered when he had first been introduced to the Horses, the Big Brothers.

The boy looked around and looked up at Shoren. "Um, sir? The ah, water pump is just around the corner."

Shoren looked at the boy. "What?"

The boy looked surprised. "Oh, I'm sorry sir. I thought you asked me for some water."

Shoren shook his head. "I didn't."

The young man nodded and bent back down to scooping hay. Shoren frowned. Could that boy be…? Shoren shook his head again and dismissed the incident. No, couldn't be.

✵ ✵ ✵

As soon as he was able, Shoren found a tailor to make him a new dress uniform to replace the one lost during his time with the Sioux. He looked down at himself. He was wearing a coat of a dark forest green. The coat buttoned up off to the left side with brass buttons. These buttons had a thunderbird imprinted on the front. There were also three similar buttons on the outside cuff of each sleeve. On his shoulders were gold epaulets. These were lined in gold with two brass buttons on top of each. A black and gold cord looped from beneath his left epaulet and around his shoulder. On his left breast he had the different medals he had earned throughout his career. There were only a few.

He wore a golden thunderbird on a black ribbon, the Order of Fidelity, first class. He had a silver eagle clutching two golden thunderbolts, the Blitz-Batel, the lighting war, second class. He had won that during a battle with the Aztlani. The Aztlani had punched through the Denver line and scattered the troops. The only warriors who had held were the Black Guard. Shoren was an over lieutenant at the time, in charge of one platoon, or about fifty men. He had rushed to reinforce the Guard with his soldiers, and several platoons followed his example. The final medal was a silver sword hanging from a red ribbon. That simply meant that he had graduated from a military academy, a physical military recommendation everywhere he went. That was especially important, since wearing one without having earned it could be punished severely.

Above, his coat had a large green-lined gold collar. This was stiff and opened up in a v-shape in front.

Finally, Shoren wore gray pants and black leather riding boots. The boots came up to about mid-calf and were heeled. He wore a black leather belt with a simple buckle on which to strap his sword. He wore a hat unique to Denver that in a different time was known as a beret. Over everything he could wear a black surcoat that would in some evoke an image of a cowboy and the Wild West, although the two terms and the image itself would have made no sense to the man wearing it.

Shoren walked up to the command building where Rekii had his General Staff. Rekii had called all of his officers to prepare them to leave Stadton. Rekii was even calling Shoren to meetings, despite Shoren's status as an officer without a command. He snorted. His rank was still legion commander, but Commander Shoren didn't actually command anything.

Shoren walked up the steps of the small building to the ancient front door. The natives of Stadton proudly proclaimed the town hall dated back to the Lost Times, but Shoren wasn't really sure of that since the Lost Times had been lost for over two millennia. The two guards opened the doors and Shoren walked right into Rekii, on his way to the meeting. The two men arrived together and awaited the others in an awkward silence. Once the others arrived, the meeting began with Rekii telling everyone he intended to go south, through Tradefield. After a cursory glance at the map, Shoren quickly noticed a much faster northern route that also ended in Tradefield. He pointed it out to Ryon, who agreed. As soon as Shoren opened his mouth, Rekii quickly changed the subject to what supplies each unit would need for the journey. Shoren swore and muscled his way to the front of the group.

"Rekii! This road," Shoren traced the road on the map with his finger, "will take us to Tradefield in half the time the southern route will take. I think we should go that way."

Rekii looked right at him, grinned, and returned to asking the unit commanders what supplies they needed. Shoren swore again. Rekii's grin grew wider still, and grew even larger when Shoren was forced to the back of the crowd.

Shoren rolled his eyes. "General, that's a dry route. We're going to want to bring extra water."

Shoren swore again when Rekii still ignored him and then again when another officer voiced the same opinion that he had. Rekii praised the other man for his foresight.

"Now," he asked, "who's willing to make sure that we have enough water for the road ahead?"

Before anyone could answer, Shoren volunteered, adding, "There is another route, sir. A faster, flatter, more shaded, wetter route."

Rekii grinned just ever so slightly before looking around. "Come on, I need somebody to take care of this water situation unless someone has a better idea, like another route."

Everyone looked around in discomfort, shifting glances and shuffling feet. A few coughed discreetly. No one looked at Shoren, not even Ryon. After a few minutes, Shoren swore loudly and left the room.

✲ ✲ ✲

Shoren thought that he'd be elated when he finally reached the massive stone gates of Denver. Instead, he sat on Fury's back, depressed, bored, miserable and unsure why he had ever bothered to come back. Rekii had decided to follow the route Shoren had laid out and then proceeded to organize it after Shoren had left, leaving Shoren with absolutely nothing to do.

As soon as Shoren was through the gates, he galloped Fury and Yakman away from the main army and toward his home in the city. Rekii probably wouldn't like it, but Shoren didn't care. Screw him anyway. Shoren was convinced that Rekii was still a psychotic killer, but so far had no evidence other than his own intuition. Rekii had acted mostly sane, although Shoren had seen him mumbling and whispering frantically to himself more than once and it didn't seem to matter whether Rekii was alone or not. The older man would also giggle at odd moments, which the rest of the general staff seemed inclined to ignore.

"Shoren!" Shoren turned back to see Ryon riding up to him, an amused grin on his face.

"What is it?"

"Where are you going? You can't just leave you know. We have to report to the Citadel, the military headquarters, don't forget."

Shoren frowned. In his eagerness to escape Rekii's clutches, he had forgotten. "I didn't forget! I haven't seen the city in a long time, and I just wanted to see more of it. I wanted to see my other friends and my family."

"Yeah, well, that might not turn out the way you think. Denver's a little different from the way you left it. Different. Better." Ryon nodded to himself and turned his horse away, lost in thought. Shoren shook his head. Was everyone around him going nuts?

✫ ✫ ✫

Emperor Richerd Jorge McCarter III sat on his huge eagle throne, staring down at his new Major General Rekii Ubel. The man had delivered some interesting news.

"So tell me again, Rekii, how it is that you found my little cousin out wandering alone in the Plains of the Sioux."

The older man bowed sardonically before once more repeating himself. "Well, Emperor (how that title grated on his tongue), I found your whelp of a cousin running from some Sioux. They were chasing him for some reason or other. After completing the last of your, ah, directives, I spotted Shoren all alone with a large war party behind him. I didn't know who he was, so I decided to investigate." Then, without a hint of irony he added, "Of course, when I learned who he was I decided to rescue him. I am, after all, a gentleman."

Richerd rolled his eyes. He had noticed the irony, but Rekii either didn't or was hiding it very well for some odd reason, if for any reason at all. Richerd couldn't tell, and it infuriated him. It was as much for that reason as for any other that Richerd smiled at his next thought. After the timely death of Richerd's father, Richerd and Rekii had worked together and consolidated political and military power into a tenuous partnership. Since then, they had spent most of their time sniping and backbiting so as to determine who the dominant power in this relationship was. So far, neither could tell.

Richerd shook his head. "Did he explain why he was in the Plains? You haven't explained that yet."

"He apparently fled from the battle of Garriton like a coward. I must say, I would not have. Later, it seems, he was captured by the Sioux. This past six months he was stuck in a mud hut or whatever the Sioux live in." Rekii laughed.

Richerd shook his head. "I imagine it would be preferable to being dead. Besides, the Sioux live in tepees. They're a special kind of tent."

Rekii grunted. "I don't care. Look, unless you're planning something special for your cousin, I owe him a debt of pain and humiliation. I will enjoy administering it."

"How? I am curious. I have to admit, when it comes to vengeance you're very clever. I want to know what exactly you have in mind for Shoren though. He is family after all."

"Well, Emperor, some things are better left unspoken. What I plan to do would shock you I'm afraid. Shock you to the very core." Richerd narrowed his eyes and pursed his mouth. In many ways, he had lived a sheltered life and more than once wondered what he had missed, what he didn't know. Sometimes, like now, he was almost glad that he didn't know. Rekii, of course, had continued running his mouth. "If you really must know, I suggest you ask Shoren yourself when I'm through, because," he said, with the air of a man making a great concession, "I won't even kill him."

Richerd frowned. What could he intend for Shoren? The young Emperor shook his head. Enough of that. He grinned.

"Major general, did Shoren recently receive a posthumous medal? I really can't remember."

Now it was Rekii's turn to frown. "Yes." He said tightly. "He did."

"What for, exactly?"

"Capturing me."

Richerd grinned. "Well, it appears my cousin is not dead. That means he cannot receive a posthumous medal. He needs to receive one in person, in a ceremony. Of course, the double lightening bolts can only be given by the major general. How...ironic. Wouldn't you say?"

Rekii looked sick. "Ironic. That would be the word."

"I want you to plan the ceremony. In it, I want you to tell the Court of Shoren's bravery and daring and how he outwitted you. Then, I want you to pin the medal on his chest and shake his hand. You won't do...whatever it is that you planned to do. I have plans for my cousin and I will not allow your petty vengeances to get in the way. Now go and prepare. I want to hold the ceremony within the week." Richerd clapped his hands. "Go on, chop chop."

Rekii looked like he hated Richerd, which he undoubtedly did. "All right. Tell me though, is that little noble woman Zarine still in Court? I was looking forward to some company."

Richerd shook his head. "No, I'm afraid she left for the countryside with her husband last month."

Rekii looked almost crestfallen. "That's too bad. I enjoyed her. Now I have to find another." He bowed to Richerd and left.

Dirty old man, Richerd thought scornfully to himself as he watched Rekii leave, never reflecting on what his harem of terrified noble ladies and expensive whores said about him.

✫ ✫ ✫

Rekii sat on his great oak bed, fuming. He didn't know why he was so angry. *That's not true,* he thought to himself, *I know why I'm angry. I just don't know why I'm so angry. Who cares if that stupid pup gets some medal? So it's a little humiliating for me. Big deal.*

The truth was that it wasn't a big deal, not in the end. Rekii had always prided himself on taking revenge on everyone who had ever wronged him. That's part of the reason he had tried rampaging in the west. The other was a firm belief that nobody who mattered, none of the generals and rich merchants who made up the nobility these days, had ever paid any attention to his thoughts and feelings and accomplishments. The fact that he never bothered over their feelings and continued breathing didn't occur to him.

Finally, Rekii stood up, dismissing the whole incident in the Imperial Palace. He had his palace now, even if it didn't have a fancy title. Rekii didn't know what exactly had convinced the previous own-ers to surrender the building and its grounds or if in fact anything had convinced them. The family may simply have been killed. It had happened before.

Rekii walked out onto the balcony that overlooked the palace grounds. His new palace came with a small hedge garden surrounded by a columned walkway on all four sides. It had large, thick walls and towers surrounding it too; the building was as much fortress as it was luxury home. Rekii admired the beauty of the gardens for just a moment. Soon enough, he turned around and began screaming at the top of his lungs for his servants to bring him some whiskey. For now, that was all that was important.

✿ ✿ ✿

While Rekii was drinking himself into a stupor and Richerd was plot-ting for even more power and authority, Shoren McCarter was sitting on Fury's back, biting his lower lip nervously. He was just down the street from his childhood home, a large marble palace. It was typical Denver, a large central building with ornamental towers and walls all around it. Like most palaces, it had a garden surrounded by columned walkways. Shoren's home had a large fountain in the very center with statues in each corner. The place sported a library, a stable and store-rooms for treasures and weapons, but most importantly, somewhere inside, was not only his mother, Lucrezia, but also Elina.

He discovered that Elina had taken to living in his mother's home about six months prior, and as far as he could tell, several small noble families had done the same. A few spacious palaces were all overrun with nobles and servants and guards, while most of the smaller ones sat empty. Most were completely closed off and were under armed guard, but break-ins remained common. No one seemed to care. The streets of the palace district had always been kept clean and neat, and Shoren remembered always being able to smell the scent of the mountain pines that grew on all the palace grounds and along the roads in specially maintained lots. Some places smelled of flowers too, and other places the scents of horses and dogs, the favored pets of Denver, filled the air. No more. Where Shoren remembered pines and flowers, he smelled nothing but ash, burnt wood and marble dust. Instead of dogs and horses, he smelled rotting flesh where the corpses of animals and people had been abandoned where they dropped. These smells permeated the empty, lifeless streets. Where people remained, the scents remained but with one addition. The new scent was fear.

"Well that was bloody profound," Shoren muttered under his breath. "Might as well dress me up in a cap and a gown and call me a poet."

Fury's ears twitched but he said nothing. Yakman was munching on some peonies and so hadn't heard him, which Shoren thought was probably for the best. He doubted the pony would have been as discreet as the mustang.

Finally Shoren swore, dismounted and unstrapped Fury's saddle girth. *~Fury!* The mustang looked up. *~Gather Yakman and head to the stable. Drop off the saddle on a table or something and head to the center of the palace. There is a spacious grassy area for you. If anyone bothers you, snort and stomp around. If that doesn't work, yell for me.*

The mustang stomped his hoof, an unspoken "yes, sir!" With an evil gleam in his eye, he quietly snuck over to Yakman and snapped at his ear. Startled, the pony kicked Fury who dropped the saddle. The two began snapping and stomping at each other until Shoren shouted and swore at them. The two horses stopped immediately and looked up, their faces perfect pictures of innocence. He glared at them. Yakman kicked the saddle with his hoof at the same time Fury tried to pick it up with his teeth. That might have started another fight had Shoren not walked over, picked up the saddle and placed on Fury's back. He didn't move again until the two very subdued horses turned a corner and vanished from his sight.

Shoren swore again before marching up the steps to the front gate of his mother's palace. No guards were in sight. He banged on the door. Nothing happened. He banged on the door again. Again, nothing happened. Afraid now and frustrated, Shoren tried to kick the damn thing in, only to hurt his foot. Too late he reflected on the folly of kicking a huge, iron-reinforced oak door. He was about to hurl a rock through a window when a man came running outside. He was obviously a servant, though Shoren didn't recognize him. His clothes were shabby but clean and he carried a small wood axe. He drew this weapon now.

"Who are you? You belong here? Get out!" He waved the axe without much skill but with great enthusiasm. Shoren laughed. Then he casually walked over to the man.

"Look, I don't know who you are but I used to live here. I'm just trying to find my family." The other man looked around nervously and lowered the axe, although he gripped it so tightly his knuckles were white. He twitched nervously when Shoren got within striking distance, but still seemed to think he had the upper hand against the seemingly unarmed Shoren.

"Look, pal, clear-ooph!" Shoren had delivered a blow to the man's throat with a stiffened hand while at the same time sweeping the man's feet from beneath him. The man fell to the ground hard. When he began to get up, Shoren wrapped an arm around his throat, grabbed the axe, and threatened his belly with it.

"What the hell is going on? Where the hell are Lady Elina and Lady Lucrezia?" The man whimpered. "Where!"

"Inside! They're fine! I just work for 'em! They don' want any strangers in the house!"

Shoren let the man go but didn't relinquish the axe. "Look, I'm Lucrezia's son and Elina's fiancé. Take me to them." The man nodded and led Shoren to a small side door.

"The main door's been bolted shut, sir. Anyone who wants to get in comes through here."

He kept looking nervously around. He positively jumped when both women stormed out of the house with several guards in tow. Shoren jumped when he saw Fury calmly walking behind them. The two women and their guards stopped in their tracks.

"Bloody hell," Shoren swore.

"Bloody hell!" the women shouted at once.

~Bloody hell! Fury shouted, along with a loud neigh. Shoren glared at him. *~What? I felt left out.*

"Shoren! What are you doing here? I thought you were dead! I missed you so much!" Elina ran over and gripped him fiercely. Then she burst into tears.

"Well, I'm not. I missed you too, by the way. I see you've met my horse, Fury."

She looked up. "This is your horse? What about the pony? This one just walked into the palace and has been following us around, and the pony's been raising holy hell in the garden with the guards." Her eyes narrowed. "What exactly have you been up to?"

"Well, I don't know what you've been told, but I've spent the last six months or so in the Plains."

"With the Sioux? How did you get there?" She shook her head. "Never mind. Let's get in the palace."

As Shoren was led through his childhood home, he was amazed to see how much it had changed in the year and a half he had been gone. The tapestries and paintings were gone, leaving only bare walls. Several doors were barred shut, and guards were everywhere.

"After Emperor Richerd came to power, the Civil Guard was absorbed into the army. Looters began breaking into shops and homes and some began to take over the palaces in the noble districts. All of the guards here are mercenaries and private security groups of veteran soldiers. Nobody has been able to clean up the city though."

Shoren was flabbergasted. "Why in the world would Richerd transfer the Civil Guard into the Army? Nobody would support him after that; the Assembly would make his reign a living nightmare."

Elina shook her head as she sunk into one of the larger chairs in the large sitting room they had come to. "The Assembly can't bother him if there is no Assembly. He disbanded it, or didn't you know?" She looked at Shoren quizzically.

Shoren's mother, Lucrezia, spoke up. "Shoren, the simple fact is that Richerd doesn't care about what happens to anyone. He's off in his palace enjoying all of Denver's riches while the empire collapses around him. The army doesn't care about what happens to the nobles because they don't come from the noble classes. The officers who do are either too terrified to do anything or simply use their own soldiers to guard their family homes."

Shoren shook his head. "That still doesn't explain why the Civil Guard is gone. Richerd didn't need to do that."

Lucrezia also sat down in one of the overstuffed armchairs. "Actually, he did. Josef's Rebellion cost well over two hundred thousand soldiers killed, and the invasion by the Koro cost another thirty thousand. Most of the surviving rebels are either hiding with Josef in the mountains or else have simply turned bandit and are raiding trade routes and supply convoys. The army has been cut in half. Richerd simply needed the soldiers."

Shoren heard the capitals thud in place. "Josef's Rebellion?"

"Major General Josef Nixon tried to lead a coup against Richerd shortly after Emperor Otto's death. Richerd used the coup as an excuse to disband the Assembly, although Josef claimed that Richerd had always wanted to do that anyway. I guess he still claims that. Not that anyone would dare say it. Richerd has had hundreds of people killed, including his own family. You're about as close a relative as he has."

Shoren's eyes widened. "That's a scary thought, given that I'm his cousin. I think it would be good to talk with Josef as soon as I get the chance."

Lucrezia and Elina looked at each other for a moment. Finally, his mother smiled. "I think that can be arranged."

CHAPTER TWENTY-THREE

Shoren stood in the massive imperial throne room. It was a far cry from the rest of the city. Whereas most of the city was dirty and breaking down, the palace had been polished until it practically sparkled. Denver flags were everywhere, as were flags displaying Richerd's personal sigil, a black eagle on a red field. Normally the eagle had a golden body with red wings and rested on a field of blue.

Shoren wondered just what exactly was coming, especially since he could see what little remained of Denver's nobility. Most of the high-ranking officers were there with their entourages. Shoren had no entourage.

If someone were to look at Shoren, one would assume that he was doing nothing more than politely paying attention to the speech the current major general, Rekii, was giving. Rekii had started by listing all of the wondrous qualities of the Denver soldier, and had then gone into painful detail about how Shoren met each and every one of these qualities. Intermixed with the fulsome praise of Shoren was Rekii's typical ranting about traitors and enemies and about how everyone needed to bend knee to the Spirits of the Sacred Mountain and about how the Spirits had appointed Richerd their shield and Rekii himself their sword. Given Rekii's sudden, violent tendencies, absolutely no doubt appeared on the attendees' faces.

Soon enough, Shoren stood to receive his medal. This meant he had to stand for another hour while Rekii muttered on about how Shoren had defeated him. As he listened to the official story of the battle, Shoren could have sworn he must have missed something, because what he remembered was absolutely nothing like the tale Rekii told. Finally, Rekii worked his way toward pinning the medal onto Shoren's chest. Shoren gave a brief speech thanking Rekii and Richerd for the honor and the guests for attending. He told everyone that his victory had more to do with luck than any particular skill of his, adding that it was pretty hard to lose a battle when you commanded twenty thousand troops and your enemy commanded only three. He ended with another thanks to Rekii, "for without Major General Rekii, this honor would not be possible." Rekii began muttering to himself again.

Just when Shoren thought the ceremony over, Richerd stood. "We see before us today one of Denver's most promising young commanders. We have a shortage of true heroes, but here stands my cousin, returned to us from the dead. As many of my officers will know, the rank of captain general has been empty for quite some time. We finally have a man worthy of the position. I hereby decree that Shoren McCarter is to be the new captain general of the entire Denver armed forces, answerable only to the major general and, of course, myself. The ceremony is over. Walk with the spirits."

Shoren stood there dumbfounded. After a few moments, his eyes found Elina's. She looked just as shocked as her fiancé. Then, she fainted.

✵ ✵ ✵

Shoren rode out on Fury's back, alone. He was heading toward a small shrine just a day's ride from Denver, at the top of one of the closest peaks. Legend held that the founders had built it so that they could see the ruins of the old Denver, which had been destroyed in some pre-Lost Times calamity. It was near this shrine where he would meet Josef, mastermind of the first rebellion against a duly anointed Emperor in two hundred years.

He had managed to get away by announcing he would be visiting the shrine alone for spiritual guidance to aid him in his new task. In reality, he would meet with Josef and then travel to the shrine, where he would in fact pray for spiritual guidance but not necessarily for the reason given. The specific reason for his prayer was what he intended to discover.

There were many large shrines in Denver, as well as temples and churches dedicated to other faiths. Religion had never really mattered to Shoren before and it continued to not matter to him now. Some of the religions dated to before the Lost Times, and some rose afterwards. Many people, like the Aztlani, were zealots and fanatics. Shoren couldn't have cared less, though he was aware that religion was a useful tool to mask his true intentions.

Lucrezia had given Shoren explicit directions where and how to meet Josef, and Shoren was quickly coming up on the small clearing where Josef was supposed to meet him. Shoren had been told that Josef's scouts would meet him there and would either take him to Josef or bring Josef to him.

As Shoren approached the clearing, he was met by a group of armored men. Their armor was Denver made but in various states of disrepair. In addition, the plate armor on some had been painted green, while other soldiers were wearing green cloth with branches and leaves tied around their helmets and torsos. All carried regular crossbows, not repeaters, and all had a variety of melee weapons. One of the soldiers held up a drawing. He looked around at the others.

"Yeah, it's him." He gestured for a couple of his soldiers to approach. He looked at Shoren and held out a black cloth sack. "I'm sorry, but if you want to see the General, you're going to have to put this on. If anything unfortunate occurs, we don't want this place to be betrayed."

Shoren nodded and reached down for the sack and put it over his head, obscuring his vision. He grinned. *~Fury?* He waited for the stallion's mental nod before continuing. *~I want you to be careful and watch out for where we go. If something happens, I'm going to rely on you to get us back.*

Fury responded affirmatively and allowed the armored men to lead him away. After what seemed like a long time they stopped.

~Are we there yet? I really, really hate being blind like this.

~We're there.

Shoren heard a shout. "Take off the sack!" He did.

Shoren looked around. He saw a few more soldiers than he had seen before. Some were on horseback with short bows and others were on foot. The men without ranged weapons mostly carried swords, axes, maces and knives, since a spear or pike's length would be a disadvantage in such a heavily forested area. In addition, there stood Josef himself, in green painted plate armor. Some of the plates were missing and his hair was longer, as was his beard. He looked like he had aged ten years.

"Well, Shoren, good ta meet ya again, though I'd rather be do'n it in happier times. When yer mother told me ya wanted ta talk, especially afta' yer promotion, I did'n know what ta think. So, what do ya want ta talk about, hmmm?"

"You have some explaining to do, Josef. Why are you in rebellion against the lawful Emperor of the Denver Empire? What the hell were you thinking? You have no troops, no supplies to speak of, and little support, Josef. I've heard that you've been raiding traders and merchants like a common bandit."

Josef snorted. "I had a lot o' support in de beginnin'. About a full third o' de army, all told. Yonder 'lawful Emperor' had little more than I did, though his was better 'quipped. De rest o' de soldiers was sitting it out, waiting ta see who was goin' ta win."

"Why though? Richerd's not exactly a nice guy, but why revolt? It doesn't make any sense."

"Richerd's no legal Emperor, and he's a whole hell o' a lot worse than 'not a nice guy.' He's been goin' 'round killing people he don' like. He's been doin' a lot o' dat lately. Look Shoren, I revolted 'cause Emperor Otto, may he rest in peace, didn' die o' natural causes. He were murdered. I were able ta prove it too, 'cause I had in custody one o' da men what did it. Horrified out o' his mind he were, when he learned who it was he'd gone and poisoned. Tol' me 'ol Richerd hired him, he did, and he showed me da money order and sure as hell it were signed by Richerd for quite a lot o' gold. Found one o' his partners too, but da damn angry mob overpowered me guards, killed him and strung him by his thumbs. Literally. Dat's a nasty way ta die, sure 'nough. I couldn' find de other fellow neither, 'cause dat blasted fool went and hung himself like a coward, 'stead of trying ta fix what he broke. It don' matter now no how, since Rekii killed de man I did have. Hired assassins ta kill de assassin. Yeah, I know. It's funny, funny like a blasted, bloody crutch." Josef turned and spat on the ground.

Shoren looked around. "So you used to have a lot of support. What happened to it? I guess you were defeated, since you're standing here in the woods instead of behind a puppet on the throne."

Josef swore angrily at him. "If I'da won, I wouldn' ha' put no puppet on the damn throne. I'd have either sat on the damn thing myself, or I'd have found some cousin o' yours ta stick on it, even if it meant inventing a new face for some poor fool. 'Course I expect he'd have been a bit of a puppet.

"Anyway, what I would have or wouldn' have done don' make no difference anyhow. I lost. I would have won. I should have. But Mekal's failure in the north was more complete than any o' us imagined. Picture everyone's surprise when one day, a bunch o' damned stinkin' Koro come marching out o' da north ta attack Denver itself wid 'ol Mekal's head on a stake! Rekii and I quickly arranged a truce ta repel de invaders and maybe den negotiate sometin' out. We pushed da northerners back, we had 'em trapped we did, you bet. De final battle wid 'em was planned perfect, just perfect." Josef's face glowed with unabashed pride.

"But something happened, something you didn't expect, didn't it. Obviously you won the battle, but you lost to Rekii."

The older man's eyes darkened. "Yeah, dat's de way it went down. Rekii would come at 'em from one direction, and I another. Perfect flanking move. We got a runner saying Rekii's troops hit a snag but not ta worry, engage in de battle. Well hell, I thought even Rekii wouldn' want ta risk the city so I loosed de dogs o' war and attacked. No Rekii. I kept fightin' but no Rekii. I'm pushin' de Koro back, I am, but at terrible cost, when de Loyalists charge out and smash inta de enemy. All de Koro die but when me survivin' men start ta celebrate, Rekii's troops begin ta slay dem all. I managed ta escape wid about five hundred and about three times dat disperses and turns bandit. De rest die or are taken prisoner. De prisoners die."

Shoren was stunned. "I don't know what…that's quite a story, Josef. What, what can I do to help?"

Josef grinned. "Go ta ya shrine. Pray. Go back ta Elina. Marry her. Develop support among de nobles and merchants, and when de time be right, don' revolt, simply force a palace coup, kill de traitors or not as ya please and install yaself as de new Emperor. Den ya can deal wid de rest as ya please."

"Josef, I'm not sure that's such a good idea…"

"Ta da future Emperor! Now git a'fore someone sees ya missing."

In a daze, Shoren climbed back on Fury. As he turned Fury around, one of the soldiers threw something into his lap. It was the black sack.

"Emperor or not, you've still got to wear that."

Shoren protested, but the soldier wouldn't bend. When he looked around for support from Josef, all he got was the general's retreating back and some booming laughter.

"I'm glad someone thinks it's bloody funny," Shoren muttered. He glared at the soldier for a few minutes, but then put the sack over his head.

Shoren knelt in the small shrine literally built into the mountain peak. Fury was just outside somewhere. Shoren tried to return to the sense of reverence he had felt only a little while earlier, but his efforts were in vain. He stood up.

He was, once more, wearing his full dress uniform, although it now was covered in decorations of office that included looping shoulder cords of a variety of colors, new gold thread epaulets with little green eagles in the center, a green and gold sash that wrapped around his waist, a shiny black leather strap that connected to his belt to hold in place a beaded "pouch" that held various ceremonial symbols of office, and, finally, uncomfortable shiny black leather boots. The damn toes and heels were even tipped in metal so as to create a clicking sound whenever Shoren walked. He hated them.

Shoren stood up and walked out. As he looked around and placed his service cap on his head, he caught another glance of the original Denver. Though he had seen it several times now, the sight never failed to take his breath away. The twisted metal ruins still reached up toward the sky in a silent plea for mercy. Shoren didn't know what weapon could cause such devastation, and he was afraid to find out. According to the monks who maintained this shrine, the very center of the city had been completely wiped clean, every building, every person scoured from the earth. The ground was cracked glass, and permanent shadows screamed their fear from the remaining walls. Moss, trees and animals lived in the more plentiful ruins of the outer city, but even after all this time, the center remained barren. Shoren didn't know whether the ground was infertile or if the memory was so great, so vivid, that even moss and rats stayed away, out of respect for, or fear of, the dead.

Unable to look anymore, Shoren walked down the lovingly maintained stone steps to the waiting monks and the larger temple and monastery. Also there was the Wall, a large stone wall with names carved into it; not names of people, but names of long forgotten places where similar devastation had been visited. New York, Hong Kong, Washington, London, Moscow, Tokyo, Geneva, Paris, Berlin, Munich, Kiev.... The list went on and on. Shoren didn't know where a single one of those cities had once stood, but he knew that every day in a tradition dating back two thousand years, the monks prayed for the souls of those dead.

They weren't praying now; at least some of them weren't. They stood waiting for him. Some of the monks followed him silently to his horse, while some strode up to the shrine. They seemed to understand his desire for silence, as did Fury when Shoren mounted him. Before he left though, Shoren took some time to thank the monks for their hospitality. The monks had been polite, albeit cold and distant. This was not the first time Shoren had seen that few wanted anything to do with Richerd's new captain general.

✲ ✲ ✲

After his time at the shrine, Shoren returned to Denver where he set himself to take up his new duties with diligence. Unfortunately, he found himself without any duties or responsibilities. What he had found for himself was an unwilling junior seat in a triumvirate the likes of which hadn't been seen in millennia, the closest approximation of which had once ruled an empire four thousand years lost and halfway around the world.

That was in general of course. At the moment Shoren found his seat, however junior, soaked in wine from a cup thrown at him by Rekii in a fit of neurotic rage.

"Calm yourself, Rekii. Your constant tantrums are unbearable. I swear, working with you is like babysitting a two-year-old and remember: I don't like children!"

That was Richerd, the Emperor. The source of Rekii's rage, and his voice rose with his anger as he spoke. Shoren watched the bickering with considerable amusement. *Of course it's funny in a weird sort of way,* he thought. *They are fighting over me.* Ah yes, Rekii was finally condescending to use understandable words again, instead of whines and half-curses. Shoren figured he might as well pay attention.

"No, no, no! I am not giving up command of half my army to this pup! As for the prissy nobles pissing their silk pants in fear of looters, I say, who cares? Forget them! The country will be better off without them! Let me guess, this is just a chance to de-fang an old wolf, huh? You want me powerless 'cause you can't pull my strings, you can't yank my chains, but you think you can give my armor to your baby cousin and lead him around on a leash! Well I won't stand for it! No more!"

"Rekii, the whole point of this is to make Denver strong, not weak. The nobles are rich. The nobles are educated. The nobles know how to run farms and factories and smithies and businesses as well as you know how to run an army. I won't cripple my country because you think it's funny to torment dainty little women. I am Emperor, and if you won't obey my orders, than I'll remove you from office and replace you with someone who will.

"The whole point of giving my cousin responsibility for the cleansing of crime and banditry in Denver is to learn, to gain experience. Maybe he will take your job in a decade or so, but not now."

Shoren laughed. This was getting ridiculous. "Actually, cousin, I don't want Rekii's job in a decade or so. Yours would do nicely, I think."

Richerd laughed. "Just so. Both of you want my job, as much as I want to keep it. Since I'm here now, you'll just have to wait. Anyway, Rekii, I'm pulling a legion, about ten thousand troops, for Shoren's command, not half your damn army. So shut up and be happy I don't actually take half your army."

"Look at me, Emperor Richerd…"

"I meant the shut up comment. I don't want to hear your voice anymore."

Rekii looked as if about to explode. His face reddened, his fists clenched, and his eyes widened. After a few deep breaths, he turned around, gathered up his papers and stormed out, slamming the door behind him.

Richerd looked over at Shoren. "Well, that was unpleasant. The legion has already been assigned to you, Shoren. I want a progress report in two weeks' time. Get to it."

Shoren saluted, turned, and walked away. As he made his way through the titanic, labyrinthine palace, he was already planning the most effective use of his new army. Soon enough Shoren reached the front outside doors to the palace, and from there went to the stables where Fury was reluctantly standing. Shoren quickly made his way to the unofficial "Temple City," an area of Denver City that was filled with the holy places of all the numerous competing faiths of the Denver.

There were numerous temples and shrines dedicated to one deity or another. Several faiths that had been popular during the Lost Times had survived and prospered, whereas others had come after. Some of the Lost Times faiths had not survived intact but had been reborn in the form of entirely new religions. Shoren, like most Denver, knew the tenets of most popular religions but didn't personally ascribe to any of them. The reason for this short trip was to check out one of the statue parks in the area to see if it was a suitable site for his marriage to Elina.

Once he found the park, he dismounted Fury but let the Horse follow him through the park. The walkways were laid out like a wheel, with a large outer circle and then a much smaller inner circle and eight spokes connecting them. Statues lined the walkways and where the spokes connected with the outer circle stood large decorated arches. There were also arches of a sort – statues of warriors holding their swords high over their heads and touching so that the statues formed a gateway – where the walkways connected with the inner circle. The center was a paved circle where various ceremonies could be held. It was nice, but Shoren wasn't sure he liked it. He'd have to decide.

✲ ✲ ✲

Shoren's first act as captain general had been to appropriate a large number of troops specifically to guard his own home and neighborhood. He had decided that his action, both real and symbolic, would make an excellent start to quelling the chaos that Richerd's reign had brought upon the city. Elina had hired workers to begin repairing the palace so that it would once more be open to visitors as well as for parties and other social events. Her example had encouraged other nobles to do the same.

Shoren rode through his neighborhood with conflicted feelings. He was glad to have the power he did, and also to act on the plan that he and Josef had hashed out, but he wasn't sure that he wanted all the trappings of the office. Certainly the uniform and power it entailed were both nice, but Shoren knew that soon enough he'd have to be traveling with armed guards nearly everywhere he went.

When he reached the palace, he dismounted Fury, removed the saddle, and watched Fury wander about the lawn. Shoren quickly walked into the small mansion to find Elina and his mother ordering workers about trying to set the thing in order. He walked over and gave them both a quick hug before suggesting they move to a private room so he could tell them about his conversation with Richerd and Rekii at the Imperial Palace.

"So he wants me to put the city back in order with ten thousand men. I don't think they'll be enough though. I'll just have to see."

Elina shook her head. "They won't be if he wants you to rebuild the Civil Guard. What you should do is clear up some parts of the city well, but leave the rest alone. That way when you give him your report, you can make sure that you get more soldiers."

"Rekii's not going to be very happy about that. Of course, he's never happy, so I don't know how much it's going to matter. It'd probably be best to take it slow. The goal isn't to take over the country, not really. If I can hold Denver, then I will control the country."

Shoren's mother spoke up. "Not necessarily. Richerd and Rekii control Denver, but they don't really control the countryside. Josef's still out there and the roads are filled with bandits. Whole divisions have simply stopped reporting back to the Citadel."

Shoren frowned. "That's not what I meant. I meant that I wouldn't need to conquer the whole country in order to become Emperor. I may have to recapture whole chunks of the country from bandits, but I wouldn't be facing an organized army."

"That's only true if you manage to kill Richerd and Rekii at the same time. Otherwise you'll be facing the same problem you did last summer with Rekii running loose. Remember Shoren, even if you kill one of them, if the other escapes the army will be more likely to rally behind that person than behind you.

"Richerd is the rightful Emperor even if he is a tyrant, and Rekii is a famous general. You'd be considered a pretender to the throne either way, more so if Richerd lives and Rekii dies, mostly because Rekii isn't as able to sway a crowd as Richerd."

"Do you really think Rekii would be more accepted as Emperor than I would? I at least am related to the Emperor."

Lucrezia nodded. "You're the Emperor's younger cousin. Your father was the previous Emperor's cousin, but they're both dead now and besides, who hears about the younger royal cousins anyway? You're father was well known, but as a general, not as a royal. Otherwise he'd always have been in Otto's shadow. Until recently, nobody had ever heard of you. Rekii on the other hand, is an important part of the established authority. In case you haven't noticed, that matters here."

Shoren nodded and began to think about how he was going to take over his own country. His mother and fiancée moved the conversation to other matters, such as when the mansion would be finished and where the wedding would be and when. He had little to add to the conversation. He was more worried about Richerd and Rekii.

✲ ✲ ✲

While Shoren was talking to his fiancée and mother, Emperor Richerd lounged on his throne, waiting for his next appointment. A herald entered.

After bowing, the man announced, "Your Majesty, a man named Francriek Pall is here to see you. He says it's very urgent."

Richerd nodded. "Of course, of course. Did you send some wine and food to the private meeting room?" The herald nodded. "Then take him there in just a few minutes."

"Yes, sir."

The herald quickly left. Richerd lazily stood up and walked to the private meeting room. Two guards stood outside the door, looking intimidating and fierce. When Richerd passed they snapped to attention and saluted. Richerd returned an indolent salute.

"After the herald and his guest arrive, don't let anyone else in unless it's very urgent. Very urgent."

The guards saluted. Richerd had no sooner poured himself a glass of wine than Francriek walked in. Francriek was a skinny man of about average height. He had light brown hair but other than a few knife scars on his hands and face he was completely... average. He had no distinguishing features whatsoever. Even his clothes were unremarkable. They weren't well made, but weren't shabby either. All in all, he was a completely forgettable man, assuming one were to forget about his special... talents.

"Take a seat Francriek, and a glass of wine. I can have some more food brought for us if you're hungry."

Francriek shook his head. "Your Majesty, this will do. I have interesting news for you. Have you spoken with the captain general since his return?"

"I have. I met with him just a few moments ago. Why"

"I fear he may not be entirely loyal to you, sire. I followed him as you ordered, sire, and he went off the course of his intended journey to the Shrine of the Lost. He met with the traitor Josef. I couldn't get close enough to hear what was said, but the meeting was brief. Shoren was brought to them hooded so he couldn't see the path, and when he left he appeared agitated."

"That's interesting, but not entirely unexpected. Shoren would have wanted to hear both sides of the events that took place when he was gone. I want to know how he managed to contact Josef in the first place."

Francriek shrugged. "I can't say for sure, but I think his mother has been in contact with the rebel for some time."

"That's good to know. Was there anything of note?"

"Only that he speaks to his horse like he would to another person. I don't know though if he's crazy or if it's simply a silly affectation. It probably doesn't matter."

Richerd pulled out a small sack and poured its contents onto the table. It was filled with small gemstones. Francriek leaned forward.

"I have something more up your alley today, Francriek. You see, there is a merchant named Sher Johaan, and he's been causing some trouble recently. You know who I'm talking about?" Francriek nodded. "Then get rid of him. Make it look like an accident. No. Make it look like it was made to look like an accident. I want that taken care of immediately."

"Of course, your Majesty." Francriek leaned forward to scoop up the gems.

"I don't think so. Those are for when you get back."

The assassin grinned. "As usual. When are you going to learn to trust me?"

"I'll trust you when you're dead, the same time I trust everyone else. Now get going!"

Richerd followed Francriek out, since his guards weren't going to let the man leave until they saw Richerd alive and well. As soon as Francriek left, Richerd called for some paper and a pen. When he was finished writing, he called for a messenger.

"I want you to take this to the captain general with the utmost haste. Do you understand?" The boy nodded and ran off.

Once the boy was gone, he sent for another one of his many spies. Now that he knew that Shoren's loyalty was compromised, he intended to have him followed at all times. This man however, wasn't going to be following his cousin. Like he told Francriek, he didn't trust anyone until after they were dead.

✵ ✵ ✵

"For the crimes of murder and banditry, you have each been sentenced by the Imperial Court to death by hanging, the sentence to be carried out immediately. Pray to whatever god you hold, and may your souls find mercy in the afterlife."

This is the worst part of my job, Shoren thought as he stepped away from the platform. There was no doubt at all that the ten condemned men here today were guilty, since they had been part of a bandit clan responsible for the murders of at least one hundred people. The trouble was that Shoren didn't know if it was going to do any good. Since Shoren had sent armed patrols throughout the city, crime had decreased greatly…in the patrolled areas. Then he would send his troops somewhere else and crime would decrease there but would increase again in the places his troops had left. It was maddening.

Shoren and Richerd had spoken and they both agreed that the gangs of men roaming around ought to be considered bandits and thus subject to the same penalties that bandits were normally subject to. Shoren thought the proclamation would scare some away, but not enough, so today was to show that the new law had teeth. It would have taken a miracle to make significant progress in two weeks with only ten thousand soldiers. This was after all a city of nearly two million citizens. Shoren knew he needed more troops.

Shoren sat in his office awaiting his new aide, Charlz Smied, the young man who had saved his life during the attack on Laramie, where he had forced Rekii out. Shoren had checked the military records he now had access to in order to discover what had happened to the young man in the two years since they had parted ways. Charlz, rather than return to an officer's school, had opted for a position as an aide to one of Rekii's generals; he would be basically a secretary and an errand boy but he would learn how the administrative side of the military worked and in a few years he would get a field position, either as an aide again, or more likely, a small field command.

Shoren had transferred the boy to his command soon after reading his file. First of all, he didn't trust the secretary and aides he had been given by Rekii. Secondly, the young man had stayed with Richerd and Rekii rather than revolting or staying put. One thing Shoren was interested in was why. Most of the loyalists he had spoken with were either fanatics or terrified, or both, and Shoren wanted to know Charlz's reasons. Hopefully, they were good.

The sergeant he had posted outside his office as a temporary secretary (the one Rekii had given him had another position now) knocked on Shoren's open office door and peeked his head in.

"Sir? Lieutenant Charlz Smied to see you, sir."

Shoren nodded. "Thank you, sergeant. Send him in."

Charlz walked in and saluted, standing at attention. When Shoren saluted back, he relaxed and took a seat when Shoren waved at the chair. He looked suspiciously at Shoren.

"You wanted to see me, sir?"

"That's correct. You were one of my officers during the campaign to capture the then rogue general Rekii Ubel. I had you sent back to Denver from Garriton before the Kirendadi and the Koro surrounded the city. I wanted to know what had happened to you."

Charlz looked at him a little oddly. "Well, sir, I imagine that you've read my file, so you know what has happened to me. When I came back I was given the option of returning to school or taking a position as an aide on some commanding officer's staff. I took the job because I thought I would learn more, as well as make connections in the military. I was promoted from lieutenant-cadet to lieutenant after the rebellion ended. I've been serving as General Koren's aide since then."

Shoren nodded. That was exactly what he had read in Charlz's file. "You are a lieutenant second class, then? Or first class?"

"Second class, sir."

"What did you do, specifically, in the rebellion?"

Charlz shrugged. "I was an aide, sir. I copied orders and sent messages and did whatever I could to make General Koren's life easier, sir."

Shoren hesitated. "Did you…did you ever consider working for the rebellion? Did you speak with anyone who did, or know anyone who did? I wasn't here for it, you see, and I didn't learn about it until I got back. I don't understand what it is that happened."

Now it was Charlz who hesitated. After a few false starts, he finally spoke. "I never considered working for the rebels and I don't know anyone who did. I know what rumor said, but I don't know the names of anyone who said anything, sir."

Shoren laughed. "This isn't an inquisition. I just want to understand why the rebellion happened. I don't want to know any names, and I don't want to hear baseless rumor. Now, would you like to revise your earlier statement?"

Charlz shifted uncomfortably in his seat. "Some people found Emperor Otto's death suspicious and Emperor Richerd's move to replace the old major general with the new one was very unpopular, especially at first. There was a lot of confusion. No one really trusted anyone after Rekii began naming dissidents as traitors and executing them. Everyone was afraid to speak for fear he'd be next. The Assembly tried to rein in Emperor Richerd and the major general, but when Major General Josef revolted, a lot of people stood behind the Emperor. There was a lot of chaos.

"When the Koro invaded, the rebellion just fell apart. First, a lot of prisoners were executed in ever more inventively painful ways. Secondly, no one really supported it any more, and the ones who did were too afraid to do anything. After the final battle just outside the city, the rebellion was finished. As for me personally, I had a secure position in the army, the worst had passed, and Denver was beset by outside enemies anyway. It still is. The Tejas are moving and they'd just love to swallow up a ton of our territory, and the Sioux are raiding too. Even if the Emperor is a horrible, evil tyrant, which I'm not sure he is, not anymore, wouldn't a Denver tyrant be better than a Tejas one? Or a Sioux, or, spirits forbid, an Aztlani one?" He shrugged. "There really weren't a lot of good options."

Shoren nodded. "I see. I think I understand the rebellion a little better now. I think you were wise to stay as an aide to General Koren." He paused. "I'm in need of an experienced aide I know I can trust. How would you like a transfer to work for me as my aide? Of course, a lieutenant second class is good enough for a regular general, but the captain general would need his aide to be at least a lieutenant first class. You would get the pay raise that goes with the promotion as well as a more prestigious duty station. I imagine working for the captain general would be better than working for a regular general, wouldn't you say?"

Charlz's eyes were wide. "You mean it, sir?" Shoren nodded. Charlz jumped to his feet and saluted. "Sir, yes, sir!"

Shoren pulled out some papers and signed them. "These are your transfer papers. Take them down to the transfer office and then to record-keeping. When you return, I'll have some orders for you to copy."

Charlz saluted, took the papers, and ran off. Shoren leaned back in his seat. Well, that was one thing taken care of. Having heard a number of sides to the story, he thought he knew his path a little better now, but only a little.

CHAPTER TWENTY-FOUR

Shoren, Richerd and Rekii, the new Denver triumvirate, sat together two weeks later to learn Shoren's progress in ridding the city of bandits. Shoren gave his report but when he requested more troops Rekii went ballistic.

He began by yelling at the tyrant-Emperor. "You see? You see? He can't do it! I said don't give him troops, Shoren's just a little pup. He doesn't know what he's doing…"

"Rekii…" Richerd tried to interrupt but Rekii was having none of it.

"'I'm going to give him ten thousand troops,' you said. 'Don't worry,' you said. 'You'll still have more,' you said. Well, I say 'phh!'"

Shoren leaned back, thinking Rekii was going to actually spit on the map. When the madman didn't, he breathed a sigh of relief. That would have ended badly.

Rekii began to launch himself into another tirade, but Richerd jumped up and shouted, "Enough! You're not happy! We get it! Don't drag your sad, sorry, anger problems into these meetings any more! I can't stand it! Now sit down and shut up because it's not your decision. It's mine! I have the power! I'm the Emperor!"

Rekii drew himself to his full height and puffed out his chest. "Just remember who you owe that to. I put you on that throne. You'd still be scheming and plotting with no action if I hadn't done your dirty work for you!"

Richerd was standing too, and quivering, his face red with rage. "Right. If I hadn't gotten you to do my 'dirty work,' I might still be scheming and plotting, but you'd be dead! They'd have laid you out and cut your head off. You'd be dead and buried and rotted and forgotten by now if it wasn't for me!" Richerd mimed a decapitation with his hand.

At that Rekii and Richerd both began screaming and hollering at each other at an even higher decibel level. Spittle flew from their mouths and papers jumped as they banged on the table for emphasis. A servant entered the room with some sandwiches and drinks for the three men, but when he saw his Emperor and the major general screaming incoherently at each other (actually, it was Richerd who was incoherent; Rekii was understandable, though his shouts largely consisted of the worst obscenities and blasphemies Shoren, not to mention the poor servant, had ever heard) he backed away, wide-eyed and terrified.

Shoren himself began to lean out of his chair, his hand on his knife. He was certain that both men had forgotten about him since he doubted he was supposed to have heard their enraged conversation. It wasn't difficult to figure out what they were talking about and he wasn't glad to hear it; in fact he fervently wished that he hadn't heard it. *Maybe I ought to let them kill each other.* He shook his head. *That's too dangerous. If Richerd lived he'd never trust me and if Rekii lived I wouldn't. Damn it.*

"Stop it! Stop it! Enough!"

His shouts went unheard. Shoren backed away in surprise and fear when Rekii jumped up onto the table and rushed Richerd. The two fought ferociously, punching and kicking and clawing but not doing any real damage. They were evenly matched. Both were tall, both were fast and strong, both practiced a variety of martial arts every day; what advantage Richerd had in youth and vitality, Rekii made up for in skill and experience. In addition, the two men weren't really trying to hurt each other, simply assert dominance.

Shoren, after a few moments of indecision (and more than a few of amusement), hurried over to the two men and tried to break up the fight. He was hit a few times by each man and he had to scream to be heard over their caterwauling, but he finally got them separated by wedging himself into the fray. Rekii backed off from Richerd and walked over to the other side of the room, and Richerd simply turned around and seemed headed for his chair.

All of a sudden, Richerd wheeled around and rushed at Rekii with a yell, but Shoren stopped his Emperor with a rather disrespectful shove.

When he then preemptively turned around to stop Rekii he found the old man nonchalantly leaning against the wall. Richerd, still breathing heavily, pushed his sweaty hair out of his face. Finally, he sat down at the table again and invited the others to join him.

Rekii did, albeit with a superior smirk, while Shoren sat down still gripping his knife.

"Can we get back to the matter at hand?" Shoren asked the two other men. They nodded, eyeing each other warily.

Finally Richerd spoke. "How many troops do we have in Denver under your command, Rekii?"

"A little under fifty thousand, your Majesty. I sent the rest away to secure our southern border."

Richerd nodded. "Good. Good. Shoren, will an additional fifty thousand men be sufficient to bring this city back under control?" Rekii started, but didn't say anything.

Shoren himself was somewhat surprised. "Ah, that would be more than enough. Well, it should be enough."

"Good. In that case, I'm ordering all the troops in and around the city to be transferred to your command. You, Rekii, will be leaving the city before the week is over to take command of all of the southern troops. I fear Tejas may be using our disunity to try to overrun our southern border. If that happens, I want them to run into our greatest general. Also, it's time we started to control the rest of the country instead of just this capital city.

"You, Shoren will bring order back to the city and Denver will be great once more. Are there any questions? No? Good. You are dismissed."

✣ ✣ ✣

Richerd watched as the two men left the small meeting room that had become the unofficial headquarters of the Denver Empire. Once they were gone he sagged in his chair with relief and shook his head. After a few deep breaths, he got up, strode to the other side of the room and poured himself some brandy.

"Well, that could have gone better."

He set the glass down on the table, the brandy untouched. *I know I can't trust Shoren, and Rekii's too much of a wild card to leave alone.* Maybe he could keep Shoren under control for a while, but not for too long. *I am going to have a short reign, aren't I? I'm losing authority; I'm losing power. One of them is going to move soon. I know it.*

He sat and thought some more but nothing came. He drank the brandy and set about pouring himself another glass when an idea came to him, an idea so perfect that he almost dropped his glass, so astounded was he with his own brilliance.

"Messenger! Messenger!"

A message runner sprinted into the room while the Emperor finished scrawling a hasty note.

"Here," he said, thrusting the note into the startled boy's hands. "Take this to the imperial scripter immediately! Have him write it out and get it to the captain general." The boy bowed and ran off. Richerd just smiled to himself, for he had found the perfect way to bind Shoren to him, and when this was all done he wouldn't need Rekii at all.

✿ ✿ ✿

Shoren and Elina were still talking about his newfound power for several days after the meeting. Shoren was half certain that a message would soon come telling him that Richerd had decided against giving him all of Rekii's troops and that Rekii was staying after all. Shoren had been completely convinced of this unwelcome outcome until he personally saw Rekii off with a small guard contingent. Then one day a message from the Emperor did come, and Shoren was stunned at its contents.

"He wants us to have the wedding in the Palace. Why?"

Elina looked at him a little condescendingly. "He wants to make you grateful for his help. He wants you to obey him. I think you should agree to hold the wedding in the Palace so that he trusts you. Then, when the time is right, you'll strike for his heart."

"He wants to host the wedding. He's asking to be my best man."

"Who else would you have chosen? Who else could you have chosen? Rekii? You can't afford to anger Richerd yet. Agree to it."

"I'll be saying he's like my brother. Besides, I was going to have Ryon as my best man."

"Look Shoren. If you don't do this, Richerd will be sure you're up to something. Right now he just suspects. He's testing the waters. If you want to put him off, agree; make him your best man. You need him to be complacent about you so that he feels safe bringing Rekii back, at which time you can kill them both in one fell swoop."

"I guess you're right. I just don't like using our wedding as a political tool."

Elina laughed. "Welcome to life in the Empire, my love. If you don't like it, change it when you're Emperor."

"I had never had such an ambition before. Damn it, I never even really imagined being where I am now."

"When do you think you'll be done with your current task of cleaning up the city?"

"With all these troops, a month, maybe two at the most."

"Then set the date for a month from now, when everyone knows your name and speaks it with fear and awe. Then we'll have the grandest, the largest and most impressive wedding anyone has ever seen; Richerd's paying for it. Make sure that Richerd trusts you. Once you know he does, kill him. It's that simple."

"You think it'll work?"

She laughed again. "I know it'll work."

CHAPTER TWENTY-FIVE

Richerd was feeling better. It was the day before the wedding and Shoren had done everything he had ordered and more. It seemed his cousin was becoming more and more docile every minute, no matter how ferocious he seemed in public. Shoren's name and Richerd's name were spoken side by side with awe, admiration and a healthy dose of fear. In his many speeches, Shoren had told the crowds of "my brother, the Emperor" and as it turned out, he was an excellent speechmaker. The best thing about this was that Shoren seemed content, almost devoid of ambition; although he did speak openly about ascending to major general. Yes, life was good.

The marriage was to take place in the Throne Room. The concept and celebration of marriage differed from culture to culture. Among the Sioux, for example, marriage was a religious ceremony attended by the whole tribe. Further east, marriage was a blending of religious and civil proceedings, and was attended by family and friends.

In Denver, the typical marriage was not religious at all. More than anything, it was treated as an alliance between two families. This was especially true among the richer nobles, since they were constantly scheming and positioning themselves for greater power within Denver society. To regular craftsmen, farmers and soldiers marriage emphasized love more than greater power or wealth. Interestingly, in most cultures, the bride married into the groom's family and took his last name. In Denver culture, either bride or groom could take the other's last name, and the couple could even separate from both families and take an entirely new name. In the marriage between Shoren and Elina, she was taking his last name, since his family wielded greater power due to his relationship to the Emperor and his position as captain general in the Imperial Army.

The Denver flags all around the throne room were being taken down to be replaced with the family symbols of Shoren's family (incidentally, that happened to be a Denver flag with a silver border, since Shoren's father was the cousin of the previous Emperor) and of Elina's family, an evergreen tree, chosen long ago because her family's business was construction and timber.

A white carpet was being rolled out for the bride to walk down, to be escorted by her father to Shoren who would be surrounded by his family right at the foot of the dais that raised the throne. On either side of the carpet temporary seating was being put up, not only for the extended family and friends, but also for guests. The last group would include powerful Denver families, religious leaders, wealthy merchants and other important people.

Richerd was looking for Shoren, but that had nothing to do with the wedding. Instead, he wanted to talk to Shoren about how to bring the rest of the Imperial Army back under his control, and what to do about Tejas, which had overrun several important fortresses and towns on the southern border. Rekii had managed to get the Tejanos to sit down at the negotiating table to talk about pulling out, but the talks were going nowhere.

A servant ran up to Richerd. "Your Majesty, the captain general wishes to speak with you. He said he'd be waiting in the smaller meeting room."

Richerd nodded and patted the boy's shoulder. *What did he want now?*

When he reached the smaller meeting room, Shoren was busy laying out maps and pulling reports out of a case. He looked up when Richerd walked in.

"Your Majesty. We've finally begun getting reports back from some of the missing troops, but a large number of them aren't where they're supposed to be." Shoren pointed to some places on the northeastern border of Denver. "The army that guards this territory is spread thin trying to guard both its assigned district and the northern border, which was stripped of troops for the invasion of Koro. Since Morken

Luviecell invaded, they've been dealing with raids by the Kirendadi. I also have a few reports of Sioux beginning to encroach on our land, and I have also heard that Tejas has amassed a large army that has moved into Navajo territory. I imagine that they might try to sneak around Rekii and attack him from the rear; or they may be moving to fight the Aztlani. That would explain why they agreed to negotiate with us. The other possibility is that they're finally moving to take over the Navajo themselves."

Richerd looked over the map for a few moments.

"What about the western border? Have we heard anything from them?"

Shoren shook his head. "I haven't heard anything from the western troops, and the riders I sent out haven't reported back in yet."

"You sent out riders?"

Shoren nodded, his face a mask. "I needed to determine what was going on over there. None of the soldiers stationed there have sent any messages back in months. They need to know what's going on over here in Denver and I need... uh... we need to know what's going on over there."

Richerd narrowed his eyes. "You didn't run this by me. What message did you send with those riders?"

"I simply told them who was in charge now. You are the new Emperor, Rekii is the major general and I'm the new captain general. The other part of the message was that the elected Assembly was no longer sitting."

"You told them that the Assembly was no longer sitting, Shoren?"

Shoren's eyes widened for a moment. "Your majesty, I simply told them that the Assembly was no longer meeting, not how or why. I am... ah... sorry if... uh... I erred. I simply thought it would be best for those soldiers to know the truth about the Assembly. If they hear the news officially from us, the soldiers will be more inclined to accept how things are. Otherwise they might rebel." Shoren's face became the image of amiability, loyalty and comradeship that it had presented for the past two months. Richerd frowned. *Had Shoren been...?*

"Your Majesty, I simply thought that had we taken the time to discuss this, we would have reached the conclusion I came to, only much later. We'd probably still be discussing what exactly to say and how to say it and the riders still would not have left. Now though, the riders are probably about halfway there, so we should start getting responses in a week or two. Which is better, discussion or action?"

"All right, Shoren, I see your point. In military matters you are the man in charge. You have to make the decisions when Rekii isn't here, but this matter isn't military. It's more political. When you want to discuss politics with soldiers, you come talk to me first. That way we can decide what the approved message will be. Do you understand the difference?"

Shoren's jaw twitched, a motion not unnoticed by Richerd. "Yes, your majesty. I'll make sure I do that."

"Good." Richerd slapped Shoren on the back as he made to walk out of the room. "So, how's Elina? She's excited about the big day tomorrow, isn't she?"

Shoren nodded and grinned. "Yes she is. She loves the dress you had made for her, by the way. She really does. I already told you I'm not wearing my uniform, right?"

"You did, and I think it's a mistake. Not everyone gets a wedding in the Throne Room of the Emperor, you know. You're the captain general and people should know that."

The younger man shook his head as he pushed open the door, having finished putting away the maps and papers. "I know you think that, but I don't want my wedding to be too politicized. Everyone already knows who I am, and they know who you are, and they know that we're in charge..."

"They know that I'm in charge. You and Rekii are my generals and you control the army, but I'm in charge in the end."

"Yes. I stand corrected. Majesty, I need to get back and get ready for the wedding, unless you have any more questions or orders..."

"No, that's fine. Get on your way, general."

Shoren nodded and hurried off. Richerd watched him drop a map, stop to pick it up and hurry off again. Richerd thought the man was still trustworthy and there was no doubt that he was competent, but his father had thought the same of him, and Richerd had thought the same about Josef, and what did that all prove? Nothing. Richerd sighed and resolved to keep a closer eye on Shoren.

✧ ✧ ✧

Shoren stood on the middle step of the dais upon which sat the Eagle Throne of the Denver Empire. Richerd himself sat on the throne in preparation to preside over the ceremony. The fact that the Emperor himself would not only preside over the wedding but was also the best man had caused a great deal of rumor among the nobles, since the Emperor usually presided at a wedding like this, but would rarely fill any other role. He wouldn't have presided over the weddings of his children but instead would have taken the much smaller role of a father in the ceremony.

Temporary seating had been set up for the hundreds of guests who attended; most of them were complete strangers to Shoren. Elina knew many of them though and hoped to gain their support by sending a personal invitation instead of a general imperial announcement.

Shoren took a deep breath. He was nervous. Elina was in the huge columned hallway that led up to the throne room and was hidden from his sight. Her father would escort her to the foot of the stairs, where Shoren would take her hand and escort her to the platform, where the wedding would begin.

The music started. Elina walked, no, she glided, out into the throne room with her father at her side. Father and daughter walked arm in arm to the music, slowly but gracefully. Shoren fidgeted until Elina reached the lowest step. At that point her father stepped back and waited until Shoren stepped down to face him. After a few moments, her father bowed and walked to the front row to sit with his wife, Elina's mother.

It wasn't until her father sat down that Shoren offered Elina his arm, which she took with a smile. They stepped up to the top of the platform. Actually Elina was gliding again, and she didn't seem to ever touch the ground, whereas Shoren was conscious of each and every step he took. Finally they reached the top, faced Richerd, bowed, and stepped apart so that they faced each other, though they continued to hold hands.

Richerd stood up and their hands fell to their sides. The music stopped.

"I would like to extend greetings to everyone to this union between Shoren McCarter and Elina Corengel, as two of Denver's greatest families are today joined as one…"

Shoren allowed the words to wash over him as he admired Elina's dress, her face, her eyes, and her hair. Her dress was all white, with a pearl necklace and little pearls sown into the gown. Unlike her distant ancestors she wore no veil, but she did have a small, white tiara in her red hair. She also wore white gloves.

Shoren himself wore his full dress uniform, just as Richerd had wanted, but Shoren wasn't wearing it for him. Elina had asked him to, and Shoren had obliged her even though he would have preferred to leave it at home. He had decided to put on the white gloves that he had planned to wear, and also the white belt and boots, a small victory, even though he felt like he was on display. Elina displayed no discomfort at all. She was radiant. She was beautiful.

Richerd stopped speaking for a moment and Elina lifted her hands to clasp Shoren's once again. He was handsome in his uniform, and she was glad that he had finally agreed to wear it, even if he had insisted on altering it. He fit in his clothes; they *belonged* on him. Beneath her radiance and air of buoyant confidence, Elina felt overwhelmed in her dress, and she was nervous in front of so many people. She felt like they were staring at her and Shoren, as if at a circus or a drama. None of them really cared, none of them really were glad to be here. She was nervous. She was scared. So much was going to change and she didn't know if she was ready despite her brave face at home.

Richerd motioned for some priest to approach the dais to bless the new couple, after which Richerd began to speak again, but Elina paid no mind. She was looking into her soon-to-be husband's eyes, searching for doubt, anxiety, fear. She saw none of it.

She smiled slightly. *That's why I love you,* she thought. *Brave, confident, strong, a little cocky, and you don't worry about things. You just do them.* She smiled again, brightly this time, and was overjoyed to see

Shoren smiling back at her. She straightened slightly, knowing they were in this together, forever.

Richerd noticed none of this, bored as he was. He was just glad that things were going well. He no longer feared Shoren, but respected him as an underling. More than anything, the wedding had got him thinking about his own wedding and his future, unspecified heirs. It would have to be a powerful marriage, of course, but he needed to find one quickly. As long as he had no heir he was a target, especially by a younger, married cousin who would soon have children on the way. That could be a problem. He would need to buy himself some time…but now wasn't the time to think about it. He needed to get through this ceremony.

Shoren was glad when Richerd finally came to the vows. Normally at Denver weddings, the best man and maid of honor had the honor of holding the rings and handing them to the couple before the vows, which they did. Shoren repeated the vows as Richerd laid them out, but before the Emperor could read out the command to say "I do." Shoren blurted out the two words of commitment, much to the delight of the audience, who laughed, and Elina, who smiled. Richerd rolled his eyes, but no one noticed that. Elina too repeated the vows as Richerd said them, and slipped the ring on Shoren's finger after Shoren slipped its twin onto her own.

"The vows having been made and the commitments exchanged, as Emperor of the Denver Empire, I now pronounce you husband and wife. You may kiss the bride."

He raised an eyebrow in amusement when he saw that they had started without him. Shoren and Elina grinned at each other as hundreds of soldiers gathered to form the traditional saber archway that the new couple walked through after every Denver military wedding. Since Shoren was captain general, the arch consisted of officers from every branch and extended from the bottom of the steps to all the way to the doors. Shoren and Elina walked through much cheering and applause from thousands of people to the reception and then to Shoren's vacated manor for their first marriage night.

CHAPTER TWENTY-SIX

John McCarter watched as the young men of his little town lifted the next section of Denver's wooden palisade wall into place. Once they were finished, they would lay out the timbers for the next section of the wall. Later, others would come in and build walkways along it and reinforce it. Others were out front digging trenches filled with sharpened stakes. The people had originally wanted to build a moat, like a castle, but John had been afraid that the still water would become stagnant and attract disease-bearing mosquitoes, and had ordered the stake pits instead.

John's little town and the people in it led a very precarious existence. John was not technically the leader of the town; instead, he simply supported the elected mayor. The trouble was that the mayor had to listen to John because John controlled the men who had the guns. Since bandits and wild animals were a constant threat, those men guarded farms and foragers and hunted themselves, so John controlled the food and the safety of those who gathered it.

In short, John controlled everything. His men policed the town. His men guarded the town and the food, and when the town needed something it couldn't make, it was John's men who got it.

John grinned and turned to walk back to his cabin when he noticed that someone had decided not to raise the American flag. He swore and stomped on over to the mayor's house, a log cabin just off the only real street, an old stretch of highway that ran through the mountains. He pushed open the door.

There stood Tom Dowling, the mayor of the town, talking to the so-called sheriff and a few of his deputies about something or other.

The sheriff was loyal to Dowling, an obvious foil to John's own men. He sneered when he looked at them.

"Why the hell is the flag down? I thought we agreed to raise it every day!"

The mayor rolled his eyes. "We agreed to keep raising the flag so people wouldn't lose faith in the country. It's been four years since the war ended, John. It's been four years since the radios fell silent. The Chinese dropped an atomic bomb on Washington, D.C. four years ago. Air Force One was shot down, with the president on board, five years ago. It's over, John. We lost. Everyone lost."

John got red in the face. "We didn't lose. We're just… down right now. The country's going to come around, Tom, and when it does, everything will go back to normal."

"It's never going to be normal again. Don't you see that?"

John grimaced. Everything Dowling had said was probably true. No, he had to admit it. Everything Dowling said was true.

"Well, Tom, if that's the case then we need to make sure that we can get the country back on its feet, or at least as much of it as we can. I think we need to make some changes around here. We need to get other little towns working together and a whole slew of other things. So we need changes."

Dowling looked at John with some degree of alarm. "What kind of changes?"

"Well, I think we need to re-gear our government. We need to set up new rules and laws and set up a real country instead of a bunch of tribes apart. And we need someone to be in charge of it all."

"Who should that be? You?"

John grinned. "I think so."

The sheriff stepped in now. "We ought to have the town decide this, and we ought to elect the man in charge instead of just deciding."

John grinned. "All right, we'll have an election. We'll have it right here. Who thinks that I should be in charge?" He raised his hand and so did the two men he'd brought inside. "Who thinks the Tom Dowling should be in charge?" With a sigh, Tom, the sheriff and his four deputies raised their hands.

Dowling grinned. "Looks like you've been outvoted John. Better luck next time."

John shook his head. "I win. Do you know why?" Dowling raised an eyebrow but said nothing. "I win because I have more men than you do. I win because my men have bigger guns than yours do. We have the rifles, the grenades, and the machine guns. You have pistols and sticks. Therefore, I win."

Dowling turned red and slammed his fist on the table. "You can't do this!"

John laughed as he walked out to his people, his troops, outside. "Can and did, Dowling. Can and did."

CHAPTER TWENTY-SEVEN

Shoren and Elina had spent two weeks at his country villa, away from the court and all of its trappings, intrigues and worries. They had come back to their (it was theirs now, not his) city palace just a few weeks ago as the new heads of the family. In the meantime, Shoren had only met with Richerd a few times, but he had received a very strange request. Richerd wanted him to recruit for the palace bodyguard, which Shoren had done with much success. The strange part, though, was that the bodyguards would be trained by Shoren and his officers.

Elina was looking at the initial reports of that training. "I really don't understand it. Richerd's letting you train his bodyguards, influence them with your ideas and beliefs. They'll constantly be surrounded by your own veteran troops. I don't get it."

"Well, he obviously wants to increase the defenses. I thought the goal was to have everything under my control because that meant that he trusts me, which I'm not sure he does anymore. What should I do?"

"Keep recruiting and training them. That's all you can do. You should leave out some things though, like the dirty tricks your veterans would know."

Shoren grinned. "That's right. If it comes down to a fight, I'm not worried. My troops outnumber his twenty to one, and what's more, mine are veterans. It won't be a problem at all."

Elina looked like she was going to say something else, but a servant knocked on the door, which she answered. The head butler stood there with a fourteen-year-old messenger from the Emperor. Elina reached down to take the letter.

"I'm sorry, ma'am," he said, shaking his head, "but this letter's got to go to the captain general himself. I'm not allowed to hand it to anyone else."

Elina sighed and rolled her eyes as Shoren reached over and took the letter from the boy, who immediately left. Shoren opened the letter and swore loudly and vehemently, ignoring the look from his new wife, as well as the shocked look from the butler, who had been leaving, and the boy, who had come running back out of curiosity. Shoren read the letter a second time and swore with even greater enthusiasm as well as with a few petty blasphemies that got the boy's eyes as round as dinner plates. The butler quickly escorted the boy to the front door, hoping to spare the child some of Shoren's more colorful expletives.

Elina on the other hand simply walked over and took the letter from Shoren. "What's wrong?"

"What's wrong? What's wrong! Bloody Richerd's sending me away from Denver, that's what's bloody wrong! I'm taking all the troops I've been training, half a legion of the Black Guard and a large contingent of other troops, and invading the Sioux, that's what's bloody wrong!"

"Do you have to? I mean, isn't there something you can do?"

"Nothing. It says 'with all due haste' which means either tomorrow or the next day. I can't change a thing because he's on that throne and I'm not!"

Elina's opinion on what Richerd could do with his throne was illegal, immoral and anatomically impossible, despite Shoren's hearty agreement. Shoren and Elina continued along this vein for some time with gusto, but all too soon Shoren found himself on Fury's back on his way to the Imperial Palace.

Richerd was, of course, unsympathetic. "Shoren, you're the captain general. I want you to go. You're the only general I've got that has any experience with the Sioux, so you'd be the one to go. I'm sorry."

"Is this really necessary though? I mean, what the hell's going on?"

"Two days ago the Sioux sacked Tradefield. It's a border town that sees a great deal of business both with the Sioux and with Tejas. We can't simply allow that sort of thing to go unpunished."

"I know. Give the Black Guards the task; they're bored anyway. Send a legion out to punish the war band responsible, but don't send in a full-scale invasion. I'm not sure we can afford one, not with Tejas breathing down our neck."

"We have to. All our neighbors will be watching how we respond. If things were going well for us, we'd invade. Even though we're in a tight spot right now, we have no choice but to commit to a full-scale invasion, because if we don't, we appear weak, and let me assure you, Tejas isn't the only nation that would love to take us over. Cali, Koro, maybe even the Navajo. We can fight the Sioux now and scare everyone else into backing down, or we can decide not to invade their homeland and as a result have to fight everyone at once a year or so from now."

Shoren frowned. "What exactly should I do?"

"Ignore the nomads unless they come at you. Conquer their static population centers — their farms, their towns and markets. After a winter they'll have to submit."

Shoren nodded this time. "I'll take care of it, your majesty. Then I'll come home."

Shoren growled to himself, thinking of how he had found himself in this hot, dry, flat, dusty place. He hadn't even fought a single battle yet, but already this campaign was proving expensive. Hundreds of tiny skirmishes against his patrols and foragers had lost him hundreds of irreplaceable men. The Black Guards had even lost a few and their frustration and rage practically radiated throughout the Denver force.

Madoc Sharon, the commander of the Black Guards, galloped his horse up to Shoren with an angry expression.

"How the hell are we supposed to kill these damn Sioux if we can't find them? What the hell are we going to do? We can't just keep chasing them around like this."

"Madoc, do you know how the Sioux coordinate all of the different tribes of all the different clans scattered throughout the Plains?"

The older man looked a little confused. "I didn't realize they did, sir."

"They do. They're not just a bunch of wanderers living in hide tents. The Sioux have a very sophisticated system of communication among all their little groups. That's how they're able to control all this territory and keep it safe on horseback. Their entire population hovers at just below one million people. They have maybe a hundred thousand trained warriors, and all of them are scattered amongst all the tribes between here and the Great Mississippi. The Sioux are not going to risk their warriors in open battle. We outnumber them, and we have better armor and weapons, so we're going to make them come to us."

"How? What makes you think that the enemy would want to engage in a large battle? Whatever you do, they'll probably just wait until they can start chipping away at our numbers again."

"They won't have a choice. The Sioux have numerous towns and villages scattered around the Plains. The people who live there farm the land, store food, keep the lines of communication open between population centers, and they keep most of the Sioux's written records, since those are too precious to risk being taken out on the nomadic hunting routes."

"I see." Madoc said, despite doing nothing of the sort. Shoren shrugged. He'd just have to see.

The next time Shoren and Madoc spoke, they were on horseback again, but this time they were looking across a field at a Sioux farming town as Denver infantry marched forward. The few warriors were gathered by the half-built gate, which was the only entrance through the hastily erected wooden wall. Shoren grinned. Unable to build a large wall to keep his troops out, the villagers had instead dug a long trench around the town and filled it with sharpened stakes. The sod had been used to reinforce the small wall that they had made, and its main purpose was to provide a safe place for the Sioux archers.

"An interesting defense, wouldn't you say, Shoren?" Madoc grinned wolfishly and eyed the Denver archers who sat hidden behind the infantry. Shoren grinned too.

Once the foot soldiers were just outside the range of the Sioux bows, Shoren ordered them to halt and gave an order for the archers to open fire. The arrows fell short. He grinned as he heard laughter among the Sioux warriors all along the wall as they stood up to mock the Denver. He gave another order. This time when the archers let loose, the arrows found their marks, piercing flesh and bone with almost effortless grace.

The Sioux up along the walls used the bows that they would have used on the backs of horses. These small bows packed a great punch and their use was one reason the Sioux had crushed invader after invader for hundreds of years. Each bow was made of strips of cross-grained wood glued together. These light, fast bows gave the Sioux horsemen unequaled killing power, but they were no match in range for the Denver longbow.

The longbow was a vicious weapon, carved from a single piece of wood and, unstrung, over six feet tall. It was an awkward weapon on the move, but from a standing position could kill a fully armored warrior at over three hundred yards. The best archers could put an arrow in a man's eye at half again that range.

Shoren saw Sioux after Sioux die on the wall and many flatten themselves to hide from a constant stream of arrows. After a few minutes of this softening of the enemy, he ordered his infantry to march toward the gate. The Sioux horsemen, unable now to rely on the archers to keep the overwhelming infantry away, would have to plug the gate with nothing but their weapons and bodies. A few warriors, unable or unwilling to wait, charged forth, only to die on the pikes of the Denver infantry. Others, having seen the deaths of their friends, charged the swordsmen, who ducked behind their huge, rectangular shields, allowed the horses to trip, quickly dispatched the fallen and defenseless riders, and moved forward.

Shoren wondered when the Sioux would realize that, in the confines of the village, cavalry would become useless. They didn't seem to have thought of it by the time the infantry crashed into the horses. The Sioux, able to fit only a few horses at once in the gateway, were also unable to kill most of the Denver with their weapons. The riders with lances could stab the man a few feet away, but were powerless to stop the Denver right next to them who were stabbing them and their horses. The ones with axes were even worse off, because they couldn't kill anyone even a few feet away. Instead, they tried to stop the men right next to them and usually did, but it was the four other Denver, the ones who had slipped in between the horses, who killed them. It only took a few minutes before the Sioux had fallen back into their village.

By this time Shoren had given the order for his archers to stop their massed volleys for fear of hitting his own troops, so now the Sioux were back up and killing his men. He considered having the archers try to pick them off but decided against it once he saw his infantry running up and down the walls killing the Sioux with their swords. It was nearly over now... ah yes, there was the white flag. Shoren quickly gave the orders for his own troops to begin taking prisoners and to kill whoever resisted. For now, it was over.

Red Wolf, the Sioux warrior, stared in dismay at the huge column of smoke that rose from the general location of the village that had just fallen. In fact, he had gotten the report of its fall only moments before. No doubt the Denver had simply burned the town and left, abandoning or killing whoever had survived the battle, if indeed there had been survivors. The enemy had taken advantage of the time it had taken Red Wolf to gather his scattered warriors into a single force, and had taken the town. He growled that now they would be reduced to chipping away at the great host of warriors through skirmishes and ambushes. He had no way of knowing that the fires hadn't come from a burning town, but merely from burning weapons, or that Shoren had no intention of leaving the village, and was actually building up the walls and gate, deepening the trenches and building a few nasty surprises for the Sioux when the inevitable effort to retake the town would come.

Shoren stood in the home of the village chief, poring over a map with Madoc Sharon and a few of his other officers. They were trying to identify ways to defend the village from the Sioux, although Shoren knew that the Sioux would need to be encouraged to attack, since they had no concept of attacking a town except as a raid, or of attacking a fortified town or village for any reason.

Shoren pointed to an area on the map.

"We need to lower the wall here. The Sioux need to think that they'll be able to retake this town."

"Sir, maybe instead of lowering or weakening the wall, we could simply dismantle the gate we set up, or else make it weaker so they attack that. When we do, we can concentrate our archers near there and force the Sioux into a destructive trap."

Shoren looked at Madoc. That was actually a good idea.

"Another idea would be to convince some villagers to run out and tell the warriors what horrible things we're perpetrating on this village, so that the hotheads push for an attack right away."

One of the legion commanders grinned. "It had best be some young women, maybe about fourteen or fifteen. All we would need to do is separate them, scream at them for a while in our language, maybe smack them around a bit, and then let them escape. We might even pay a few to whisper rumors to the others about all the horrible things we're going to do. That'll set the enemy screaming for our blood."

Shoren nodded. "Once the young warriors get all pumped up, they'll be ready to fight immediately. An older, wiser warrior will be in charge though, so he'll probably try to wait until he's ready."

"That's all to the better, sir. If whoever's in charge doesn't want to move right away, the young bloods'll either confront him and his supporters, or fight us on their own. Either way, things are easier on us."

"Not necessarily. We want them to try to take other towns back as well, so we can kill them again and again. Remember also, if they start killing each other, then we don't get the large battle that the Emperor wants."

Madoc snorted. "To hell with a large battle I say. A whole mess of dead enemies is good enough for me. Besides, we might be better served if we just killed the war chief and claimed a victory."

"The Sioux don't work that way. Killing the war chief would simply mean another warrior would be in charge. We'll be better off with a large, politically disruptive battle that we win with a lot of famous warriors on their side getting killed. That'll be more shocking."

"If you say so, sir."

"I do." Shoren looked over at the guards standing outside the doorway. "You two! Find the chief's daughters and a few other teenage girls. Bring them to one of the empty houses and find some guards for them." The two men ran off. Shoren looked at his officers. "I also want you to find some of the more clever girls that we might convince to whisper lies to the other girls, or else convince them that they're warning the girls. Make it work."

The officers saluted and marched out of the room, all except Madoc Sharon. Shoren began to roll up the maps when the big man laughed.

"What's so funny, Madoc?"

"Remember when we went to capture Rekii? In different and happier times?"

"Madoc, that was only a couple of years ago. The times aren't that different."

The big man grimaced and shook his head. "Yes, they are. Three years ago we wouldn't have been out here trying to placate our bastard Emperor's temper. Three years ago we wouldn't see the walls of Denver lined with the heads of so-called traitors, and a hundred Black Guards wouldn't have died impaled along the road to the capitol. Hell, two years ago you wouldn't have given an order like the one you just gave. Of course, you wore a much plainer uniform then. You also had less that could be threatened."

"This is a dangerous topic, Madoc."

The big man held up his hands. "I know, I know. I just hope that you haven't forgotten how things used to be, that's all. Of course, I'm getting up in years and all oldsters like to reminisce about the past." Madoc shrugged.

"You're not that old. You've got to be what, ten years my senior? That's really not that old."

"Not for you, but for the Black Guards, I'm as old as the mountains themselves. I don't expect to get too much older."

"Right. Well, try not to die any time soon, and I'll keep in mind what you said. Deal?"

Madoc grinned. "Deal."

The two men shook hands and Madoc slipped out the door, leaving a very confused and troubled general staring at the maps before him.

✲ ✲ ✲

A young Sioux warrior sat on his horse, looking at the occupied village under the light of the moon. He wasn't a Horseman, just a regular warrior, though he hoped to make a name for himself in the upcoming battle. His name was Wind in the Grass and as he sat watching the village, fiddling with his lance, he saw some people ride out from a low section in the wall. Even from this distance he could see that they were two and three to a horse.

Wind in the Grass looked around. No one else was with him, so he'd have to be the one to investigate. He shoved his lance in the leather case that sat behind the saddle, drew his bow and galloped toward the riders who fled.

Very curious now, he galloped to chase them but the mysterious riders tried to speed up. They almost got away when one of three sharing a horse fell off. Wind in the Grass laughed as the others stopped further away. He would get there first.

"I have you now, whoever you are."

To Wind in the Grass' surprise, the rider turned out to be a young girl. Not only that, she was a pretty girl although her looks were spoiled by the fear written on her face. Of course, she was also very dusty and her clothes were all torn. When he approached, she screamed, picked up a rock and chucked it at his head.

"Whoa! St-stop it! I'm not here to hurt you! I can help."

The girl calmed down a bit at the familiar sound of the Sioux tongue.

"You're here to help us?"

"Yes. Actually, I thought you were Denver raiders or something. Are you all right?"

Sagging with relief, the girl said she was. Wind in the Grass leaped down from his horse to help her up, and called to her friends who warily rode over.

Once they had gathered around him, he introduced himself with the added-on title "of the free Sioux warriors." The girls, all of whom were in their early to mid-teens, only a few years younger than himself, were all very impressed. When he showed them a helmet that he had taken from the first Denver soldier he had killed, they were astounded. Naturally, he didn't tell them that his first kill was his only kill, or that the man had been squatting over a latrine when Wind in the Grass had shot him in the back of the neck. What he did tell them was that he was certain that the upcoming battle to save their village would bring him even more glory.

The girl who had fallen off, named Prairie Flower, winced when Wind in the Grass mentioned the attack.

"They have a lot of big soldiers. More than we do, I'm sure."

Wind in the Grass smiled. "We have a lot of warriors too. We'll beat them for sure."

"But… the Denver are really big and scary, and they wear a lot of armor. They have some who are all black: black armor, black weapons, black clothes… they're really scary!"

One of the girls, Dances in the Sun, began to cry. When Wind in the Grass tried to comfort her, she just cried some more, saying that the Denver were evil, evil demons and were going to do horrible things to all of her friends back in the village. He tried to get her to explain, but she couldn't. Her older sister, Smiles a Lot, simply told him that the Denver had gathered all of the villagers and separated them: the elders from the young, parents from children, boys from girls, women from men. The younger women and older girls were being kept together, and apart from everyone else; the others were at least allowed to see each other during the day when they worked, at mealtime, and when they slept.

"I don't get it. Why would the Denver do that?"

"I don't know, to confuse everyone?"

Wind in the Grass shook his head. "No, no. That's not what I meant. What about the young women?"

Prairie Flower looked him in the eyes. She spoke very softly. "Why do you think?"

His eyes grew large and round. "They can't do that! Can they?"

She shrugged. "They have the swords and spears. They can pretty much do whatever they want. We need to get to your camp soon, but uh, how many warriors do you have?"

Wind in the Grass grinned and puffed out his painted chest. "Many tens of thousands of brave Sioux warriors." He put his hand on her shoulder but she grimaced, started to move away, but stopped and looked at the ground. "We'll kill all of the evil Denver and rescue your friends and families before the Denver have the opportunity to lay a single filthy hand on anyone. You'll see."

The other girls clapped and cheered, but Prairie Flower simply climbed on her horse with Dances in the Sun behind her while a misty-eyed Smiles a Lot sat behind Wind in the Grass. Prairie Flower skillfully turned her horse away, not a mustang, Wind in the Grass noted, but a Denver thoroughbred razorback. She waited until the young would-be hero caught up and pointed the way before galloping off, but she couldn't help but send one final glance back at the nameless village.

Red Wolf, leader of the entire Sioux Army, wished with every fiber of his being that he hadn't called his war council to listen to those girls' story. The older warriors were outraged at the atrocities this younger generation of Denver would commit as well as stunned that the prior generation, the commanders and general, would allow such a thing, and the story simply confirmed the tales the younger ones had heard. Of course, no one listened when he insisted that the general was that Shoren McCarter, the only foreign Horseman, or that the village couldn't hold all the troops that they had seen before.

Naturally no one listened to him. All they saw was an army in control of a Sioux village, and they wanted to go in and reclaim it. No one thought about why no reinforcements had come from nearby villages, none considered that a village of about two thousand couldn't hold twenty times that number of soldiers, which left unanswered the question of where those men had gone, and none considered the other impossibilities of the story.

"Look," he said, in a desperate bid to convince the warriors from doing something drastic, "the Denver don't operate this way. They don't separate people. That only creates fear and panic. They don't scream and beat little girls, and they definitely don't steal them away from their families to whore out to their soldiers. That would be against their law, and whatever else they do, the Denver obey their laws."

"So how do you explain these girls' story then? Are they lying?" One of the younger leaders asked.

"No. I think they were tricked. Tell us again, Prairie Flower, how you escaped."

The girl looked down demurely and nodded. "Well, it was at night. One of the black armored Denver was yelling at us but I don't know what he said. One of the older girls translated and said we'd better get some sleep, because tomorrow would be a busy first day. She also said that once the traders arrived, they were going to ship us back to Denver, where they would sell us.

"Anyway, I was really scared, but later that night I saw that the door was unlocked, so I woke up the others in my room and we fled. When we got outside, we walked along a bit until we saw some horses, so we took them, snuck around to where we found a gap in the wall and just rode on through. That's when we met Wind in the Grass."

"That would be the young man who brought you here."

She nodded.

"Listen to me, young lady. The Denver don't take slaves. They don't sell, buy or own slaves. The very prospect is as offensive to them as it is to us. They don't take young women or any women for that matter for the desires of their soldiers. Do you understand?"

"Yes, but…"

"Did the Denver at any point tell you that they would punish anyone left behind if you escaped?"

"Uh…no."

Red Wolf nodded. "These stories are just stories then. They want to goad us into attacking a fortified position before we're ready."

One of the other leaders spoke up. "Red Wolf, I really think we need to take these stories seriously. I know you've dealt with these people in the past, but they have a new Emperor now. From everything I've heard, this Richerd is a real nasty character. He may have changed the laws."

Red Wolf mulled this over for a moment. "That's possible," he said slowly, "but not likely. I don't think the Denver people would accept such a drastic change so suddenly. But even if it is true, an assault on the village now will accomplish nothing except to kill our brave warriors. It'll be a slaughter."

"We have to rescue our people! We just have to!" One of the youngest leaders stood up. "If we let the Denver monsters hold our people in captivity any longer, then their blood will be on our hands. Our hands!" He held up his hands for emphasis.

"A battle now will accomplish nothing. We need more men, and we need time to build the same machines the Denver use. Any other course will lead to a massacre."

"You may be afraid to die, Red Wolf, but I am not. If the mechanical wizardry you want to conjure isn't soon built, then I will lead my warriors with or without the rest of you."

"As will I!" The younger warriors echoed the shout all across the tent, all of them glaring defiance at their elder comrades. The older warriors glared right back at them until the younglings stalked out of the tent, one by one.

Shoren and Madoc both laughed when Charlz brought them Commander Jorgez's report on the Sioux. After sitting idly by for two weeks, the Sioux were finally moving. That wasn't quite true. Not all of the Sioux were moving. That morning about a third of the fighting force had mounted their horses and begun galloping to the fortified village. Shoren had begun to think that his plan wasn't working, that common sense and experience would prevail; but it seemed that bravery, a sense of justice, and the Sioux spirit of independence had won the day. It wasn't long before the warriors would begin pouring over those hills in numbers most Sioux would think overwhelming. Shoren laughed again, this time to himself. Those Sioux were walking into a trap.

✧ ✧ ✧

Wind in the Grass galloped his horse to the front of the host of Sioux warriors, not in any formation but in a great writhing mass of horses and men. Like the others all around him, he had been filled with rage at the plight of those young girls, and ashamed at the cowardice of his war leader. He wanted to take part in the battle and kill many demons, as the Denver were now called, but in the back of his mind he kept hearing Red Wolf's warning that while the Denver were bastards, they were sneaky bastards. That had to be why his hands shook as he held the reins of his horse.

There was the village. He would need to decide whether he wanted to use the bow or the lance. He decided on the lance. He wanted to see his enemy. He rode quickly and saw with the others the Denver warriors hastily throwing up a wall against them. It was only a few feet high though, and wouldn't get any bigger in the time it took the Sioux to attack. The Denver threw down their shovels and grabbed their weapons before hastily assembling in formation.

Like every good cavalry soldier, Wind in the Grass looked on infantry with a bit of disdain. Doomed to marching and fighting on the ground, they would never know the glory of combat between two riders. When he neared them though, the Sioux boy was struck by how ferocious they looked. They were dressed all in black with a variety of hooked, bladed, and spiked weapons. Their armor was thick and terrifying, and it made the troops look completely inhuman; which was of course the idea. Elongated shoulder spikes, a horned helmet shaped like a skull and other deformities completed the image of demonic warriors from the depths of hell sent to earth for murder and plunder.

Wind in the Grass briefly wondered why they had been building with their armor on, but stopped worrying when he skewered a Denver on the end of his lance. *So, these demons can be killed*, he thought. For a moment he had wondered.

The fighting outside the wall was short but savage. The Denver quickly broke and fled for the safety of their buildings. *Old Red Wolf's losing his touch. Today, I become a hero*, Wind in the Grass thought. With every other Sioux warrior he chased them inside, gleefully and with a triumphant shout.

He was one of the first in, so he saw the formation of more troops in the village square. He was about to holler an attack when an arrow whipped past his ear and thudded into the man beside him. Wind in the Grass turned around. To his horror, what had been a glorious charge of brave warriors had turned into a pile of corpses, all punctured by Denver arrows!

The warriors still outside the walls panicked and fled, only to be chased down by Denver cavalry pouring around from the other side of the town. Here on the inside though, black demon warriors, and their smaller, sleeker counterparts, rushed out from the alleys on every side to smash into the Sioux with spear and sword and axe and pike. Wind in the Grass felt his horse die beneath him.

He quickly got to his feet and used his lance to stab the leg of an onrushing demon soldier. The man used his huge blade to snap the lance in two and pulled out the end stuck in his leg, and just as Wind in the Grass drew his knife, the big man used his equally big sword to tear out Wind in the Grass's throat. As he lay dying, the boy screamed silent rage at those black demon bastards. *They tricked us! They tricked us! Those sneaky...*

Prairie Flower looked at the corpses in disgust as she walked her way to the foreign general who spoke her language.

"I delivered the Sioux into your hands, General. Just as I promised."

The foreigner nodded. "Yes, you did. I thank you for that. Now here is your son, just as I promised." A black demon soldier handed her an infant boy.

She took her baby and raised her eyebrow. "What about the rest?"

"Just as you said before, the Sioux Plains are no longer a safe place for you. These five Black Guards," he spoke the requisite words in his own language, "will escort you safely to wherever you wish to go."

Prairie Flower, holding the infant son of her dead husband, mounted the thoroughbred razorback the general had given her and rode away with the soldiers, knowing that whatever happened, she would never see her beloved Plains again.

CHAPTER TWENTY-EIGHT

Shoren looked back at the town he and his army were leaving behind. He had won a victory there, not a small victory but not a large one either. The Sioux were not defeated. All he had killed were some young hotheads and their leaders. He shook his head. He had his soldiers inspect the bodies, and he had been surprised to discover that the enemy dead counted fewer than three thousand! In addition, most of those killed weren't the experienced ones; these were the younger war leaders and the younger warriors.

Immediately after the battle, Shoren had ordered that the bodies be collected and organized, both Sioux and Denver. He had lost only a portion of what the Sioux had – about two hundred and fifty men, which was a little under his pre-battle estimate. But he was angered that not all of the Sioux had fallen into his trap.

"Of course, I knew that at least the more experienced ones would see the futility of attacking a fortified position. Now I'm going to need to try something else."

After a few more moments, he reached out and touched Fury's mind. *Fury?* The Horse snorted and shook his head. *Fury? Fury!* The stallion snorted louder this time and stomped his hoof before walking on, silently. Shoren sighed. The Horse was mad at him for embarking on this campaign in the first place, although he claimed to see the necessity for it, and he was especially mad at the trick Shoren had played and was even more upset at its success. Fury had thought the Sioux were smarter than that. Shoren explained that many of the Sioux warriors were smart enough to not fall for his trick. *~Besides,* he had said, *the Denver organize and hierarch everything to the hilt. The Sioux are much more individualistic.* The Horse didn't seem to care.

At least I did the best I could with the bodies, Shoren thought to himself. After organizing the corpses to see who had died, he ordered the Denver bodies burned and the Sioux laid out so that the Sioux could deal with them when they retook the town. This would have both the effect of not angering the Sioux by doing the wrong thing, or in this case, anything, and would slow them down as they stopped for the funeral rites.

He had recorded as best he could who the Sioux were; not there names, he had no way of knowing that, but what accoutrements they wore and thereby their potential rank in the Sioux Warrior Brotherhood, which took the place of a typical organized military. He expected to learn more as time went on. The villagers had been completely uncooperative in telling the difference between a badge of rank, tribal symbols and other identifying marks, but he hadn't really expected their help. The really interesting thing was that many of the villagers had no idea what he was talking about.

When Shoren ordered the army to make camp for the night, he gathered his officers together and searched out the best new target. Several wanted to capture another village and try the same trick. It worked once, after all, why wouldn't it work again?

Shoren's concern was exactly that; it had worked once. Maybe he hadn't slain as many warriors as he had hoped, but he had killed a good number of them. If he tried it again, could the Sioux be goaded into attacking again, or would they strike right away, or try to starve him out? That last option could very well succeed, especially if the town's food stores weren't full. The trouble was that the Sioux didn't keep the extensive underground warehouses of food that the Denver did; they simply didn't need them.

In Denver, a certain amount of each harvest was always preserved in huge, cold, dry, underground storage rooms, against the possibility of some disaster. Since the Denver had a large population gathered in small areas of land, a famine or other natural (or not so natural) disaster would hit them hard. The Sioux didn't have to worry so much. Hunting and foraging would be enough to sustain their people until times got better.

Shoren took another long look at the map and traced the road his army was taking. He also looked at the positions the other columns were taking across similar roads or paths. Shoren had split the army of fifty thousand men into four large battle groups. Three legions on their own, and his own group with twenty thousand. The goal had been to increase the speed of all four armies, and Shoren believed he had a place where the four armies could meet and fight the Sioux head on.

He gestured. "I want to draw the Sioux into a stand-up fight this time. We won't be able to trick them the same way again, but we might try. This town, Minisanti, maybe we begin to fortify it, trick the Sioux into laying siege. Then the rest attack and break the siege."

Madoc scratched his head. "Maybe we ought to just burn the damn thing down. That would get them all riled up for a straight fight."

"Maybe we trick the Sioux into coming straight at us, but we come at them from two sides. That way they don't run away." That was Charlz who had spoken. Shoren had been teaching him battlefield tactics and he learned with incredible enthusiasm.

Madoc leaned forward with excitement. "We'll take the town, wait until the Sioux are within striking distance and then burn it. Or maybe we raze the town beforehand and attack the Sioux when they're investigating."

Shoren frowned and cocked his head for a moment before speaking. "Maybe we should, all fifty thousand of us. We would be very visibly setting up to lay siege to the town. When the Sioux reach us, and we'll have plenty of time to prepare when we see them, we'll fight a pitched battle and crush them. Then we can go home."

One of the decalegion commanders spoke up. "What about trophies, sir? Won't the Emperor want some physical proof of our victory?"

Shoren shrugged. "We might be able to capture some prisoners, although that would spawn more attacks by the Sioux, which is counterproductive to our mission here, or maybe Minisanti will have something we can take. Either way, we'll bring home something."

Red Wolf, war leader of the entire Sioux army, also looked at a map spread out before him. He was looking at his map a few days later than Shoren, but of course, they had each studied their respective maps every night for several nights now. He didn't have to see a place where he could gain a victory to soothe his brat of an emperor's wounded pride, or trophies with which to impress his people with his own greatness. All that Red Wolf saw was another catastrophe that he needed to deal with, and if this catastrophe was anything like the last one, then he was between a rock and a hard place. *Actually*, he thought to himself, *he was between a steel sword and an iron tomahawk.*

Red Wolf growled low in his throat and wondered if the demon general even knew how devastating his trick was. He knew it was a trick now too. Several villagers spoke of how they had all been separated, and of what they had thought happened to the girls and women, but it seemed that all of the women who were taken had simply been confined until the day of the battle, at which point they had simply been released. No one had been hurt. No one had been touched at all.

Some of the girls, including that Prairie Flower woman, had simply disappeared. Red Wolf ground his teeth at the thought of her. She had been instrumental in leading his troops to disaster, and the last time anyone saw her she was in the company of some of those black demon soldiers.

The trouble was that the defeat had scared away hundreds of the younger braves who stayed behind, and most of the reinforcements he should have gotten by now were nowhere to be seen. Whether their chiefs had kept them away, or whether they had stayed away themselves, or had tried to come but had met some nasty fate between here and their tribes he didn't know. All that mattered was that they weren't coming, and now all the Denver troops were joining together to attack one of the Sioux's most culturally valued towns. The town had been built a thousand years ago over the ruins of an abandoned town, and contained some of the Sioux's most valued artifacts. He wondered if the demon general knew that.

Shoren glared at the reports of his scouts and cursed creatively for several minutes. The foul-mouthed general looked up when Madoc

Sharon walked into the room. The Black Guard Captain's eyebrows rose.

"I suppose I should come back at another time?"

Shoren almost gestured to make him leave, but shook his head. "No, this is important. I've just gotten word that the Sioux army has more than doubled to nearly thirty thousand. All the Sioux in the southern Plains." He shook his head. "I didn't think they'd manage it."

Madoc nodded, thoughtfully. "At least when we win there won't be any real resistance for a good long time. Richerd will have his victory and we'll be able to go home."

Shoren nodded. "This time we'll be taking considerably more casualties than we did last time. The most important thing is not to break formation. If we let the battle collapse into a bunch of little fights, then we'll probably lose. Sioux lancers will beat heavy infantry any day of the week, one on one."

"What about our own cavalry? I think we could probably swing them out from the sides, flanking the Sioux in order to force them down onto our infantry, where the bastards' horses'll just spike themselves on our pikes."

Shoren grinned. "That's a good idea. Arrange for our heavy lancers to spread out wide but only seven or eight riders deep so that they can entrap the Sioux when they charge."

"If we do that, then the Sioux will be able to break through if they concentrate in any given direction other than straight at the main force."

"They won't try to escape. All they'll want to do is kill us, and they going to do their best to get that done. Most of those warriors will die in battle instead of fleeing or surrendering."

"That will only make them even more dangerous."

"It will also make them dead."

Madoc scratched his head again. "Even if they all die, which is by no means a sure thing, what will be our losses, do you think? Our troops may be heavily armored and they may carry pikes, but they are still infantry standing against a charge of lancers."

"They'll be unarmored lancers carrying wooden lances, and not all of them will be lancers. Some will have axes, others clubs, and others still will be using bows. As long as we're able to trap them, we'll not only win but we'll win with very minor losses once we unhorse the bastards."

Madoc shrugged. Hopefully everything would go as planned, but even if it didn't, they wouldn't lose. Given that the Denver had the advantage of technology, numbers and initiative, it would take a miracle for the Sioux to defeat them.

✲ ✲ ✲

Shoren sat in his tent talking with Madoc. They had just reached Minisanti, and everything was ready. A servant had just brought some wine when Chralz walked in. He saluted.

"Sir. I have the list you wanted."

Shoren nodded and took the list. He scanned it for a moment and looked up. "Wait just a moment, Charlz? Have some wine." He gestured and went back to reading the list. After a few minutes, he looked up.

"Charlz, do you know why I asked you to find all the platoons and companies led by a low-ranking officer?"

Charlz kept his face perfectly still, but his voice quivered with curiosity. "No, sir."

Madoc grinned. So did Shoren. "Well, Lieutenant, an ambitious officer needs experience not only at the administrative level but also in the field. You've served as a good aide, but this platoon needs a commander. You'll have the position, and if you do well, the rank to go with it. Do you want it?"

Charlz nearly burst with excitement. "Sir, yes, sir!"

Shoren grinned. "I thought you would."

✲ ✲ ✲

"It's going to take a miracle to beat the Denver," Red Wolf muttered as he stared out over the Plains where the enemy was gathering, "If only we had more warriors and some of their catapults with the flaming missiles to throw into their ranks. That'd shake 'em up."

Running Eagle laughed. "If anyone had those, Red Wolf, the Denver would, or at least they'd have some and we'd have some. Those things are just nasty. Besides, who would use them? We sure don't know how."

"I just wish we had some advantage here. The only thing we have that I can see is speed and that's not going to win this kind of battle."

Running Eagle shrugged. "We don't have to fight now. We could just keep harassing them."

"Until when? Until all our people are under their control? Until they move more troops in here than we can defeat? Unless we halt them now, we're dead and dead for good."

Running Eagle shook his head. "Can we negotiate? What exactly do they want? Or do we even know?"

"For what reason do you think they're here, hmm? They want to conquer us, and they'll be able to do it too. Maybe if we sent messengers down to Tejas to get them to invade the Denver…"

"They already have, and the Denver stopped them. Major General Rekii has been fighting them and negotiating with them for months now. Tejas might try to pull something later, but right now they'll be able to get trade concessions from the Denver. That makes Tejas money while giving the bastard demons freedom to conquer us without distraction."

Red Wolf nodded. "Even if we stop them here, they're going to send more troops followed by settlers. It will take a while, but eventually they'll overwhelm us. If we don't stop them, then they can threaten our capital and make the conquest go that much faster."

Running Eagle sighed. "Either way we lose, don't we. We just have to hope that we kill enough of them to slow them down while they wait for reinforcements. That might be enough time to pull together a new army and halt them again, or maybe even to attack deep into their country. If their citizens feel threatened, then the army will have to stay to protect them."

"Or it will make them scream for revenge. Either way, I doubt we'll live to find out."

Running Eagle could only nod.

✥ ✥ ✥

Captain General Shoren began buttoning up the padded vest that would protect his chest and arms from the blows of his enemies' weapons. He already wore the light cotton pants with the sewn-in chain mail and would soon pull the mail hauberk over his head. The mail on his torso would protect his joints and the gaps between the banded plates his armor consisted of. His legs, which made use of more solid plates, had greater gaps, so the mail there was of much greater importance.

He looked across at the banded breastplate. It had thick shoulders, and the whole chest, belly and shoulder protection were all connected as a single piece of armor. The bands tied up the middle of the front and back, basically as two separate halves but connected by a wide leather strap riveted to both pieces. When he pulled the cuirass over his head he was able to tie up the leather strings that fastened the front of the armor but required the help of a servant to tie up the back. All of the armor pieces were covered in intricate bronze designs and symbols of Denver.

He strapped the forearm and upper arm plates and pulled on his armored leather gauntlets after two servants finished strapping on the leg and boot plates. The metal only protected the outer leg while leather covered the chain on the inner leg so as not to injure the horse.

Finally, Shoren picked up his helmet. Unlike the much plainer original helmet, Shoren's new helmet, made specifically for this campaign, was as intricate as the rest of his armor. The helmet was shaped like an eagle, with the head sticking out over the top and the back swooping down. The bottom lip covered the back of Shoren's head and was shaped like the tail feathers and claws. The wings swept forward to form cheek guards and a small steel faceplate, literally shaped like a grimacing face from the nose down, was tied to the wings.

He walked out of the tent, the hem of his green general's cape swirling around his ankles. Madoc, seeing Shoren emerge from the tent well armed and armored, hurried up to his general and saluted. He too was wearing his armor and weapons. The two of them looked at each other.

"Well," Shoren asked, "are we ready?"

Madoc Sharon nodded and saluted. "As ready as we can be, sir. The troops are lined up, the cavalry is in place and the archers are well stocked. All we need is the Sioux to show up and your order to attack."

Shoren nodded. "Today we'll make our victory, and then we can go home. Richerd will have to be satisfied with that."

Madoc nodded and hurried away as fast as he had arrived, no doubt to ensure that all of his Black Guards were in place. Shoren himself hurried to the small corral set aside for Fury. The Horse was already saddled and bridled, although Shoren had no intention of using the reins unless he had to.

~Fury? Are you ready?

The Horse snorted. *~Of course I'm ready. Did you think I'd let someone else carry you into battle?*

~No, I just wanted to make sure that you were all right.

~Look, Shoren, I'm not pleased that you're going to crush the Sioux warriors here today. I'm not pleased with any of this campaign, although I am glad that you've decided to fight your enemies head on instead of using trickery.

Shoren nodded. *~Then let's go.*

Shoren mounted the Horse, who stomped his hooves, snorted and galloped off toward the battle.

In another, smaller camp, Red Wolf was similarly talking to his own Horse, Fire in the Wind.

~Are you ready? Is your song ready?

The Horse nodded. *~Do you think that today is the day we die?*

The warrior nodded and stroked the Horse's mane. *~Yes, yes I …* "Yes, I do."

~Then I am glad that we will die defending the Sioux. Our ancestors have been called on before to do this and we too will make the sacrifice. If your axe is sharp and your lance is strong, then you should have no fear.

"My only fear is for my children, my wife and my people. I fear for what the Denver will do to them when they win."

~You fear our sacrifice will be in vain. I fear this too, but we have to trust to those who follow to keep the demons from our people. Even if we slow them for a time, then we will not have died in vain.

The warrior nodded. "I hope your words prove correct, Fire in the Wind. If they don't, then our nation will be destroyed for the second time, and this time we may never come back."

The warrior mounted the Horse, shouted a few orders and galloped into history.

Shoren stood next to his horse on a hill that gave him a bird's eye view of the entire battle. Even though Fury had been disappointed that they wouldn't actually be fighting, the Horse had been glad at least to see the great battle.

Shoren saw the massed power of the Denver heavy infantry and the reinforcing strength of the Black Guard in the center and on the edges, and Madoc was surely among them. The black however was very much outweighed by the silver of the steel. If the Black Guard was, as they claimed, the blade on Denver's military spear, then the legions were definitely the shaft that gave it power and he the hand that guided it.

Far off, to each side of the battlefield, was Shoren's heavy cavalry, waiting for his orders to charge and create a box for the Sioux, to drive them right into the infantry. A sound in the distance reached his ears. It was a battle cry, howled in unison by men and horses. They were coming.

Unlike before, the Sioux didn't worry about anything but reaching the Denver as quickly as they could. Sioux lancers readied their weapons; warriors raised their axes and other blades above their heads. The flag bearers, whose falling flags would be the cavalry's sign to charge, glanced at him nervously.

"Not yet," he whispered. "Not yet."

Once within range of the longbow, Sioux horses and Horses began to fall, not from arrows but from the hidden caltrops that tore up their hooves. As warriors dismounted to help their steeds, arrows rained down on them, driving the survivors ever forward.

Shoren looked at the two flag bearers.

"NOW!!!"

The flags dropped and the cavalry charged. The Sioux were nearing the infantry…

"Defensive positions!"

Bugles trumpeted and the infantry dug in their feet, set forward their shields and awaited the impact. It came with a crash and an initial falling back of Denver troops, but most of the first wave of lancers and horses were impaled on Denver pikes and spears. Riders were hurled off their mounts to die at the hands of waiting Denver swordsmen.

The fiercest fighting was around the Black Guards, since the enemy had concentrated around them. Their formations stayed structured but the outside troops were being whittled away. The Sioux had formed into teams of three to four men who would all concentrate on the same soldier. They stabbed one man together and then stabbed him again; he died. Then they moved on to the next man.

Shoren ordered the archers to stop firing. All the Sioux were throwing themselves against his men, and the arrows were now in danger of taking out his own cavalry. The longbowmen and crossbow men, including those with rapid-fire crossbows, all backed up further upon the hill. The crossbows stayed silent whereas the longbows began their deadly work in earnest now. They were shooting to pick off individual targets, not firing deadly arching masses of arrows.

His cavalry now slammed into the sides and rear of the Sioux army; the enemy was completely encircled. Yes, they were outnumbered, outmaneuvered and overmatched. Sioux died by the hundreds and then by the thousands. Soon it seemed that there were more Sioux corpses than there were fighting and breathing Sioux warriors.

The fighting wore on and on. At one point one of the formations broke and the Sioux threatened to break through the line until the Black Guard plugged the gap at great cost of their own lives. Later, a Sioux arrow flew through the air and whisked past Shoren to land harmlessly in the dirt. He gave orders for the archers to be ready to smash any breakthrough with a volley of arrows; some broke through but never en masse.

A few of those Sioux rode like madmen through the archers, who mostly fled, to reach Shoren, his General Staff and the messengers. One warrior leaped off his horse with two long knives, one in each hand, and ran at Shoren, who quite neatly slashed off the nearest arm. The man took no notice and pressed on until a slash to his belly all but cut him in half. Fury tore out the throat of a second man with his teeth. He howled triumphantly, glad to have taken part in the fighting.

Shoren saluted the Horse and looked at the battlefield once more, ready to issue more orders, but he found a cheering mass of Denver instead! The fight was over. He had won.

~*By the Spirits, Shoren! We won! We won! I didn't think you could do it, but you did! You smashed the largest single Sioux fighting force in centuries!* The Horse carried on for some time, even after Shoren had clambered on his back and galloped his way to the field. He barely noticed. He had won!

CHAPTER TWENTY-NINE

That night, Shoren camped victoriously a few miles away from the battlefield. His troops continued to celebrate deep into the night. They had reason; out of fifty thousand soldiers, he'd lost less than half a legion. The Sioux, on the other hand, had easily lost seven or eight times that number. Out of all those men not a single warrior was known to have run away. The Denver had achieved total victory.

Charlz had also done well. His platoon had been in some pretty thick fighting and he had impressed his men. Shoren made a mental note to promote the boy to over-lieutenant soon. He could see bright things in that young man's future.

Though Shoren was giddy with joy, he worried about what to do with this victory. He had met the army his friend Ryon had been leading in the north; apparently it had swung south to meet Shoren's. Ryon had won a similar, though smaller, victory in the north. Ryon seemed filled with the possibility of glory beyond his wildest imaginings, and riches as well. Supposedly there were hills filled with gold out there, and Ryon had spoken of claiming them for the empire.

While Shoren merely sought to soothe the pride of a man he hated, Ryon sought the approval of a man he idolized. This was the situation when Ryon mentioned orders Richerd had issued before he left, orders that continued the campaign.

Shoren stared across the table at the lower ranking general.

"What do you mean, move against the Sioux City? What good could that possibly do?"

"We don't 'move against' it, we destroy it. We're going to burn it to the ground, Shoren."

"What is the use?"

Ryon shrugged. "We destabilize the Sioux. We destroy them and pave the way for total conquest."

Shoren leaned forward so suddenly that he startled the servant bringing him chilled wine. "It appears I was mistaken as to the goal of this campaign. I thought we were to defeat the Sioux in battle so Richerd could claim a bloody victory and show everyone that we're still strong. We can't afford a war of conquest. Hell, we could barely afford this short, damn thing. Tell me I'm wrong!"

Ryon's mouth tightened. "We have our orders, sir."

Shoren growled, wishing he had never told Richerd about that city. The bloody, filthy bastard had just asked where it was and Shoren had pointed to a map and now Ryon wanted to destroy it, had orders to raze it to the ground, and Shoren had shown them how! Damn him!

Well, he still had friends in that city, not least the Great Shaman who had gotten him out of there before the others could murder him. He never knew what became of her. With every other horrible act and twisted trick he had committed in this campaign, he'd be damned if he'd…

"Captain General! Captain General McCarter!" Madoc shouted, snapping him out of his reverie and reminding Ryon that Shoren had both rank and breeding on his side. By the way Ryon's mouth tightened, he didn't like it for all the gold in Knox's Castle.

"Well, captain general," Ryon began, stressing Shoren title, "what are your orders?"

"No."

"No?"

Shoren nodded. "That's right, no. I am the captain general and I refuse to follow these orders. We're going home and if you don't like it, then take it up with the Emperor. In fact, I have a few choice words for him myself."

Ryon shook his head. "I was afraid you were going to say that, old friend."

"What does it matter? I give the orders here and you take them. Tomorrow morning both armies will turn around and go home and that's final."

Ryon stood up, whistled, and three men wearing armor like a Black Guard's appeared. In fact they had the tattoos, but the chest plates were painted red and over their hearts was an imprinted black eagle in a white circle. The rest of the armor was black, although the insignia was on their red capes and red oval shields.

Shoren and Madoc looked at each other in alarm. "What's going on here?"

Ryon looked a little sad. "As the newly appointed head of the Imperial Security Police, I place Captain General Shoren McCarter under arrest for dereliction of duty and treason. I'm sorry, old friend."

Shoren drew his sword at the same time Madoc threw himself at the policemen, screaming "Assassins! Protect the general!" Two of Shoren's Black Guards rushed in and stabbed at Ryon's goons.

Shoren kicked the table between himself and Ryon, who hissed in alarm when he leaped out of the way. Shoren swung his sword. "Burn in hell, old friend!"

Ryon slashed with his own sword. Shoren blocked it easily. The two swung at each other again, slashing and cutting, neither landing a blow, neither taking a wound.

After the initial blows of rage, both men settled in for a long fight. Each man knew the other's strengths and weaknesses. They had been best friends for decades, and had spent countless hours dueling each other. They were of even skill, and the informal rule in those bygone days was that eventually one of them would "die." But now the rule had changed. This was for keeps.

Ryon back-stepped out of the tent to avoid a slash at his head. Shoren just managed to block his riposte. Shoren thrust, but the blow was a little wide and he knew it. Ryon knew it too and blocked it with ease. He slashed at Shoren's legs but missed and sliced a ragged hole in the tent wall.

The two men circled one another with their swords up, each looking for a weakness. Time seemed to stand still. They leaped at each other at the same time, each aiming his sword for the other's head.

When the swords met sparks flew and they fell back. Ryon fell to the ground but before Shoren could kill him he lashed out with a leg and tripped Shoren.

As soon as Shoren was on the ground, Ryon hurdled forward and punched him in the face. Shoren's vision blurred as Ryon grabbed his jacket collar and punched him again and again. He could feel blood pour out of his nose down his face when he kneed Ryon in the groin, pushed him off, and began pummeling him with his fists.

After a few blows Ryon was dazed, and his attempts to fend off his former friend grew feebler and feebler but when Shoren tried to hold him still, the other man bit his hand. Hard. Shoren clutched his bleeding hand and stood up rather unsteadily, but he was able to kick Ryon's jaw so hard some teeth fell out.

Shoren picked his sword up off the ground where he had dropped it. Ryon didn't try. Instead, he drew a long-bladed dagger and weaved past Shoren's sword, lunging at his old friend's throat. He missed, but managed to cut a deep gash across Shoren's left shoulder.

Shoren punched Ryon with his free hand and stomped on his foot before backing away. The other man also backed away, this time to pick up his own sword with which he darted forward to cut a small slice across Shoren's leg. He bought that slice at terrible cost however. With Ryon's sword reaching and low, Shoren brought his straight down to hack at Ryon's right shoulder. Ryon screamed and fell down.

Shoren looked at the wound. The sword hadn't been able to cut all the way through; the arm was still attached, but useless. Ryon, though in considerable pain, switched his sword from his right to his left hand and charged at Shoren with a series of wild slashes. Shoren backed out of range, rolled forward to one knee and cut.

He felt resistance as his sword cut through flesh and muscle before slicing through Ryon's insides. He felt the blade puncture Ryon's stomach. He pulled his sword out and stood upright.

Amazingly, Ryon was still alive. In too much pain to scream, he simply lay crumpled on the ground. Shoren shook his head and used his sword one more time, a merciful killing cut across the throat.

Shoren tried to catch his breath when the tent flaps stirred. It was Madoc.

"Well," he said. "It looks like General Ryon has died. Of course, since the traitor Shoren is covered in blood, I have to assume he's mortally wounded and died escaping." He shrugged. "I guess if the only person around here is a corpse, no one will steal this bag." He produced a duffel bag which he set on the ground. "Of course, if anyone does steal it then I'll never know who. The guards at the stable are probably drunk too, damn them. It's a good night for horse thievery.

"Oh yeah, the young Lieutenant, Charlz? He'll make over-lieutenant before the day is out. I'll make sure of that."

Shoren nodded wearily.

"I guess it's up to me to get this army home without any other stops along the way. It's bad luck when both generals die suddenly."

Shoren hefted the bag and discovered his armor. When he went to the corral where Fury was staying, there were, as Madoc had said, no guards. After a brief conversation, Shoren mounted the Horse and rode away in the darkness. No one stopped him.

Some distance away, the only Sioux survivor of the battle stood grieving. Fire in the Wind, the Horse of Red Wolf, nuzzled his rider's broken corpse and howled his grief and rage into the night.

Miles away, Shoren shivered.

The following account, written long after the time of Shoren and his exploits, was lifted from *Rise and Decline of the Denver Empire* Volume IV, American Empire Library, New Denver.

> It's not known how Shoren escaped into the night after being branded traitor, or what his intentions were; but it is known where he went. He traveled to Cheyenne Mountain, a mountain peak held sacred by his own people and many others in the region. Why he went there is unknown as well, although many historians suspect the influence of his sentient horse, Fury Fidelis, as records indicate that Shoren was not a particularly religious or spiritual man. At least, not yet.
>
> Whatever he expected, he didn't find it. Instead he came into contact with the Survivors, the only civilization west of the Mississippi to survive the nuclear holocaust following the outbreak of World War III. He was captured and imprisoned for trespassing, and it was there that he discovered the greatest secret in two and a half thousand years; and began his journey into history.

Shoren dismounted Fury and stepped into the cave. A few minutes of exploration told him that there was nothing to be found.

~Nothing in here either, Fury. Are there any more?

Yes, I just found another cave. Remember, the legends say that you'll find a smooth rock face with glyphs all over. It's got to be here somewhere.

Shoren nodded and walked to the mouth of the cave. When he got there, four massively tall green armored figures blocked his way. He drew his sword and they pulled out intricate metallic rectangles that they held like weapons. One of them said something and Shoren raised his sword. The same figure spoke again and one of the objects spat flame. Shoren felt something bite him in the leg.

He fell to his knees and saw the same figure pull out a small orb, squeeze it and mist began to pour out. He felt sleepy and vaguely heard Fury screaming. He felt more than heard a deep rumble and saw a great flash of light as he was picked up and carried away. The pain became overwhelming and he passed out.

The End.

ABOUT THE AUTHOR

Matt Moriarty was born in California and raised in Cincinnati, Ohio. He attended Archbishop McNicholas High School, where he had occasional trouble with his English courses (due at least in part to his preference for reading science fiction and fantasy rather than the dry and boring textbooks). A history buff, Matt owns well over a thousand books covering a broad range of topics – and has read most of them. He enjoys chess, camping, and backpacking, and became an Eagle Scout (scouting's highest rank) at the age of seventeen. He also enjoys discussing philosophical dilemmas and obscure historical events with his younger brother.

Matt began *Echoes of the Past*, his debut novel, when he was seventeen and still in high school. Now a student at Northern Kentucky University, Matt is hard at work on the second novel of his *A History of the Future* trilogy.

Made in the USA
Charleston, SC
12 November 2010